I'm Still Standing II

Angela D. Evans

authorHOUSE®

AuthorHouse™
1663 Liberty Drive
Bloomington, IN 47403
www.authorhouse.com
Phone: 1-800-839-8640

Published by AuthorHouse 2/20/2012

ISBN: 978-1-4685-5491-5 (sc)
ISBN: 978-1-4685-5490-8 (e)

Library of Congress Control Number: 2010906184

Chapter 1

ANA CAME RUNNING INTO THE house.

"Mom, Mom."

"What is it baby?"

"I met my sister."

"What are you talking about?"

"My father's daughter. She was in the lunch room."

"How do you know she's your sister?"

"Me and Karen was talking and Rosalyn, that's her name, when she walked pass us. Karen commented that she looked like me. At first I didn't think anything of it. Then these kids started bothering her. She looked scared. I don't usually talk to freshman, but I felt sorry for her. I went over to help pick her things up. When I went over I asked her what was her name. She was scared. I told her it was alright. I led her to my table. She told me her name. When she said her last name I looked at her. I asked her what was her father's name was. When she told me I was shocked. At first I wasn't sure if I should say anything and then I thought this is my little sister. I hugged her. She looked at me as if I was crazy. Then I told her that her father was my biological father. She continued to stare at me. I waited patiently."

"You?"

"Mom. I guess it was a shock. She thanked me for helping her and then left the lunch room."

"Well does she look like you?"

"A little I guess. That is so weird. I have a sister. You know I use to wonder what she looked like. If she talks to me I will take a picture of her. I better tell TJ so he don't try to talk to her."

"He's younger than her."

"Only by a year and he's in the same grade. She wouldn't know that he's younger. Girls be looking at him and he is interested in girls."

TJ came in the door.

"Hey mom. Hey Ana."

"Hey TJ. Come here."

"What?"

"Come here. I have to tell you something."

"What?"

TJ walked into the kitchen where Margaret and Ana were standing.

"I met our sister today." TJ looked at Margaret with confusion and then fear replaced it.

With anger in his voice TJ asked, "Ana what are you talking about?"

Margaret began, "Come sit down." TJ walked over to the island and sat down. "Ana was adopted by your father. Her biological father had a daughter. She is really no relation to you."

Although TJ still had a confused look on his face his relief was visible.

"What's her name?"

"Rosalyn Ware."

A smile washed over TJ's face.

Ana asked, "What is that smile for?"

"She's hot. I know her. She's real shy."

"TJ you can not be attracted to her and you can not even think of talking to her."

"Why not?"

"Because she's our sister."

"She's not my sister."

"But she's mine and you're my brother."

"She and I do not have the same biological parents."

"That's nasty."

"No it's not. She's not my sister."

Ana pushed TJ and then stormed out of the kitchen.

TJ looked at Margaret. He smiled and shrugged his shoulders. "Mom she's not my sister."

"TJ although she's not your sister it just seems inappropriate because she is related to someone in your family."

"Ok mom I won't pursue her. But she is hot."

TJ went up to his room. He got on his computer and turned the webcam on. Rosalyn was on line.

"Hi TJ."

"Hi. You want to meet tonight?"

"Do you think we should?"

"More than ever. I'll meet you at the usual spot. About nine?"

"Ok."

The two completed their homework together. When they were done TJ heard Margaret call up stairs for everyone to come down for dinner. TJ told Rosalyn that he would see her later. They disconnected and TJ left the room.

As he walked down the hallway TJ ran into Ana. Ana explained to TJ why he should not make any advances toward Rosalyn. TJ pretended to understand. Ana placed her arm around TJ's neck and thanked him for understanding.

During dinner the family made light conversation. Rosalyn was not mention.

After dinner TJ went up to his room. He put a blanket in his book bag. He watched the clock on his computer.

Although the children were now teenagers Margaret and Thomas continued their nightly ritual. At eight thirty Thomas and Margaret knocked on his door. TJ slid the bag under the bed. Thomas and

Margaret entered the room. They hugged and kissed their son and said good night. The couple then went to Ana's room. When TJ heard his parents go into their room he gathered his things. TJ opened his door and peeped out. When he didn't see or hear anyone TJ left out of his room, closed the door quietly behind him and eased down the stairs. TJ eased out the back door and headed to his destination.

A half hour later he had arrived at an abandoned house. He eased inside, watchful that no one else was there. He lit a candle, took the blanket out of his bag and laid it on the floor. TJ walked over to the window, sat where he could see out of it, but not where anyone could see him.

After fifteen minutes he thought that he had been stood up.

Just as he was about to get up Rosalyn walked into the house. TJ walked over to her and put his hands on the side of her shoulders and lightly kissed her on the lips. They moved over to where TJ had laid down the blanket. They sat down onto the blanket.

It was visible that Rosalyn was nervous. TJ had watched a lot of movies with confident men playing leading rolls. He tried to be like them. TJ took Rosalyn's hands and kissed them.

"Don't be nervous." (TJ shield his nervousness. This would be his first time as well) "You care about me right?"

"Yes, but I don't know."

"What don't you know? We snuck out to do this. I really want to be with you."

"I want to be with you too. Do you think that we're ready?"

"Yes. You know every girl in the school has done this. What are you waiting for? I care for you. Come on don't leave me hanging."

"TJ."

TJ kissed Rosalyn, She returned his affection. After kissing for a while TJ hands started roaming.

"Are you sure we should be doing this?"

"Rosalyn you are the only girl. Don't you want to be like the other girls? I really want to do this for you."

Rosalyn laid back. TJ laid down next to her. He remembered what the men did in the sex DVDs that his friends had given him to watch. He began touching Rosalyn the way he saw the men on the movies. He was impressed when what he did to Rosalyn seemed to please her.

She had finally let her guard down. Rosalyn melted under TJ's touch. TJ continued to practice what he remembered. After two hours TJ felt like a man. He and Rosalyn cleaned up and they parted their separate ways.

TJ returned home. He opened the back door. He cautiously looked around. When he saw the area was clear TJ went upstairs. He tip toed down the hall to his room. When he entered his room TJ looked into the mirror. He smiled at himself, feeling different, like he had graduated into manhood. TJ took off his clothes in front of the mirror. He looked at himself. He was amazed how different he felt. He put on his robe and went to take a shower. When he returned to his room TJ got into bed. His cell phone went off. He answered the phone in a low tone.

"Hello."

"Hi."

He smiled.

"Hi. How do you feel?"

"Different."

"Did you like it?"

"Yes." TJ smiled.

"Good. I wanted your first time to be special. I wanted you to remember it in a good way."

"I will. TJ."

"Yes."

"How did you learn to do those things?"

"Practice." (He lied)

"Have you had many?"

"I can't tell you that. I don't brag."

"That's why I chose you to be the one."

"I'm glad you did."

"Was I alright?"

"You were perfect."

TJ laid back onto his bed. He felt proud. TJ and Rosalyn talked until dawn.

The next day TJ woke up. He went into the bathroom. As he was coming out Thomas pass him. He said good morning. TJ returned the greeting. His father looked at him curious. TJ wondered if it was that noticeable.

"What?"

"Did you change your hair?"

"No."

"Is your hair longer?"

"No dad. Why are you asking me this stuff?"

"It's something about you." Thomas stood there for a few seconds and then he walked up to TJ and took him by the arm. Thomas pulled him into his room. "Why didn't you come to me?"

"What are you talking about?"

"TJ I know you had sex."

TJ looked at his father in disbelief.

"Dad."

"Don't lie to me. I know the look. I hope you used a condom."

"Dad."

"Don't dad me. Did you?"

"Yes."

Thomas smiled at his son and wrapped his arm around his head. Thomas sat on TJ's bed.

"So were you nervous?"

"A little, but it was her first time too. She didn't know it was my first."

"How is that?"

"I didn't tell her. She chose me because I implied other wise."

"And you were able to pull it off? I was so nervous my first time."

"I got tips."

Thomas looked at his son questioning.

"What do you mean?"

"Some of my friends showed me DVDs."

"What?"

"Nothing out there dad."

"I would like to continue this talk, but I have to get to work and you school. Promise me you'll come to me if you need to talk."

"I promise dad."

Thomas got up and hugged his son again.

"Be careful."

Thomas walked out of his son's room. He went down the hall and downstairs. Thomas went into the kitchen. He got his coffee mug and then kissed Margaret. Thomas then left for work. Ana was downstairs. She asked TJ if he wanted a ride with her to school. He yelled down yeah. After a few minutes TJ came downstairs. Margaret gave him lunch money. TJ kissed his mother and then ran out the door. He got into Ana's car.

"Come on."

"Ok, I'm here."

Ana pulled off. Ana turned on the radio. She and TJ sang along. When they arrived at the school Ana turned the car off. She reminded TJ not to flirt with Rosalyn.

"No worries." He smiled and then walked off.

When TJ got to his locker he opened it. A note fell out of it.

It read, "*TJ remember no one is to know.*"

TJ thought "That's fine with me. I just didn't want to be a virgin anymore."

Throughout the school day TJ went to each class feeling anew. He didn't feel like a little boy anymore.

Ana saw Rosalyn at lunch. She invited her to have lunch with them. As they ate lunch Ana drilled Rosalyn about their father. Rosalyn told Ana that their father had married her mother when she was three years old. Rosalyn told her that she was the flower girl in the wedding. Ana couldn't believe how much she craved to hear about this family.

After school while she drove home Ana felt a little guilty about wanting to know about Rosalyn's family. Ana pulled up in front of the house. She got out of the car and went into the house. No one was home. Ana went up to her room. She pulled out her photo album. Ana looked through it until she came across a picture of her biological father and mother. She stared at it, wondering what kind of man he was. Ana laid back holding the photo album to her chest. She closed her eyes and tried to remember him. Tears formed in her eyes because she couldn't remember. Ana turned over to her side and cried. Ana tried to quiet herself when she heard a knock on the door.

"Yes."

"It's mom. Can I come in?"

"Yes."

When Margaret walked into the room she sensed something was wrong. She walked over to the bed and sat down.

"Ana what's wrong?"

"Nothing."

"Have you been crying?" Margaret placed her hand to Ana's face so she could see it.

"Something's wrong."

"I don't want to talk about it."

"It may make you feel better."

"But it may make someone else feel bad."

"Talk to me Ana."

Ana told Margaret about her conversation with Rosalyn. Then Ana asked Margaret if she would tell her about her biological father. Margaret got up. She held her hand out.

"Come downstairs with me and help me so I can start dinner. I'll tell you about your biological father."

Ana took Margaret's hand.

"You sure you're okay to talk about him?"

"That was a long time ago. There are no bad feelings. Come on."

Ana got out of bed. She and Margaret walked hand in hand down the hall. As they were going downstairs TJ was running up them. TJ spoke, hugged and kissed his mother and then went into his room. When they entered the kitchen Ana sat down. She sat up straight ready to hear about this man she had once called her daddy.

Margaret began, "Where should I start? I guess the beginning is best." Margaret smiled. "I sound like your grandmother. When I first met her that's how she started. I didn't know her that long, but it seems like a life time." Ana gave Margaret a curious look. "That's a story for another day. Well let's see, when I met your father I was in a lonely place. He was charming and he paid me attention. I was all alone. My adoptive mother, who I didn't even know that I was adopted had past away. I was all alone in the world. Steve your father came at a time when I was in need of someone in my life. He was intelligent."

"Were you in love?"

"No." Ana looked confused. "At one time I believed that I was. I even thought that we would get married."

"What happened?"

"Well we dated. Things were serious. I thought he would ask me to marry him after I got pregnant. That didn't happen. He asked me to move in with him. I couldn't do that. Crazy right, since I was having sex with him."

"Was he your first?"

"Yes."

"Did you have any doubts having me?"

"No. I thought that now I have someone to love me. I never thought your father ever did. Maybe when we were dating it was too much for him. We were never meant to be."

"What about dad?"

Margaret looked at Ana and knew what she meant.

"When I met your dad it was immediate attraction. He was so handsome." Ana noticed Margaret's face light up. "We didn't date long before we realized that we were in love. He asked me to marry him."

"How did dad come to adopt me?"

"Well, with your father living with Shirley and she being pregnant you saw him as starting a family and you weren't included. Your dad asked you if you wanted him to be your father. You thought about it a few minutes and then said yeah."

"How old was I?"

"Three years old."

"Three?"

"Yes. You were a very bright little girl."

"So my father just agreed to it?"

"It took a little while before he agreed, but eventually he said yes."

"How was I with TJ?"

"We included you in everything we did. We didn't want you to ever feel on the outside and your dad loved you as if he had help create you."

Ana got up and hugged Margaret. Just then Thomas came home. He walked into the kitchen.

"What's this?"

Ana walked over to Thomas and kissed him on the cheek.

"I love you daddy."

Ana walked out of the kitchen. After Ana left Thomas asked, "What was that about?"

"Ana met her half sister the other day."

"Oh."

"She just wanted to know about Steve and what happened, so I told her."

"So how does she feel about everything?"

"You saw it, she loves her dad."

Margaret lightly kissed Thomas and then went back to preparing dinner. Thomas came up behind her and put his arms around Margaret's waist. Margaret caressed his hand. Thomas kissed her on the neck. He left the kitchen and went upstairs.

When Margaret had finished cooking she called them all down to eat. As everyone ate the children talked about their day in school. Thomas brought up graduation. Ana explained that she wanted to go away to school. Thomas asked her what she wanted for a gift. She excused herself and was gone for a few minutes. When she returned Ana handed a brochure to Thomas. Thomas looked at it.

"What's this?"

"Look at it."

"What is this?"

"A cruise. That's what I want for graduation. I want us to go on a cruise."

"Really? You want us to go on a family vacation?"

"Yes. We've gone so many places and I would like us to go on one more trip. We may not get this chance again."

"Why do you say that?"

"Me and TJ are growing up and I'm graduating. I'll be going away."

"What you've moved away already?"

"I am going off to college and I will be starting a new life."

Margaret interjected, "Well I guess we better book the cruise."

"Really? Thank you so much. Can I bring Karen?"

"You need to ask her parents and have them call us."

"I'll call her now."

Ana jumped up. She hugged Thomas and then Margaret.

TJ chimed in, "Wow this is going to be great. I wonder if they'll be girls there?"

Thomas responded, "Slow down. Oh we were suppose to have a talk."

"I know all about it."

"Son that talk we had years ago was just an introduction, like sex talk 101."

Margaret interrupted, "What is this?"

"Something between me and my son. It's talk." Thomas winked at TJ.

"Well my two men help me with cleaning off this table."

The three cleared the table. After the table had been cleared TJ went up to his room. Thomas stayed with Margaret and help clean up.

After they were done Margaret and Thomas went up to their room. They discussed the trip. Margaret told Thomas that since she was off the next day she would make the arrangement for the vacation. Thomas left their room and knocked on TJ's door. TJ told him to come in. Thomas sat on the bed. TJ had been on the computer. He minimized the site that he was on and turned his focus to Thomas.

"Hi son."

"Hey dad."

"Son there is a lot of misguided info out there."

"I know what's good and what's bad."

"Do you really? You have to be careful, looking at porno. Some of that stuff is over the top and you really need to be careful trying some of that stuff and don't get too much into watching it. You can become addicted and then that will be a problem. You need to wear condoms always."

"Dad I know."

"TJ you need to really be careful. This is a big step. So are you dating this girl?"

"No."

"No? How old is this girl and why did she choose you."

"She didn't want to be a virgin anymore. She's a year older than me. She thought that I would know what I was doing and that I would keep it a secret."

"You're not dating?"

"No."

"Why not? What kind of girl is she?"

"She's a nice girl. She was the only virgin in school and didn't want a guy who would tell."

"So you were the deserving guy?"

"Yes. What can I say?"

"TJ this is serious. You have to be careful."

"I am dad. She doesn't want a relationship."

"She says that now, but sometimes when you have sex emotions happen."

"It won't with this girl. It was just the one time. We're not going to be a couple."

"So you don't plan to have sex with her again?"

"I don't think that's something she wants."

"I don't understand."

"We're friends. I did a favor for my friend."

Thomas looked at his son with confusion.

"Son I don't know what kind of girl this is, but you need to be careful. Sometimes things start out one way and then it drastically change and you're wondering how you got there."

"Well dad (TJ put his hand on his father's shoulder) you don't have to worry about that happening to me."

"I hope not." Thomas got up. He kissed his son on the forehead. "Good night."

"Good night dad."

Thomas walked out of TJ's room. He knocked on Ana's door. She opened it. Thomas kissed her on the forehead and said good night. Thomas went into his bedroom. Margaret was in bed. As he got undressed Margaret asked, "How was your talk?"

"Apparently TJ thinks he knows more than his father."

"They are at that age. He'll come to you if he needs you....."

Thomas went into the bathroom and turned on the shower. After he had gone into the shower Thomas thought back to when he was his son's age. Thomas realized that he was very much like his son at that age. Thomas finished showering and then dried off. He got into bed and moved close to Margaret. He placed his arm around her. Margaret placed her arm on his.....

After his father had left his room TJ returned to the computer. A message was waiting on the computer. It said, "Are you there?"

TJ typed, "Yes. My father wanted to have a talk."

"Kind of too late."

"Well we talked before."

"Is he the one who taught you what you know?"

"No, research."

"Research?"

"Yes." TJ smiled.

"I don't understand."

"Don't worry about it. You liked what we did right?"

"Yes."

"So, this was a one time thing right?"

It was silent for a while.

"TJ don't get me wrong. I just wanted to fit in. I didn't want to be the only, you know. I didn't think further than the one time."

"Well let me know if you ever need my services."

"I will."

Rosalyn and TJ continued their chat throughout the night. At midnight they logged off.

The next day TJ passed Rosalyn in the hall. They spoke nonchalantly. TJ noticed she was with new girls. More popular girls. He smiled thinking that he had something to do with it.

The next few weeks TJ noticed how much Rosalyn had changed. He noticed that she seemed to have grown up. She dressed more like a girl and not the way she had before their encounter. She was hanging out with Ana's friends. He presumed Ana was looking out for her now. TJ shivered at the thought of them being sisters. He reminded himself that they were not related. TJ hoped that she may one day want to be with him again......

As the school year progressed Ana and Rosalyn were getting closer. Rosalyn came over a few times. On one occasion when Rosalyn was there late Thomas noticed an uneasiness in TJ. Thomas asked TJ about it, but he told his father that he was imagining things. TJ went up to his room. Although it had been months since his encounter with Rosalyn he could still remember every thing about that night. He long for that moment to come again, but feared it wouldn't. He tried to move on, but had not found any girl that he liked. Although TJ was in the ninth grade he was a year younger than the other ninth graders because he had skipped a grade and the girls seemed to be interested in older guys....

One day Ana brought Rosalyn home after school. Margaret was home. Ana asked if Rosalyn could go with them on the cruise. Margaret told Rosalyn to ask her parents. Rosalyn called her parents while she was still there. Her mother wanted to meet Ana's parents. Steve did not remember Margaret's married name, so when he agreed to meet with Ana's parents he had no idea who they were and didn't realize Ana was his daughter. They arranged to come to dinner to meet this new friends family.

Saturday came and the Gibson family prepared to have company. Although it had been many years since Margaret had seen Steve she was nervous and curious as to what the years had done to his looks. Dinner had finished cooking. Ana helped Margaret with placing it on the dinning room table. Ana was nervous and excited to meet her father. Thomas seemed cool and relaxed, but underneath it all he was anxious. Thomas wondered if Ana would feel different once she meet her father...

At five o'clock the doorbell rang. TJ went to answer it. Rosalyn was the first person that TJ saw. He smiled trying not to appear too happy. TJ tried not to show any feelings whatsoever. He didn't want anyone to know the depth of his relationship with Rosalyn.

"Hi Rosalyn."

"Hi TJ, these are my parents."

"Hi, come in. Mom."

When Margaret came out of the kitchen into the living room Shirley and Steve got up. When Steve looked, Margaret saw the surprise look on his face. Margaret walked over. She hugged Shirley and Steve.

"Please sit down."

Looking at Margaret, Shirley realized who she was.

Margaret I remember who you are. I saw a picture of you once. I can't believe it. It's a small world. I always wanted to meet you, but Steve said that he didn't think it was a good idea. Does Ana know?"

"Yes."

"I wanted Ana to meet Rosalyn, but when your husband adopted her I figured that was that. I thought we would never see her again and look at this. It's a good thing that we didn't have a boy and they met and began dating."

TJ shifted his body. Just then Thomas came into the room. He walked over to Shirley, bent down and lightly kissed her on the side of her face and then shook Steve's hand.

Margaret introduced him to Shirley and Steve. Thomas said, "How are you? Would you like a drink?"

Margaret said, "Thomas you could bring them into the dinning room. TJ go up and get your sister."

Just as TJ got up Ana came downstairs and was entering the living room. As she entered the living room everyone was on their feet. Ana spotted Shirley first. She spoke to her. Then she saw her father. She stood there frozen. Steve not realizing it walked over to his daughter and put his arms around her. Ana returned the embrace. Tears filled her eyes. For several minutes everyone stood watching the embrace. Not wanting to disturb them Thomas, Shirley, TJ and Rosalyn left them to have this moment. When Margaret came into the dinning room she asked the whereabouts of Steve and Ana. She was told that they were talking privately. Thomas placed the drink in their prospective places. Rosalyn tried to lighten up the moment and began talking about the trip.

Steve still holding Ana walked over to the love seat. He tried to wipe the tears from her eyes.

"Don't do that. You're too pretty for that. I'm sorry I wasn't in your life." Ana laid her head on his shoulder. "I wanted to be. I'm not going to make any excuses, I thought it might be better this way. You had someone who loved you as much as I did and wanted to be a father to you. Your mother and I were starting a new life with other people and didn't realize you would miss me. I have to admit, I wasn't always there. Please forgive me."

While hugging him Ana said, "I did miss you. I thought you didn't want me."

"I always wanted you."

"Did you?"

"Of course. I love you Ana. I could never stop loving my baby girl. Has Thomas been good to you?"

"Yes. He's always been wonderful. I couldn't ask for a better dad." She looked up, afraid that she had offended him.

Steve smiled.

"Don't look like that, that's what I wanted to hear. I'm happy that Thomas was good to you. We better go. We can talk more at another time."

Ana wiped her face. The two walked in with Steve arm around

Ana's shoulders. When they entered the room everyone looked at them. Nothing was said. After a few seconds Margaret asked everyone to hold hands. She said a prayer and then they began to eat.

On occasion TJ glanced at Rosalyn. He tried not to be noticed. During the meal Thomas and Margaret went over the plans for the cruise. Shirley and Steve agreed to allow Rosalyn to go with them.

After dinner the children left the dinning room.

Steve said, "Ana has grown up to be a beautiful young lady. You did a good job. Is she a good student?"

Proudly Margaret and Thomas simultaneously said, "Yes."

Margaret went on to say, "She's on the honor roll. She is so smart. Ana loves school. She's been accepted at a good school and have been given ten thousand dollars in scholarships."

Steve looked at Shirley and then at Thomas.

"I would like to give ten thousand dollars towards Ana's first year. I would like to also pay half towards her graduation gift."

Thomas just stared at Steve in disbelief. He then looked at Margaret.

Margaret said, "Thank you for your generous offer, but you don't have to do that."

Steve looked at Thomas. Thomas saw something in Steve's eye.

"Please let me do this. I know it's not expected. I know I signed my rights over, but that doesn't mean that I stopped loving my daughter. I do love Ana very much. I missed so many important moments in her life. Let me do this."

Thomas looked at Margaret. He gave her an approving look.

Thomas said, "Ok."

Steve reached out and the two men shook hands.

"I'll need the figures for the trip."

Steve pulled out a blank folded check.

Thomas said, "You don't have to give us the money right now."

"It's fine. I like to take care of things while it's on my mind."

Thomas gave him the figures. Steve made out a check for half of the trip for Ana, the cost for Rosalyn and added the ten thousand dollars. He made the check out to Margaret…

As it got late Shirley announced that it was time for them to leave. The women hugged and the men shook hands. Margaret excused herself and went up to Ana's room. She knocked on the door. Ana told her to come in. Margaret told Rosalyn that her parents were getting ready to leave.

Rosalyn went down to her parents and asked if she could spend the night. They responded that she could if it was alright with Margaret and Thomas. The couple said that it would be fine....

Ana and Rosalyn stayed up late, talking and laughing about boys. They fell asleep at one in the morning...

Two hours later Rosalyn awakened. She looked around. Rosalyn realized where she was. Rosalyn eased out of bed. She left out of Ana's room. She looked down the hall. The house was quiet. Rosalyn opened the first door and saw an empty bedroom. She walked a few feet and opened another door. She saw TJ laying in the bed. Rosalyn walked over. She just stood there watching him sleep. She undressed and then crawled into bed with him. Rosalyn laid next to him for a few minutes. She was nervous and began thinking of retreating. TJ changed positions, landing his hand across her body. Without opening his eyes he touched her body, sending sparks throughout her. She laid there continuing to be quiet and still. TJ smoothed his hand lightly down her face. He moved closer and then kissed Rosalyn. Without opening his eyes he continued making love to her. He continued his tour of her body. Their bodies tensed, TJ kissed Rosalyn and after a few minutes Rosalyn eased out of his bed. She went into the bathroom in the hall. She showered and then dressed. Rosalyn returned to Ana's room. She got back into bed. Rosalyn laid awake thinking of how good TJ made her feel. She smiled and fell asleep...

The next morning Rosalyn and Ana awakened. Ana asked if she was hungry. Rosalyn told her that she was. They went downstairs. Ana fixed them both a bowl of cereal and they went into the den. Shortly after TJ came downstairs. He made a bowl of cereal and then headed to the den. When he walked in he was surprised to see Rosalyn there.

"Good morning."

"Good morning."

"What are you doing here?"

She smiled, "I stayed over."

"Oh."

Ana got up to leave the room. "I'll be right back." She looked at TJ. "Remember what I told you."

"Yeah Yeah."

After she left out TJ gave her a questioning look. Rosalyn smiled.

"I thought that I was dreaming. So that was real?" Rosalyn continued to smile. "I thought you didn't want to do that anymore."

"TJ I didn't know Ana was your sister. After that first time when I went to school you were walking by and one of Ana's friends said that you was her little brother. I started thinking about what that made us and then realized that we weren't related. When I got here and saw you it was so hard to compose myself. I saw how you looked at me. It turned me on. Last night when I woke up and realized where I was I found your room. It wasn't planned. I saw you asleep. I wondered if it would be the same as before."

"Was it?"

"Even better, because even in your sleep, you're great. I didn't realize it until we were done that you were asleep."

"I promise if you give me a chance it'll always be that way."

"We have to keep this a secret."

"I know"....

A month went by and Rosalyn had not made any request of TJ.

June came and all everyone talked about was Ana's graduation, what they were going to do during their Summer vacation and the up coming cruise......

Graduation came and excitement was in the air. Margaret took Ana to shop for a graduation dress and clothes for their trip. Rosalyn and Karen accompanied them. After they were finished shopping Margaret took the girls out to lunch. The group so excited when they came home TJ heard them and came downstairs. Margaret handed TJ a bag with clothes for him. He spoke to all of the girls. He briefly looked at Rosalyn. She gave him a small smile. What caught his attention there was something in the way she looked at him when she smiled, he couldn't make it out....

The big day came. The house was busy getting everything together. The group planned to leave for the airport right after graduation. Margaret ordered sandwiches. Ana left early for rehearsal.

After school Rosalyn went to the auditorium to meet up with Ana.

She stayed with Ana until it was time for them to line up. Rosalyn then went to meet up with her parents…. When the ceremony got on it's way both families looked for Ana. As each name was called everyone clapped. When Ana's name was called both families stood, clapped and yelled her name. Ana looked over at them and smiled. Margaret took her picture.

Before graduation the family had chosen a place to meet after graduation. They didn't have much time to spare between graduation and the flight.

After the last name had been called, the principal released the graduates and said good night. The family went to their meeting place. When everyone was there they took turns hugging Ana.

When Steve hugged her he whispered in her ear, "I'm proud of you. Here's a little something for your trip."

"Thank you. You didn't have to my parents told me that you helped with my tuition for a year and you gave towards my vacation."

"I wanted to."

"Well thank you."

"You sound like your mother."

"Do I?"

"Yes. Enjoy yourself. Love you."

"I love you too."

Chapter 2

STEVE AND SHIRLEY HUGGED EVERYONE and then left. The group walked to Thomas' car. They got in and he drove to the airport. Everyone talked excitedly as they traveled to the airport. An hour later they arrived at the airport. Thomas parked in the long term parking lot. The group hurried to the airport entrance and checked in. They found their gate and then sat down. Margaret asked if anyone was hungry. They all were. She pulled out the sandwiches and everyone ate. TJ volunteered to get drinks for them. Thomas accompanied with him.

When TJ and Thomas returned the airline announced that they were beginning to board. The group stood up and got in line. Once on the plane they quickly found their seats. TJ put his ear plugs in his ears and looked out of the window. Thomas and Margaret talked amongst themselves. The girls laughed and discussed the graduation, what some of the girls wore, their up coming adventures and then questioned Ana about her future away from them.....

Two hours later the plane landed and the group went to the port. They boarded the ship. Everyone was excited. They took pictures and then went to their rooms. When Thomas and Margaret entered their room they closed the door behind them. Thomas took Margaret into his arms and kissed her.

"What was that for?"

"You know our children are older now. They don't need us. I'm sure they will find their own entertainment. How about we spend some time just the two of us."

"That will be nice. So what do you have planned for us first?"

Thomas kissed her again....

The girls talked excitedly among themselves. They looked over the activities book. The three changed into bathing suits and headed to one of the pools. When they got there the girls noticed TJ in the pool. They took off their wraps and ran and jumped into the pool. They swam over to TJ. The four played around in the pool. A little while later others joined them. The teenagers played in the pool for hours. After some time the group got out of the pool. They found lounge chairs around the pool and relaxed in them.

When it began to get late Ana told them that she was going to her parent's room. Karen, Rosalyn and TJ left with her. When they got there Ana knocked on the door. Margaret answered the door.

"Come in."

Ana said, "This is a nice room mom."

Karen said, "Yeah Mrs. Gibson this room is even bigger than ours."

Ana asked, "So what are we doing tonight?"

Thomas came out of the bedroom. He walked over to Ana and put his arm around her shoulders.

"We were planning to go down to dinner in a hour."

Ana said, "We better go and get dressed."

Margaret said, "We'll come to your rooms in an hour."

The four teenagers left. The three girls ran around their room looking for something to wear. When each young lady found the outfit they were going to wear they hurried and got dressed. Shortly after the girls were dressed they heard a knock on the door. Karen opened the door. TJ walked in. They sat and talked about what they were going to do the next day. A knock on the door interrupted the teenagers conversation. They jumped to their feet. TJ opened the door. The group left for dinner.

When the group arrived at the dinning hall they found a table to fit the six of them. Another family joined them. There was a young girl the same age as TJ. He found her attractive and from the way she looked at him knew that she was interested, but he still wanted Rosalyn. He tried not to show any interest. The families introduced themselves and made light conversation.

After dinner the teens left and returned to their rooms. They changed and met at the club for teens. The young girl from dinner came over to TJ.

"Hi. Remember me? I'm Francis."

"Hi. I remember."

"Would you like to dance?"

"Sure."

Francis took TJ by the hand and they walked onto the dance floor. They danced together most of the night. A few times TJ noticed Rosalyn watching them. After the club closed Francis lightly kissed TJ on the lips. Ana, Karen and Rosalyn saw her. As they walked to their rooms Ana and Karen teased TJ about her being his girlfriend. TJ told them to stop. He could tell Rosalyn was uncomfortable with their words.

TJ arrived at his room first. He told them good night.

When the girls arrived back in their room they talked for a while and then drifted off to sleep....

Two hours later Rosalyn awakened. She looked around. She saw that the other girls were asleep. Rosalyn threw jeans and a top on. She eased out of the room and lightly closed the door behind herself. Rosalyn looked back at the door and then continued on. When she got to TJ's door Rosalyn stood there for a minute and then heard something move in the room. Rosalyn lightly knocked on his door. Rosalyn thought maybe he didn't hear her and was sort of relieved. She thought maybe he wasn't alone. As she turned to walk away the door opened. TJ looked surprised when he saw her.

"Hey. What are you doing here?"

"I didn't mean to bother you. I woke up and couldn't go back to sleep, so I thought maybe you would still be up and you could keep me company."

"You're not bothering me. Yeah, I was still up and yes I would love some company. Come in."

Rosalyn came into the room.

"This is a nice room."

"Yes I like it. Did you have fun tonight?"

"Did you have fun? I saw your little friend."

"I would have preferred to dance with you."

"Really?"

"Yes. But that can't happen right?"

"No."

TJ went to his Ipod and turned it on. He held out his hand. Rosalyn walked over to TJ. A fast song was playing. TJ took her hand and twirled her around. They began to dance. Two songs played and then a slow song played. TJ took her by the hand and pulled her to him. He held her to him and they began to move.

"Do you like her?"

"Who?"

"That girl."

"Francis?"

"Oh Francis. Do you like her?"

"I like everyone."

"You know what I mean."

"Rosalyn, I don't know her."

"You didn't know me and didn't you like me?"

I haven't thought about it. Let's just enjoy now. You didn't come in here to talk about her did you?"

"No."

"So, let's not."

The two slow danced. TJ hands began to roam.

"What are you doing?"

"I like the way your body feel."

"Just dance."

"I am. What I can't touch you now?"

"I just want to enjoy this right now."

"Ok."

A fast song began to play. TJ released Rosalyn and walked over to his Ipod. He changed the song to another slow song and then walked back over to Rosalyn. He put his arms out and Rosalyn went into them. They danced until the song went off.

"Rosalyn can I ask you a question?"

"What is it?"

"How do you feel about me?"

"I like you."

"How much?"

Rosalyn looked down.

"It doesn't matter."

"Yes it does. I really like you. I want to be with you."

"You know we can't."

"But we have."

"We can't do that anymore."

"If we're careful."

"Where is this going to lead?"

"Why does it have to lead anywhere?" Rosalyn looked at him curiously. "Didn't you say that we weren't trying to have a relationship?"

"Yes, but."

"What you've changed your mind?"

"I don't know."

"Don't you enjoy what we do?"

"Yes."

"Then what's the problem?"

"You can go with anyone"

"So can you and I wouldn't be able to say anything. Why can't we just enjoy each other?"

"I don't know."

"Well it's getting late and I think you better get back before you're noticed."

"I guess so."

Rosalyn walked towards the door. TJ caught her by the hand. He held her hand and moved closer to Rosalyn. He moved his face close to hers. When she didn't move he kissed her. As he kissed her TJ continued holding Rosalyn's hand. TJ realized that Rosalyn was into the kiss. He stopped for a second and said, "Put your arms around me." Rosalyn obeyed. "Doesn't this feel good?" Rosalyn didn't speak. TJ kissed her again. They kissed a few minutes and then Rosalyn pulled away abruptly.

"I have to go."

"Ok." TJ smiled. "Thanks for the dance." He let her hand go.

TJ followed Rosalyn to the door. She opened the door and walked towards her room. TJ watched until she entered the room. He went back into his room. TJ got into bed. He layed in bed thinking about Rosalyn. After a while TJ drifted off to sleep....

Rosalyn changed her clothes and then got into bed. She laid in bed thinking about her conversation with TJ. Rosalyn thought to herself how she liked being with TJ. She knew that no one would understand. She decided that she'll enjoy whatever it was that they had until someone else came along. Rosalyn soon drifted off to sleep.....

At ten o'clock Thomas knocked on the girl's door. Karen came to the door.

"Good morning. Are you young ladies going to stay in bed all day?"

"No Mr. Gibson. We were getting ready."

"Mrs. Gibson and I are on our way to the dinning hall."

"Ok, we'll be right down."

"Fine. See you there."

Thomas walked to where Margaret was. She was talking to TJ. He had dressed and was ready to leave with them. As they walked to the restaurant Thomas questioned him about what he did the night before. TJ told him about the club. When they arrived at the restaurant they noticed the family from the night before sitting at a table. The woman waved at the Gibsons and made a motion for them to come over. The Gibsons walked over to their table and sat down. The families discussed going on tour together....

A half hour went by before the girls showed up. The girls spotted the group and joined them. The group greeted them. Once the girls had gotten some food they discussed returning to the club and everyone decided to go on shore together.....

After breakfast the group joined others from the ship and went on shore. Francis made a point of showing much attention to TJ. TJ noticed the looks that Rosalyn gave her. Rosalyn stayed neutral.

Everyone gazed at the beauty of the island. After their tour the group was given the option to remain at the shops. Many of the travelers stayed. They looked around. The girls purchased a couple of shirts from the local vendors. As time past the group was reminded of their ships departure. They met up with their tour guide and returned to the ship. The group split up and everyone returned to their rooms....

Shortly after TJ heard a knock on his door. He opened it. He was surprised to see Francis standing there.

"What are you doing here?"

"Are you not happy to see me?"

"I apologize. I am just surprised to see you."

"I told my parents that I was going down to the pool. They wanted to rest. Can I come in?"

"Do you think it wise?"

"Why not?"

"Do you think your parents would approve?"

"No, but my parents are not here. Come on, let me in. Don't you like me? What I'm not pretty enough?"

"I didn't say that. I don't want you to get into trouble."

"Well if no one sees me than I won't get into trouble. Let me in."

TJ stood aside. Francis walked in.

"So what were you doing?"

"I was just laying down, listening to music."

Francis walked over to the bed and picked up the Ipod. She put it to her ears and began dancing. Francis took the ear plugs off and pulled them out of the Ipod. The music filled the room.

"Dance with me."

TJ remained still. Francis danced over to TJ and danced in front of him. Francis put her arms around TJ's neck. She continued to dance. Francis lightly kissed TJ on the lips.

"Dance with me."

After a few minutes TJ began to dance. When a slow song began to play TJ stopped dancing. Francis again put her arms around TJ. She moved slowly to the music. TJ looked at her not believing the situation. He placed his hands on her hips and moved with her. When the song was over they remained locked in each others arms. Francis looked up at TJ.

"TJ do you think that I'm pretty?"

TJ looked down at Francis.

"Yes."

"So why don't you act like it?"

"Have I pushed you away?"

"No, but if I don't make a move you show me no interest."

As TJ looked down at Francis he thought of Rosalyn. He questioned if he was betraying Rosalyn. He thought, "Are we a couple? Have we devoted ourselves to each other? No we did not. She doesn't even want to get into a relationship with me."

Francis broke his concentration.

" TJ."

"I'm sorry. Aren't you suppose to be at the pool?"

"Yes."

"Are you dressed for it?"

Francis stepped back and unbuttoned her blouse. TJ pointed to a chair. "Sit down while I change." TJ took a pair of swimming trunks out of his suite case. He went into the bathroom. After a few minutes TJ emerged from the bathroom in a t-shirt and swimming trunks. "You ready?"

"Yes."

TJ and Francis left the room and headed to the pool. When they arrived Ana, Rosalyn and Karen were there. Again TJ noticed the uneasy look on Rosalyn's face. She tried to act as if nothing changed, but it was noticed. TJ heard Ana ask her a few times what was wrong. Rosalyn told her that she was just tired. They continued to splash around for a while. TJ and Francis had only been there for an hour when Ana announced that they needed to get dressed for the captain's dinner. The group left the pool and headed to their rooms.

Once in the room TJ pulled out a suit that his mother had packed for him. He took a shower and dressed. He left his room and headed to his parent's room.

When TJ arrived at his parent's room he knocked on the door. Thomas answered the door. Instead of allowing TJ into the room Thomas came out and closed the door.

"What's up dad?"

"I just wanted a few minutes before your mother comes out. I noticed that Francis is taken with you and also Rosalyn." TJ looked at Thomas surprised. "What you think parents can't see these things? Well we do. You have to be careful. You must respect these young women. Is Rosalyn the one?"

"The one what?"

"Your first experience? Have you too been intimate since?"

"Dad."

"I hope you're being careful. TJ do you think that you should pursue her? She's your sister's sister."

"Dad I haven't pursued any of them. They have come to me."

"You must be responsible. You don't want anyone getting hurt and you don't want to get into anything that you're not ready for."

"I know what I have to do."

Thomas put his hand on TJ's arm. "Just be careful."

"I will."

The two went into the room. Margaret came into the living room. Thomas walked over to Margaret.

"Baby you look beautiful."

"And you two men are very handsome."

Margaret walked over to TJ. She placed her hand on the side of his face. "Sweetheart you be careful with these girls." TJ looked at his father. "Don't look at him. Mothers have eyes. You be careful not to break those girls' hearts. Dose your sister know that Rosalyn is taken with you?"

"No."

"Then you better keep it as a crush and not let it get any further."

"Mom."

"Don't mom me. Listen. I don't want you and your sister becoming distant."

TJ and his parents left the room. As they headed to the dinning room the three stopped off at Ana's room. Thomas knocked on the door. Ana answered the door. Thomas looked at his grown up daughter. He remembered when she was a little girl and how Ana liked to get dressed up. Thomas leaned in and kissed her.

"You look very beautiful."

"Thanks dad."

Margaret asked, "Are you guys ready?"

"Yes mom."

TJ looked at Rosalyn. He wanted to tell her how pretty she looked, but didn't want to draw attention. Rosalyn noticed the look and acknowledged it with a look of her own. The group continued on their way. When they arrived at the dinning room the group quickly found a table. Shortly after Francis' family arrived, they spotted the Gibsons and walked over to them.

"Can we join you?"

Thomas answered, "Sure Malcolm. Have a seat."

The two men shook hands. Francis and her family sat down.

Francis glanced over at TJ. He tried to acknowledge her without anyone noticing. When he looked her way TJ noticed the desperation in her eyes. He smiled slightly. He thought to himself how he was attracted to both girls. He enjoyed Rosalyn's company. She was only a year older than he but she seemed much older. TJ then thought of how they had made love twice and how he had felt afterwards. He thought of Francis. He knew she was a virgin. Not that she had told him, but the way she acted. He remembered Rosalyn before they had made love. He wondered if Francis wanted the same thing that Rosalyn had wanted from him.. ....

The group ordered drinks and then their meal. Everyone talked about the tour they had gone on earlier in the day. The adults made plans to go out to a club after dinner. The teenagers confirmed their plans.

After the meal the group talked a while longer and then left the dinning hall. Everyone parted and went back to their room.

After changing clothes the group met up at the clubs.

Thomas and Margaret enjoyed Francis parents' company. They danced and talked with their new acquaintances....

TJ danced with his sister and the other three girls. They circled around him. At one point several other girls joined them. TJ danced one on one with a few of them. Rosalyn took this opportunity to enjoy herself openly with TJ. They danced to a few songs. When a slow song was played Francis cut in. TJ looked at Rosalyn as if to apologize. Francis wrapped her arms around TJ's neck. He placed his hands on her lower back. As they danced TJ thought about the situation. TJ resolved that although he and Rosalyn had something, the fact was they weren't dating and Francis didn't know about them. She laid her head on his chest. When the song was over TJ thanked Francis for the dance and went to sit down. Francis followed him. Ana walked over to TJ.

"TJ I'm leaving. Are you ready?"

"No."

"Will you be alright?"

"Yes."

"Francis are you ready?"

"No, but my parents said I have to leave with you."

"Well I guess you have to go."

Francis got up. She smoothed her hand over TJ's arm.

"Bye TJ."

"I'll see you."

The girls left. Two of the girls that had circled TJ earlier came over to his table. They asked him to dance. TJ got up and then walked onto the dance floor. The three danced together until the club closed. The girls walked back with him to his room. They asked if he wanted to go swimming the next day and he accepted. The girls said good night and were on their way. TJ went into his room. He went into the bathroom. TJ turned on his Ipod and went into the shower. After taking a shower TJ heard a knock on his door. He wrapped a towel around himself and went to the door. TJ opened the door.

"We didn't mean to bother you, we were just checking to make sure you were alright?"

"I'm fine mom. I was just getting ready to go to bed."

Margaret kissed TJ on the side of his face.

"Good night."

"Good night."

Thomas said good night and then they walked off. Thomas and Margaret made one more stop at Ana's room and then returned to their own.

A half hour later TJ heard a knock on the door. He got out of bed. TJ opened the door. When he opened it Francis was standing there.

"What are you doing here?"

"I couldn't sleep."

"Well I was about to go."

"I'm sorry. I didn't mean to disturb you."

TJ felt bad for how he spoke to Francis.

"Come in."

"Are you sure?"

"Yes come in. You can sit in that chair."

Francis came into the room and sat on the bed.

"Do you have a girlfriend?"

"No."

"What about us?"

"I don't know you."

"We can get to know each other."

"Why are you so interested in me?"

"I told you before. I like you."

"I can't make any promises."

"So can we talk after we go back home?"

"If you like." Francis laid back onto the bed.

"Why are you over there? Come sit by me."

TJ walked over to the bed and sat next to Francis. Francis sat up. "TJ kiss me."

TJ turned towards Francis. He moved towards her and she met him the rest of the way. They began to kiss. They sat next to each other for a while kissing. This time TJ made the next move. TJ leaned Francis back. They laid next to each other kissing. TJ unbuttoned Francis' blouse. He looked down at her.

"You are very pretty."

"Do you really think so?"

TJ kissed her again.

"Have you ever?"

Francis turned her head.

"Would you like to, with me?"

Francis looked at TJ.

"TJ."

"I'll be gentle. Don't be afraid."

"Do you really like me?"

"Yes."

"Ok."

TJ kissed Francis again. He caressed her body. He tried to be extra gentle since he knew she had not planned to do this. TJ made a point of making sure Francis enjoyed her first time. TJ kissed Francis as he caressed her body.

"How do you feel?"

"Good."

"Are you ready?"

"Yes."

TJ kissed Francis. Francis held him close. When they had completed their journey TJ laid next to Francis. She kissed him on the lips.

"TJ."

He whispered yes as he tried to catch his breathe.

"Have you made love to many girls?"

"Why?"

"Because it seems like it. How did you learn to do those things?"

"It's a secret. Did you like it?"

"Yes. Can we do it again?"

"Sure......"

Francis left TJ's room at five in the morning. The rest of the cruise Francis and TJ were inseparable. Rosalyn looked on, but did not say anything. The last night of the cruise TJ and Francis promised to keep in touch. Francis stayed in TJ's room until four in the morning.....

The next day the families got their things and prepared to leave the ship. When they arrived at the airport TJ and Francis stayed together. They boarded the plane and were able to sit together. TJ enjoyed Francis' company.

After some time TJ fell asleep. Francis watched as he slept and hoped that he would keep in touch.....

When the plane landed at the airport the families separated. Although TJ and Francis wanted to kiss each other goodbye they didn't want anyone to know about their relationship.......

When the family returned home TJ began a Summer job. Ana worked and saved money to take with her to school. TJ and Francis kept in touch, but she lived too far and there were any buses to take to visit each other. For a while they talked on the phone almost every night.

Chapter 3

At the end of August Ana packed her things. The family went with her to check into school. Although Ana wanted to stay off campus her parents insisted on her staying in the dorms for her first year. TJ was impressed with the dorms, the idea of being on his own, not to mention the women. He and his parents stayed the night at a hotel and then left early in the morning.

Ana had a room to herself. She decorated it like her room at home. It was still early so she went out for a walk. Ana spoke to a few passerbys. She then returned to her dorm room. Ana called Karen. Karen had decided to stay close to home.

"Hi Karen."

"Hi Ana. How are things?"

"Well I just got here. It's beautiful. There's not many people here yet."

"I miss you already."

"Me too.

"Do you regret going?"

"No. No way. Once school begins I won't miss home as much."

"So have you seen any cute guys?"

"I'm not here for that."

"I can't believe it. You went through all of twelve years of school. I know you are not going to go through college the same."

"I have plans. The male species is second on the list. Once I achieve my goals then a family will be the next thing on my list."

"I can't believe you."

"Why?"

"You don't know what you're missing."

"You can't miss what you've never had."

"I can't believe that either."

"I never dated, how could I?"

"You don't have to date."

"That's not me."

The two girls talked for hours and then Ana told Karen she was tired. The two hung up….

The next few days Ana got ready for school. She prepared her books for class.….

School got on it's way and Ana proved to be as good a student in college as she was in high school. On occasion Ana went to parties with some of the girls she met in class. There were a few guys that tried to talk to her, but she stayed focus….

TJ was now in the tenth grade. He was no longer the underclassman. He had grown taller, more handsome and had worked out during the Summer. TJ had become more confident. He had not talked to or seen Rosalyn since they had returned from the cruise. When he returned to school TJ stopped talking to Francis as they once had. There were a few girls who showed interest, but he did not pursue them. TJ joined the track team. He and his friends, Marcos and Tim made a pack to win a scholarship and go away to school. TJ continued to make good grades. TJ was offered to skip another grade, but he turned it down. He wanted to experience high school….

As the school year progressed Thanksgiving was coming up. Ana and her family were excited that she was coming home for the holiday. Ana informed her parents that she was bringing a friend home.

Margaret set up the guest room. Thanksgiving week Thomas and Margaret went to picked Ana up at the airport. When she came out of the gate they rushed over to her. They hugged their daughter. Ana returned their embrace and then introduced Paula to her parents. They hugged Paula as well. The group walked to Thomas' car and got in. Thomas drove home. When they arrived home TJ came running out of the house. He hugged his sister.

"Wow. You miss me?"

"Of course. I don't have anyone bugging me."

"Look at you. You look taller and what's these?"

"I've always had these."

"No, you've gotten bigger."

"Whose this lovely lady?"

Ana gave him her usual back off look.

"This is my friend Paula. She's from school."

TJ kissed her on the side of her face.

"Nice to meet you."

"Nice to meet you too."

Ana said, "Let me show you to your room."

Paula and Ana went upstairs.

"Hey how old is your brother, he's cute?"

"He's fifteen."

"Jail bate."

"Remember that."

"I can't believe he's only fifteen. He is definitely going to be a lady killer."

"I'm going to take my things to my room. I'll be back."

"Ok."

Ana walked to her room. When Ana opened her door she looked around the room. Although she had only been gone just a few months it seemed much longer. Ana missed her home, but enjoyed her independence. Ana put her things away. When she was done Ana called Rosalyn. On the third ring Rosalyn picked up the phone.

"Hello."

"Hi."

"Ana."

"Yeah it's me."

"How's school?"

"It's fine. I'm home."

"For real?"

"Yes."

"Can I come over?"

"Of course. I'll come pick you up."

"Ok. I'll be waiting outside."

"Alright. I'll leave now."

The two hung up. Ana got her keys. She went to the guess room.

She told Paula where she was going. Paula asked to go. They went downstairs. Ana told her parents that she was going to pick up Rosalyn. Ana and Paula left. She told Paula about Rosalyn being her sister. When Ana arrived at Rosalyn's house she and her father was outside. Ana got out of the car. Her father walked over to Ana and hugged her.

"How are you?"

"I'm fine."

"How's school?"

"It's good."

"Grades."

"They're good."

"Dean's list?"

"Of course."

"Good girl. I knew you would do well."

"I still have a ways to go."

"You will do fine."

"Thank you."

"Thank you for forgiving me."

"There's nothing to forgive."

Rosalyn came over. "Ok break it up." Rosalyn hugged Ana. "Hi Sis."

"Hi. How are you?"

"Great since you're back."

"What you miss me?"

"Yeah. School isn't the same since you're not there."

"How are things?"

"I'm in the tenth grade now and after you made a point of letting everyone know we were friends no one bothers me."

"That's good. Come on."

Rosalyn yelled behind, "See you dad."

Steve waved.

Ana and Rosalyn got into the car. Ana introduced Rosalyn to Paula. The three women talked as Ana drove home. As she drove her cell phone rang. Ana answered it. It was Karen. Karen was excited and asked Ana to come to get her. Ana hung up with Karen. She drove over to Karen's house. When Ana arrived at Karen's house she called her on the cell phone. Karen answered. Ana told Karen to come outside. Karen came running out of the house. Ana got out of the car and the two hugged.

"Hey girl."

"Hey yourself."

"You look good."

"So do you. Let's go."

The two got in the car. Ana drove off. She introduced Karen to Paula. The girls talked and laughed as Ana drove home. When they arrived at Ana's dinner was ready. The girls sat down and ate. They chatted throughout the meal. TJ glanced at Rosalyn for a few minutes. She had not seen TJ since they had returned in July. She couldn't believe that he could get any more handsome. Once TJ caught Rosalyn look at him. He gave her a slight approving smile.

After dinner the girls went up to Ana's room. The girls talked into the night. It was late when the girls crashed on Ana's floor.

TJ had a difficult time falling asleep. He could not believe that seeing Rosalyn would bring up old memories of them being together. After Francis he had not been with any other girl. He had talked to Francis throughout the Summer and kept busy by working out and working at his part-time job. Now he laid there remembering the last time he was with Rosalyn. TJ got out of bed and went downstairs to the basement, where he had set up a small gym. TJ began working out. He worked out until he was exhausted. As he walked upstairs TJ stopped for a minute. He wondered if Rosalyn was asleep. After a few minutes he continued on to his room. When he opened the door Paula was in his room. TJ looked at her confused.

"I guest you're wondering what I'm doing in here."

"Yeah."

She walked towards TJ.

"I woke up and couldn't go back to sleep. I came out of the room and thought of going down to your den to watch TV, but then I thought that maybe we could do something to get me back to sleep."

TJ backed up.

"How do you know that I would be interested?"

Paula unbuttoned her blouse revealing a purple lace bra. Her breast were full. She ran her hand down the middle of her breast. She then stepped out of her pajama pants revealing matching panties. When Paula got close enough to TJ she asked, "So are you interested?"

TJ thought about the question. He started looking at Paula from her feet, slowly moving up to her face. She was very pretty and had a beautiful body. She was curvy and well developed. When he finally made it up to her eyes Paula ran her hand down the front of his body. Paula could feel without even looking down at TJ was turned on.

With an uneasy voice TJ asked, "Do you think Ana would approve of this?"

Paula looked down at TJ's pants. TJ remained still. She unbuckled his belt, unfastened his pant and then unzipped them. She let his pants drop. She looked up at TJ and smiled.

"She don't have to know."

Paula pulled TJ boxers down and commence to caressing him. She moved him towards his bed. She lightly pushed him to a sitting position. She did not kiss him as he thought she was headed. He sat there looking down on this older girl doing what he had only seen on the x-rated tapes. He continued to watch as this girl, thinking that she had obviously done this before. He wanted to make her feel as good as she was making him feel, but couldn't bring himself to stop her. Paula continued until she sensed TJ would not be able to hold out any longer. She got up and removed her lingerie. Paula laid back in TJ's bed. He moved up to her and they began to kiss. TJ caressed Paula's body. He wanted to make sure that he did not disappoint her. He knew that she was different from the other two girls. She was experienced and expected to be satisfied. He remembered some of the movies that he had watched. TJ tried some of the moves. When Paula called out his name he knew that he had succeeded. TJ joined Paula and met her pleasure. Afterwards he laid there quiet a few minutes. As he was about to move off of her Paula stopped him. She put her hands to his face and kissed him passionately. She released him and TJ laid back. He was silent, not knowing what to say. He was amazed at how good he felt. TJ had never felt that much pleasure before. After laying there a while Paula rolled over on her side. She smiled at TJ and told him how good he made her feel. She kissed him. They kissed for a while and then her hands started roaming. TJ allowed her to lead. He was amazed at how she was so comfortable with this. They made love until dawn. Once TJ was asleep Paula eased out of his bed, went into his bathroom, showered and dressed. She blew a kiss to him as she closed his room door. She went into the guest room, not wanting to draw attention to her coming back at that time of morning. When the others woke up they dressed. Ana left her room and knocked on the guest room's door. Paula told her to come in.

"Hey."

"Hi."

"What are you doing in here?"

"I woke up last night. I didn't want to bother you so I came in here."

"Well get up I want to go shopping."

"What time is it?"

"Ten o'clock."

"Dag. I don't usually sleep this late. Give me a half hour."

"Ok, I'll be back."

Paula got up. She picked out a pair of jeans and T-Shirt. Paula went into the guest shower. As she showered Paula thought of TJ. She thought of how he allowed her to take the lead. She thought how he will make some woman a wonderful lover. After she was dressed Paula left the guest room and went into Ana's. They went downstairs.

Margaret had prepared breakfast. The girls sat at the kitchen table. TJ came down soon after. He spoke to everyone and fixed himself a plate. Everyone chatted as they ate. Again he noticed Rosalyn watching him. He tried not to make any expression. He also noticed Paula watching him and when she saw him look at her, she licked her lips in a provocative manner. He quickly looked down, not wanting to show any emotion. When the girls were done eating they got up from the table and left. TJ finished eating and then went back to his room. TJ turned on his Ipod and put the ear phones in his ears. He laid down. Before drifting off to sleep he thought of Paula. He couldn't believe this college girl had sex with him, that he didn't have to ask or persuade her. He smiled to himself and thought how great college life must be….

TJ was sleep for a couple of hours when he was awakened by the laughs of the girls coming up the stairs. TJ lowered the volume of his Ipod. He heard Paula laugh. Although he did not see her he knew it was her voice. He became excited. He got up. TJ changed into sweats and went down to the basement. He began lifting weights. He had only been down there a short while when Ana and the other girls came downstairs. They joked around with him and then followed Ana into the rec room. As TJ continued to exercise he could hear the girls playing games. TJ went back up to his room and showered. He put on lounging pants.....

At dinner Margaret ordered pizza. They put in a movie and the family together with their guest watched them. They ate pizza and drank soda. After the movie was over Margaret announced that she was going to church on Sunday and if anyone wanted to attend with her she would be leaving at seven o'clock. Everyone went upstairs. Ana and the girls went into her room and TJ in his. Thomas and Margaret stayed downstairs a while longer watching another movie together....

Several hours later they went upstairs. Paula told Ana that she was tired and wanted to sleep in the guest room again. Ana and the other girls said good night to her. Paula told Ana that she sometimes sleep hard. She told her that if she happen to come to her room and knock and she doesn't answer don't about worry it. She said that she'll get up on her own and be ready to go to church. Paula said good night and left Ana's room.

After closing the door Paula looked down the hall and listened to make sure Ana's parents were not still up. She then went to TJ's room. Paula lightly tapped on TJ's room. TJ came to the door and opened it. Paula placed her hand on his chest and gently pushed him into the room. She locked his door. TJ was still amazed at Paula's behavior. They spoke no words. Paula kissed him while moving him towards his bed. She gently pushed against his body causing him to lay back onto the bed. Again she performed the acts from the night before. She then asked him to return the favor. TJ had seen it done on all of the movies that he had watched and he had done it to both Francis and Rosalyn. As he began Paula instructed him of what felt good. After a while she pulled him up. She laid him back and climbed on top of him. Paula and TJ made love until day break. Again she kissed TJ and eased out of his room.

At six Ana called Paula's cell phone to wake her up. Paula answered. As she showered Paula thought of how TJ had touched her. She rushed and threw on her stockings and a dress. She combed her hair and then went to Ana's room. The other girls were still dressing. Ana asked Paula how she slept. Paula smiled and said she slept wonderfully. Ana was happy that Paula was feeling comfortable in her home. After the girls were dressed they went downstairs where Margaret was waiting. TJ came down dressed in a suit. The girls looked at him. Karen commented how one day he was going to break some hearts. Both Paula and Rosalyn looked at him admiring his good looks. Ana told the girls that she would drive them. Thomas drove Margaret and TJ. When they arrived at the church the group parked next to each other. They exited the cars and went into the church. They all sat together. Before the minister began to preach he acknowledged Ana being in the congregation. While the minister preached TJ tried to stay focus on the word, but his mind kept drifting off to his time with Paula.

When the minister was finished with his sermon he closed and everyone began leaving. The group went out to lunch. During lunch TJ caught Rosalyn looking at him. He did not show any emotion. Thomas happened to see her as well. He looked at TJ questioning. TJ gave him a look as to say I don't know....

Once they returned home the girls went up stairs to change. TJ went into his room to change. While changing he heard a knock on the door. TJ opened the door. Thomas asked if he could come in. TJ moved to the side. Thomas asked TJ if anything was going on with him and Rosalyn. TJ told him no. He told his father that other than the looks she had not approached him and he had not made any advances. They talked a little while and then Thomas left TJ's room.

TJ finished changing. He checked his emails and after several hours went down to the basement. The girls were down there. TJ joined them in a couple of games of pool. He then left that room and went into the weight room. Just as he was about to start lifting Rosalyn came into the room. She got on the elliptical machine. TJ joked with her asking if she knew what she was doing. Rosalyn in turn asked him the same question. TJ began lifting the weight. On occasion, in between his rest period he noticed Rosalyn staring at him. He did not say anything. He would put his head down. When he was finished TJ got up. As he left the room TJ looked back and said, "Next time maybe you can spot me."

Rosalyn smiled, but said nothing.

TJ went up to the kitchen. Margaret told him to get cleaned up because dinner was ready. TJ went up to his room. He went into the bathroom and turned on the shower. He got into the shower.

Margaret called downstairs to the girls telling them dinner was ready. Paula told them that she had to go to the bathroom. She said that she would be down in a few minutes. The other girls went into the kitchen to help Margaret. Paula went up to TJ's door. She checked the door. It was unlocked. Paula went into the room. She locked the door behind herself. Paula heard the shower. As Paula walked towards the bathroom she began taking her clothes off. She opened the shower door. TJ's back was turned towards her. She eased into the shower. TJ quickly turned. Paula smiled. She put her arms around TJ and kissed him.

"What are you doing?"

"I figured we could get a little workout before dinner."

"We don't have the time."

"Yeah we do."

Paula kissed TJ again. With her caresses TJ no longer protest. A half hour later Paula was on her way downstairs. A few minutes later TJ came downstairs. He sat down.

The girls laughed and chatted. Margaret noticed that TJ was quiet. After dinner when everyone had left the kitchen Margaret asked TJ if he was alright. TJ told her that he was just tired. Margaret told him that he should get to bed early and not be on the computer so late. TJ told her alright. He went up to his room. After going into his room TJ heard a knock on his door. He went to answer it. TJ opened the door.

Ana asked, "Can I come in?"

"Come on."

Ana closed the door.

"Are you alright?"

"Yeah, why?"

"You've been kind of quiet since I came home."

"I'm just tired."

"Are you getting sick?"

"No. I've just been up late."

"You're not feeling uncomfortable with Rosalyn here?"

"No. I'm fine. Nothing's wrong."

"TJ."

"Yeah?"

"If you two want to talk to each other I guess it would be alright."
TJ looked at her confused. "I know what I said before. It will seem weird
for me, but you're right, she's not your sister and no relation. I don't want
you feeling bad because of my hang up."

"No everything is fine. It's not you. Thank you for that."

Ana walked over to TJ and hugged him.

"Ok, before I leave to go back to school I'm going to give Rosalyn
the green light if she's interested."

"If you want, but I don't think she's interested."

"I just want you to be happy."

"I am. Trust me."

"Are you talking to someone?"

"No, but I'm fine."

"Ok. I just had to check on my little brother."

"Good night."

Ana left. TJ laid back down and closed his eyes. He fell asleep. He
was tired from his long nights with Paula. TJ had not been asleep long
when he felt something. He looked under the cover and saw Paula. At
first he just looked at her unbelieving. Then he thought, "How can I
turn this girl away? She is a man's dream, besides she will be gone and I
will be wishing that she was here. TJ pulled Paula up and kissed her.

"Now that's what I like."

"Paula do you have a boyfriend."

"No. It's been a long time."

"What made you do this with me?"

"You look good."

"How did you know I would go along with this?"

"I figured what male wouldn't and then I can be very persuasive."

TJ thought to himself, "You're right about that.

"Can we cut the talking, we only have a few hours?"

"One more question?"

"What is it?"

"Are we going to do this every night until you leave?"

"Could be."

With that Paula resumed her prior position. TJ laid back and
enjoyed Paula....

Every night after everyone was in their room Paula would quietly sneak into TJ's room…. Thanksgiving came. Steve and Shirley came over for dinner. When they got ready to leave Rosalyn left with them. She kissed and hugged her sister. She said goodbye to her sister, TJ and their parents. Rosalyn and her family left.

Paula made an excuse to go to bed early, saying that she wanted to be rested for their Christmas shopping.

This night was different. Paula talked during their time together. Paula told TJ that she wished that they could be together for more than this moment. This night she laid in his arms for a few minutes before getting up and going back to her room. TJ had also thought about how he was going to miss his time with Paula. He turned over and went to sleep. At two in the morning TJ heard a knock on the door. He threw his shorts on and went to the door.

"You want to go with us Christmas shopping?"

"Sure."

"Get dressed. I'm going to wake Paula."

"Ok I'll meet you downstairs."

TJ showered and then threw on some clothes. When TJ got downstairs no one was there, so he leaned back and closed his eyes. Just then Ana called his name. TJ jumped and then got up. They all got into Ana's car. Paula sat in the back seat with TJ. They made a point in sitting far apart. TJ took this opportunity to get some rest. He leaned his head back and closed his eyes. Paula couldn't help watching him sleep. This is one thing she had not done with him. She watched as his chest rose and fell. Paula wanted to kiss him. She remembered how he had kissed her, how soft his lips were. Paula licked her lips as if tasting something on them. She couldn't believe how taken she was with TJ. Paula wished that he was older, then she could actually form a relationship with him. She knew he had many years of growing up and experiencing life. Paula leaned her head back, but continued watching TJ.

Forty-five minutes went past. Ana announced that they had arrived at the mall. She pulled into a parking space. Everyone exited the car and walked towards the mall. TJ stayed with them for a little while and then went off on his own. They agreed he would meet them in two hours.

TJ found a gift for his mother, sister and father. He happened to see a trinket that reminded him of Paula. He noticed that she had a chain. TJ purchased the trinket. When he was finished shopping TJ went to where they had agreed to meet. He had an hour to wait. TJ called Ana and asked where she was. She wasn't too far. He met up with her and she gave him her car keys. Paula told her that she was tired and asked if she could wait in the car with TJ. Ana told her it was fine. Once they were out of site Paula put her arm in his. They walked to the car. They got in the back seat. TJ turned his Ipod up and leaned back. Paula leaned back on her side of the car. She closed her eyes.

"TJ you asleep?"

"No."

"You know I really like you."

"Really?"

"Yes. What you thought that I could have sex with just any guy?"

"I don't know."

"Well I don't. Do you like me?"

"Yes. You're very pretty and you have a great body."

"Do you think?"

"Yes. Paula do you mind me asking how old you are?"

"I'm nineteen."

"You're a freshman?"

"Yeah. My parents didn't have money for me to start school right away, so I had to work and save. I didn't want to take a lot of loans."

"You work and go to school?"

"Yes. I have work study. I get some grants, but it's not enough, so I do take out loans. Do you plan to go to college? That's a stupid question."

"No it's not stupid, but yes I plan to attend. I also plan to look into scholarships to take some of the burden from my parents. I've already started applying."

"You're in the 10th grade right?"

"Yes. I skipped eighth."

"So you're real smart?"

"Somewhat."

"Wow, good looking and smart."

"Thank you."

They became silent. TJ drifted off to sleep. Paula didn't go to sleep. She thought about what TJ told her about scholarships. They were out in the car a while before Ana and Karen returned. They tapped on the window. Ana was relieved when she saw that TJ was asleep on one side of the car and Paula was on the other side.

Paula reached over and opened the door. TJ remain asleep. When they returned home Paula hung out the rest of the day in Ana's room.....

Friday night the girls went out to a club. The girls danced all night. When they returned home the girls remained in Ana's room.

Saturday they got their things together. At eight Paula told Ana that she was tired. She went into her room. She laid in bed debating whether to go to TJ's room and have one last night with him. She toss and turned for an hour. She wondered what he was doing and if he was even in his room. Paula wondered if everyone was in their rooms. She finally got up. She opened her door and listened. When she didn't hear anything Paula quietly went to TJ's room. Paula tap lightly on his door. She checked the lock. It was open. Paula slowly entered the room. She closed and locked the door. As she had in the past Paula removed her clothes, but this time left her lingerie on. TJ had his eyes close and ear plugs in his ears. Paula went over to the other side of his bed. She slid in beside him and rested her head on the empty pillow next to him. TJ awakened and looked over. He looked surprised to see her. TJ took the ear plugs out of his ears.

"You look surprise to see me."

"I am, kind of. You didn't come last night."

"I couldn't get away. Are you happy I'm here?"

TJ got up. He went into his draw. "I told you, you didn't need to do that."

TJ looked back at her and smiled. He handed her a small box. "What's this?"

"Open it. It's just something that reminded me of you."

Paula sat up. She excitedly opened it. Paula smiled and then hugged TJ.

"It's beautiful. I love it. Thank you."

"I saw your chain."

Paula touched her necklace.

"Yeah I bought it, but didn't have any money to have anything put on it."

"Do you really like it?"

"I love it. I've never been given a gift before." TJ looked at her unbelieving. "Really. No guy ever thought enough or maybe didn't have the money to give me anything." Paula took her necklace off and placed the charm on it. She then put the necklace back on. For the rest of the night Paula showed her appreciation. For the first time she laid her head on his chest and fell asleep in his arms. She slept just a few hours and then awakened. Paula lightly kissed TJ on the lips and then got out of bed. She dressed and then left the room. Paula went into the guest room. She got her clothes ready to leave. Paula went into the shower and washed the week away. Paula laid down and went to sleep. When she awakened Paula got up, gathered her things, made up the bed and went into Ana's room. Ana was not in there. Paula picked up her things and went downstairs. Ana, Karen and Margaret were in the kitchen. When Paula came into the kitchen they said good morning.

"Good morning. Why didn't you wake me?"

"I didn't want to bother you. You seem like you were a little home sick, so I figured I'd let you rest."

"Thank you. I'm fine. I had a wonderful time."

Margaret said, "We enjoyed you. Come back soon."

"I'll try."

Ana ran upstairs and knocked on TJ's door. He came out of his room.

"I'm leaving little brother."

TJ hugged her.

"I'll see you Christmas."

"Come down and say by to Karen and Paula."

"I'll be down in a minute."

TJ took a quick shower and brushed his teeth. He then went downstairs. TJ spoke when he entered the kitchen. He walked over to Paula. He hugged her and told her it was nice meeting her and that he hoped to see her again. Paula returned his embrace trying to keep it casual and told him that it had been nice. She lightly kissed him on the cheek. Thomas came into the house. TJ helped him take the luggage out to the car. When everyone was in the car TJ waved. He watched as they drove down the street. When they were out of site TJ went back into the house. As he closed the door the phone rang. TJ ran to answer it.

"Hello."

"Hi TJ?"

"Yes."

"Did they leave yet?"

"Ana just left. Maybe you can call her on her on her cell phone."

"I didn't call for her. I called for you."

"What's up?"

"I'm around the corner."

"What are you doing there?"

"I had my father drop me off, but I didn't come in. I wanted to see you. Open the door."

TJ went to the door. When he opened it TJ saw Rosalyn come down the street. He held the door open. While he waited for Rosalyn he watched her as she walked over. When Rosalyn made it to the door TJ backed up and they entered the house. They went up to his room. TJ sat on the bed and motioned for Rosalyn to sit in his deck chair. She sat down.

"So what's this about?"

"I talked to Ana and she said that if we wanted to date she wouldn't stand in our way."

"So what are you saying?"

"I was just wondering."

"Rosalyn we haven't talked since June. You barely speak in school. What's this all about?"

"I really haven't seen you. After seeing you this week I would really like to get to know you better. Before we were experimenting."

"What about now? What will we be doing now?"

Rosalyn looked at him curiously.

"Are you seeing anyone?"

"Why do you ask me that?"

"You seem different."

"How?"

"I don't know. Maybe more mature?"

"Really?"

"Yes."

"So you think you want to date me?"

"Only if you want to."

"I don't know. That's moving kind of fast. Let's just get to know each other and take it from there."

"Would you like to do something?"

"What do you have in mind?"

"Remember we talked about working out. I would like to get a hard body."

"Go down stairs and I'll be right down."

Rosalyn left TJ's room. He quickly took a shower washing the night before off of him. He put on sweats and then went down to the basement. Rosalyn was laying on the weight bench. TJ adjusted the weights. He then instructed Rosalyn to stretch. He helped her loosen up. Rosalyn took in his smell and remembered their time together. TJ showed no sign of attraction to Rosalyn. He was dedicated in his exercise routine. When they were done the two relaxed and talked about school.….

After several months TJ and Rosalyn decided that they were good friends.……

When Ana returned to school she noticed that Paula had become a better student. Ana asked what brought on the change? Paula told her TJ. Ana looked at her curiously. Paula told Ana that he gave her valuable information. Again Ana was relieved. She had never seen anything, but Ana thought Paula was attracted to TJ. She worried that TJ would pick up on it. Ana noticed that Paula seemed happier. Paula told her that she had gotten another scholarship. Ana was happy for her because she had been struggling throughout the school year…

On their last day of school Paula came to Ana with tears in her eyes. Ana asked Paula what was wrong.

"I'm pregnant."

"Really?" Ana couldn't believe it. She hadn't seen Paula with anyone.

"We're friends right?"

"Yes. I'll do whatever I can to help you. Do you plan to keep it?"

"I'm too far along. I have to keep it."

"What about giving it up for adoption?"

"Maybe I should. The father isn't ready. Should I tell him or just give the baby up?"

"I don't know."

"Doesn't he have the right to know?"

"He might want to keep it. Are you prepared for that?"

"I'm not prepared for this. I didn't mean to get pregnant. I have plans."

"Did you take precautions?"

"I have my own method."

"Was condoms included?" Paula looked down. "Paula."

"I'm sorry."

"What about him? He has a responsibility."

"He didn't ask for this. He didn't expect anything. Please forgive me, I came onto him."

"You don't have to apologize to me, you didn't do anything to me."

Tears formed in Paula's eyes.

"Yes I did. I violated your trust." Ana looked at Paula confused. "Ana should I tell you who the father is?"

"If you want."

"Ana please forgive me. I'll do whatever the family wants." Ana remained quiet. Ana stared at Paula not believing that she had gotten herself in this mess and didn't understand why she was asking for her forgiveness. Ana knew she had high standards, but didn't feel like Paula should feel incline to live by her ways. "Ana I'm going into my sixth month." Ana still did not make the connection. She still looked confused.

"Six months? I don't remember you with any guys."

"I know. I kept it secret."

"Why?"

"Because you wouldn't have approved."

"Why, is he a creep?"

"No. He's a good guy. He's really nice and smart."

"So why wouldn't I approve?"

"Ana, he's younger than me."

"How much younger?"

"He's in high school."

Ana looked at her. "High school?"

"Yes."

"What, he's a senior?"

"No."

"Junior?"

"No."

"Paula, you're not serious. He's a freshman?"

"No, he is very handsome. He doesn't look as young as he is."

"Paula I can't believe you. You not only messed with a boy, but you didn't take precautions and got yourself pregnant."

"I know and I'm sorry."

"Do you think that you should put this burden on this kid or his family?"

"I don't know, but I think this guy wouldn't want his child in this world and not know it. What if this child end up dating their sibling."

Ana thought about her situation, her sister.

"Then tell this kid. Just be prepared. I'm sure this kid and his family is going to be destroyed."

"Again I'm sorry. Ana before I tell these people, I want you to know that you have been a good friend to me and I haven't so much. Would you like to know this guy's name?"

"Do I know him?"

"Yes."

"What's his name?"

For a moment Paula just stared at Ana. Tears formed in her eyes. After fifteen minutes of silence Paula said, "It's TJ."

Tears formed in Ana's eyes. She shook her head no.

"Yes. Ana I'm sorry. I didn't mean for this to happen. I'm so sorry."

"Paula he's just a kid. Why?"

"I was attracted to him. I was lonely."

"But he is my brother. Did he come on to you?"

"I know. He didn't. I came on to him. I'm so sorry."

Ana felt for Paula. Although she was angry Ana felt compassion for Paula. She thought to herself how she would not have wanted to be in Paula's shoes. Ana walked over to Paula and held her. Both girls cried. They cried a few minutes. Ana pulled away.

"Paula it's not for me to forgive you. It's not for anyone to forgive you. I think you need to come home with me. This isn't something you tell someone over the phone."

"I don't have the money to go."

"I'll pay your way."

"Thank you."

Chapter 4

ANA CALLED THE AIRPORT AND checked her flight.

"Let's go. I'll get your ticket when we get there. Do you want to call home now?"

"No. There's no need. She's put me out."

"Because of the baby?"

"Yes."

The cab came. The two girls got into the cab. They were quiet during the ride. When the girls arrived at the airport the cab pulled up in front. The girls got out. They gathered their luggage and went into the airport. Ana paid for a one way ticket and then checked in. They were able to sit together. The two girls hurried to the gate. When they got to their gate the plane was boarding. They quickly found their seats. Once the plane was on it's way Paula closed her eyes and fell asleep. Ana sat with her eyes closed thinking about Paula and her family situation. She wondered how TJ would take it and what he would want to do…...

When the flight arrived the two girls readied themselves. The two girls hurried off the plane and then went to baggish and claimed their luggage. After claiming their luggage the girls spotted Thomas and Margaret. Both girls walked up and hugged them. As they walked to the car Ana saw the curious look that Margaret gave Paula.

Margaret asked, "How was your school year?"

Ana answered, "It was great. Next year can I live off campus?"

"We'll see. So Paula are you with us for the Summer?"

"If you don't mind."

"No, we don't mind. Do you need a job?"

"Yes. I planned to look for one tomorrow."

"Ana always work at the hospital with me, if you like I can get you on."

Ana chimed in, "Mom, Paula would need to do light work."

Margaret looked at Ana in a questioning manner. On the way home Ana talked about the school year and the courses she had singed up for. She tried to keep her mother's mind off Paula being there and not thinking too much about why. Ana talked about the school year throughout the ride.....

When they arrived home forty-five minutes later, Ana told her parents that they needed to talk. Ana looked at Paula. She told Paula to go into the family room. Ana asked her parents to come into the kitchen with her. When they went into the kitchen Ana told her parents that she needed them to stay in the kitchen for a few minutes and that she would be back. Ana went up to TJ's room. She knocked on the door. When he answered the door Ana hugged him.

"Hey baby brother."

"Are you alright?"

"I'm fine. TJ I need you to come down to the family room."

"Why?"

"Just come on."

Ana took TJ's hand and they walked down the hall.

"What's going on?"

"You will see soon. Just follow me."

Once they got downstairs Ana squeezed TJ's hand.

"What's wrong with you?"

When they walked into the family room TJ immediately saw Paula. He took a step back. Ana felt it and put her hand behind his back.

"TJ I'm alright. I'm not mad. Paula needs to talk to you."

TJ looked at Paula wondering what was going on.

Ana said, "TJ sit down."

"I'm fine. Paula what's up?"

"TJ I'm sorry."

"For what? Why did you tell? I thought this was between us."

"I didn't mean to."

"You females talk about dudes talking."

"I only told because I had to."

"Why did you think you had to?"

"TJ please don't be angry at me. I didn't mean you any harm."

"So what is this? Ok you told my sister. She's not angry, so what do you want now?"

Ana interrupted, "TJ Paula needs you to listen to her."

"I am. I'm here."

"She's going to stay here for the Summer."

TJ looked at Paula.

"So you're saying that you want us to stay away from each other. Ok I got it. Anything else?"

"TJ that's not it."

"So Ana what is it?"

With tears in Paula's eyes she said, "TJ I'm pregnant."

Ana looked at her brother. He looked as if the wind had been let out of him. He was pale. He didn't say anything.

"TJ I'm six months. I haven't been with anyone else."

TJ walked over to her. Ana watched her baby brother. Her heart went out to him and she was proud of him. He took Paula into his arms.

"I'll get a job and I'll help take care of our baby."

Through tear drenched eyes Paula looked at TJ in disbelief.

"You want me to have it?"

"What else is there?"

"I thought maybe we could give it up for adoption."

"No."

Paula and Ana looked at TJ in amazement.

"TJ I don't want to quit school and you're still in high school."

"Paula I can't give my baby up. I can finish school sooner. They offered to skip me. I can double up."

"That's not fair to you."

"It's not fair (TJ looked down at Paula's stomach and pointed at it) that the baby can't know it's parents. If you want to walk away it's fine, but I want my baby."

"TJ."

"No. When you have the baby I will take it and raise it myself."

"How do you know your parents will support this?"

"If they don't I'll figure something out."

Ana eased out of the room. She went into the kitchen where Thomas and Margaret waited anxiously.

"Mom, dad follow me."

As they followed Ana, Thomas asked, "What's this about?"

"You'll see."

Before Ana and her parents entered the room Paula asked, "Are you sure about this?"

TJ rubbed Paula's stomach.

"Paula this is my baby. It's a part of me. I made this. I can't explain it, but I can't give it up. I love it."

Tears rose up in Paula's eyes again and she began to cry. Tears filled up TJ eyes. He held Paula and she held onto him. Ana and her parents came into the room.

Margaret asked, "What's going on?"

TJ looked up. He look at his father. Thomas' heart went out to him. He had a feeling what his son was about to say. Thomas moved closer to Margaret. He moved behind her and wrapped his arms around her. She held them unsuspecting. TJ held Paula closer, yet tighter.

"Mom, dad Paula is pregnant with my baby."

Thomas felt Margaret's body give way. He held her so no one would know. Margaret looked at TJ, then at Paula and then at Ana. She waited for them to burst out laughing. Then Thomas spoke.

"Paula are you sure?"

"Yes Mr. Gibson. I'm six months."

Margaret looked at the two of them.

Then she said, "Six months?"

"Yes maim."

"So what's your plan?"

"I'm keeping it mom."

Margaret looked at her son, not knowing whether to be angry at him or proud of him taking responsibility. She then looked at Paula.

"TJ do you know what this mean?"

"Yes mom, I'm going to finish school sooner, get a job and still go to college. I will just have to go to a college near home. Paula will return to school after she has the baby. She's going to continue with her plans."

Margaret looked at Paula with confusion.

"Mrs. Gibson I am sorry for being irresponsible. I told TJ that I would put the baby up for adoption. I never intended to destroy his life."

Margaret sat down. TJ looked at Paula.

"You haven't destroyed my life. You changed it. It's not a bad thing. It may seem like it right now, but things will work it's way out."

Thomas looked at his son. He was proud and amazed at the same time.

Margaret said, "Thomas what do you have to say about all of this?"

Thomas looked at TJ.

"I'm proud of my son. Yes these kids have gotten themselves into a bind, but it's not the end of the world. Our son is being responsible."

Margaret looked at her son and this lost girl with tenderness.

"Look you two are going to finish school. TJ is right, we are not letting this child leave this family. Ana I don't know if you remember your grandmother. You were young when she died. TJ she had been dead a year before you were born. Ana you were adopted by your father and you just found out that your biological father had a daughter. Your brother wanted to date your sister, this happened because we didn't keep in touch with your father. I was adopted. It is a long story, not for now, but I found out on my eighteenth birthday. I was devastated. For a long time I was angry. My adoptive mother died soon after telling me and I was too angry to reach out to my biological mother. This left me all alone and lonely. I will help take care of the baby while you guys go to school. What about your parents or have you told them."

"Mrs. Gibson my parents kicked me out."

"I'm sorry. You can stay here with us. There will be nothing going on here, Understand?"

"I promise Mr. and Mrs. Gibson."

"Both of you are going to finish school as planned. Paula if you want to go out on your own my son has decided to take on the responsibility of bringing up his baby. You can live here as long as you like. We will help you as much as possible. TJ you understand what you have decided to take on?"

"Yes mom."

"Ok, Ana and TJ get Paula set up in her room. I'll go prepare dinner."

Ana and Paula started up the stairs. TJ grabbed Paula's bags. He followed them. When they got in the room TJ put the bags down.

"Ana can I talk to Paula alone?"

"Ok." Ana left the room.

TJ sat on the chair. He pulled it up to the bed. He put his hands out.

"Sit down." Paula took them. "Paula is this ok with you? I didn't mean to take over."

Paula let go of his hands. She put her hands on the side of his face.

"TJ you have been perfect. You're handling this better than I have. You are going to make some woman a wonderful man. I wish this was a different time in our lives. I have to ask. Are you sure you want to do this? After I have the baby I want to go back to school."

"I know. I'm not going to change my mind. Have you been to the doctor?"

"Yes. I went to a free clinic . They gave me prenatal vitamins and I've been taking them." TJ looked at her. "I didn't know what I was going to do, but I knew that I didn't want anyone to get an unhealthy baby, that's the least I could do after being so irresponsible."

TJ put his arms around her. She went into them. They stayed that way a few minutes.

"Paula it's wonderful being with you. Can I?"

"Sure."

TJ rubbed Paula's stomach.

"There's really my baby growing in there?"

Paula placed her hand on the back of TJ's hand.

"Yes."

TJ looked up.

"I just felt the baby."

"Really?" TJ stayed still, with his hand on her stomach.

"Yes. I don't think that you can feel it yet."

Ana came into the room.

"What's going on?"

TJ answered, "I was trying to feel the baby move."

Paula said, "I felt the baby move."

"Really?"

"Yes, but I don't think anyone else can feel or see it until I'm a little further along."

"Are you hungry?"

"A little."

"I think my mother is just about finished cooking."

The three went downstairs. Margaret had just finished cooking and begun placing the food in dishes. Ana began to help. Paula sat down.

"TJ go up stairs and tell your father to come eat."

TJ left out of the kitchen and went up to get his farther. When TJ knocked on the door, Thomas told him to come in. TJ entered the room.

"Son come in."

"Dad dinner is ready."

"I'll only be a few minutes." TJ sat down. "It was honorable for you to keep the baby and want to raise it. You should understand that it's a huge responsibility and there are some things that you are going to have to give up."

"I don't do anything or go anywhere anyway."

"No not now, but there may come a time that you may want to go out with your friends and you're not going to be able to because you have to stay with your baby."

"I'll be alright."

"I know you will. I just want you to know what you are giving up, but I can't tell you only life can show you."

"You sound like mom now."

"That's from years of being with her. TJ do you care about this girl?"

"I do."

"Not love."

"No. We were just enjoying each other."

"Without precautions."

"I know you told me. I know it's not an excuse, but I thought she had taken care of it. I mean she was older and was experienced."

"Well I guest experience doesn't mean all that much."

"Yes."

"Are you sure you want to stay home? Me and your mother will take care of the baby if you want to go away to school."

"Thank you dad, but I want to take care of my child. I did this. You told me to be responsible so now I am."

"I didn't mean it in this since."

"But it's still my responsibility."

"Yes it is."

"Then I will be responsible."

"Ok. Just know we're here."

"I know. Thank you dad."

Thomas put his hand on TJ's shoulder.

"Let's go downstairs."

Thomas and TJ went down to the kitchen. The table had been set and the females were sitting around it talking. When Thomas and TJ sat down Margaret ask them to take hands. They bowed their heads and Margaret said a prayer. They pass the food to each other and then began to eat.

While they ate Margaret told them the story of Ann. She explained how Ana got her name and how she came to meet Thomas. The kids listened, amazed at what Margaret shared. It made Paula feel better about her choice about walking away. She was confident that the baby would be in good hands and be happy.

That night Paula went to bed and prayed. She thanked God for blessing her with this family and asked him to watch over her baby....

When Monday came Margaret took Paula with her and Ana to work. A week later Paula started work.....

She and TJ became closer as her pregnancy progressed. TJ accompanied Paula to her doctor's visits. Paula and TJ spent a lot of time talking about the baby and their future plans....

A month had gone past. Paula and TJ were left home alone. Paula had gone up to her room. Her door was opened. As TJ walked pass the baby kicked.

"TJ."

TJ came into her room.

"Yeah."

"Come here." She patted the bed. TJ sat next to her. She reached over and took his hand.

"What are you doing?"

"Just be still." She placed his hand on her stomach. After a few minutes the baby kicked again. TJ looked at Paula.

"It's the baby."

"Really?"

"Yes."

"The baby kicked." TJ looked at her.

"Yes."

TJ sat there continuing to hold his hand on her stomach. The baby kicked again.

"This is great. Thank you."

"Thank you."

"For what?"

"Being so great about all this."

Paula lightly kissed TJ on the lips.

"What was that for?"

"I just wanted to thank you."

"You don't have to. Both of us did this."

"TJ."

"Yeah."

"Do you think that you can hold me?"

TJ looked at Paula and saw the sadness in her eyes. He knew this must be a lot for her. He turned his body and placed his arms around her. She placed her head on his chest. Tears rolled down her face. TJ heard her sniffle. He pulled back and looked at her.

"Don't cry."

"I don't mean to."

TJ smoothed his hand down her face. He kissed her.

"TJ."

He looked at her.

"No."

"What could it hurt?"

"My parents."

"They're not here. They won't know. I need you to hold me."

"I am."

"TJ it makes me feel better."

"Paula."

"Please….."

TJ left Paula's room before his parents came home. He went into his room and showered. He couldn't believe what he and Paula did. TJ thought about their relationship. He laid in bed.....

The next month TJ tried to figure out his relationship with Paula. Whenever Paula and he were alone they would go into her room. They figured that Paula couldn't get any more pregnant than she already was.....

In Paula's ninth month after they had sex TJ got down on his knee. He took her hand.

"TJ thank you for being such a good guy. You don't love me. We both started out just enjoying each other. That's what we are still doing. I know I coax you into having sex. Thank you for not making me feel bad. It's wonderful that you are willing to give up your life, but I can't let you do any more than you're already doing. I love you for being the special guy that you are, but I'm not in love with you, not what is needed for a good marriage." Paula smoothed her hand over his face. "Let's just continue enjoying each other. Come up here....."

Two weeks later Paula started having pain. TJ was home alone with her. Paula tried to do what she was told. The pain continued. TJ instructed her to time her contractions. As the contractions got closer TJ called his mother. She instructed him to call a cab. TJ did as he was instructed. When they got to the hospital TJ helped Paula walk into the hospital. He gave the nurse Paula doctor's name. Paula was taken to the examining room.

As the doctor was checking her Paula got a strong contraction and then her water broke. After she was cleaned the doctor checked Paula and determined that she was ready to give birth. They wheeled Paula to the birthing room. TJ was nervous. He did as he was instructed. The baby was coming quickly......

By the time Margaret and Thomas arrived at the hospital their grandson had come into the world. TJ was ecstatic that he had a son.

Soon after the birth Paula was moved to a private room. While they were alone TJ bent down and kissed Paula. He thanked her for his son. Paula couldn't believe TJ's reaction. She felt relief that she was no longer pregnant. TJ got on his knee. He took Paula's hand.

"Paula."

"TJ don't. You are doing enough by raising our child. You've given up enough. I can't take your youth by making you a husband. I've taken enough. Now get up."

Just as TJ was getting up a nurse brought his son into the room. She pushed the baby to the bed.

"You have a beautiful baby."

Simultaneous TJ and Paula said, "Thank you."

After the nurse left TJ picked his son up. He began talking to him and then asked, "Would you like to hold our son?"

Paula was hesitant and then she answered, "Bring him here."

TJ gently placed their son in her arms.

"He's beautiful TJ."

"Of course, he has a beautiful mother."

"TJ you are the sweetest guy I've ever met."

Just then Ana, Thomas and Margaret walked into the room.

Margaret said, "Sorry we didn't make it."

"TJ was perfect."

Thomas looked at him. He patted his son on the back.

Margaret walked over to Paula.

"May I?"

Paula lifted the baby. Margaret took the baby. She walked over to Thomas.

"Look at him. He's beautiful."

"Of course, he's my grandson. Oh that sounds old."

"That does. I'm Nana."

Everyone laughed.

Ana asked, "So what is my nephew's name?"

Paula looked up at TJ.

Thomas said, "He's going to be the third."

Ana said, "Tommy Jay."

Everyone looked at Ana and then agreed on his nickname. The group stayed until the end of visiting time. TJ kissed his baby before he left. After his family left the room TJ walked over to Paula and kissed her on the lips. She returned his kiss. After he left tears filled her eyes. Paula realized that she was in love with TJ. She hadn't meant to. Paula got out of bed and picked her son up. She began to talk to him. "Sweetheart I didn't mean for any of this to happen. I love you and your daddy loves me. But we can't be together because he's too young.

He like you have a whole life ahead of him. You're going to stay with him and his family. I have to make a life for myself. You are going to be in good hands. I promise." Paula kissed her son. She held him to her breast and fell asleep…. Tommy Jay awakened. She realized that he was hungry. She got up and got his bottle. Paula sat down and fed her son. The nurse came in to check on her.

Soon after the doctor came in. He checked Paula. The doctor told her that she was able to go home. After he left Paula called Ana. She told her that she was being released. After getting off the phone Ana knocked on TJ's door. He walked over to the door and opened it.

"Hey, Paula's getting released today."

"Can you take me to get her?"

"Sure."

"Give me ten minutes."

"I'll be downstairs."

When TJ came downstairs Ana was in the kitchen.

"I'm ready."

Ana got up and they drove to the hospital. When they got up to Paula's room she and the baby were dressed and ready. She and Ana carried their bag. TJ carried his son to the car. He strapped him in and sat in the back with him.

When they got home Margaret and Thomas were there. They welcomed Margaret back and celebrated Tommy Jay's first day there. TJ helped Margaret up to her room and his family followed close behind. When Paula opened the door she was surprised. The bed had been moved over so a crib and table could be placed in there. Although the baby slept in Paula's room many nights TJ came in to get the baby and feed him to give her a chance to rest.

The next week Ana got ready to return to school. She told Paula that she would be waiting for her when she return to school. Margaret and Thomas agreed to let Ana have an off campus apartment….

They drove down with her to check the apartment out. When they arrived at the rental office the manager took them out to see it. The area was nice and the outside of it was clean. There wasn't anyone hanging outside of it. Inside was also clean. It had a small kitchen, living room and two bedrooms. She was to share the apartment with Paula. It actually proved cheaper than the dorms. Steve was still contributing to

Ana's education. Margaret and Thomas stayed with Ana a week to make sure everything was in order. They purchase an inexpensive bedroom, living room set and kitchen furniture. They also purchased a months worth of grocery....

While they were away from home TJ and Paula took care of Tommy Jay. TJ felt as if he and Paula were a couple. A couple of nights they drifted off to sleep together while waiting for the baby to fall asleep. They awakened together and bathed the baby together. There were also a few times when TJ wanted to be intimate, but Paula resisted the temptation. Paula now realized that she had to somehow fight her urge to be any closer to TJ. It was hurting enough knowing that she would be leaving soon and one day he would decide to be with someone else. Paula knew that her emptiness and need to fill it had cost a lot. She looked at her son and hoped that these loving people will be enough so he would turn out healthy, not like his mother, needy. Paula watched TJ as he cared for his son and knew not to worry......

TJ had decided to go to school on line so he could be there for his son the first year. After six weeks Paula left. She kissed her baby and told him that she loved him. When she hugged TJ he knew that she loved him He returned the embrace and then let her go.... Thomas and TJ drove Paula to the airport. After she went to her gate he and his father returned home. TJ went up to his room. After an hour alone he went downstairs to the kitchen where his parents were. He asked permission to move into the guest room. He told them that he did not want to move the baby from what he was use to. His parents knew that he wanted to keep a piece of Paula even if it was just the room she slept in. They told him it would be ok. TJ immediately moved what was most important to him into his new room. His first night there TJ smoothed his hand over the side of the bed that Paula slept in. He laid on that side trying to remember the feel of her. He closed his eyes and remembered her face, her smiles. His eyes became wet from the memories. As if the baby sensed it he awakened. TJ picked him up and laid Tommy Jay on his chest. Holding his son TJ finally fell asleep......

The next morning Margaret awakened. As she was walking pass TJ's new room Margaret heard the baby. She knocked, but got no answer. Margaret checked the door knob. It wasn't locked. She opened the door.

Margaret saw that TJ was still asleep. Tommy Jay was still in his arms. As Margaret went to take the baby out of his arms TJ awakened.

"Hi mom. I got him."

TJ got up. He held the baby to his chest, trying to soothe him. TJ went downstairs. Margaret followed TJ down to the kitchen.

"TJ I'm proud you have been responsible, but you don't have to do this by yourself."

"I know mom. I'll let you know when I need help."

As TJ fixed Tommy Jay's bottle Margaret played with him. When the bottle was ready TJ and Margaret talked while he fed his son....

Months went by and Thanksgiving was coming up. TJ was excited. He figured Tommy Jay would get to spend some time with his mother.

The week that she and Ana was to come up Paula said that she needed to study. Margaret noticed TJ's disappointment. She sat down and tried to bring him comfort.

When Ana came home she picked up Karen and Rosalyn.

When they came over they were surprised when TJ came downstairs and was carrying the baby. They gathered around TJ and the baby. Rosalyn looked at TJ. He couldn't make out the expression.

Rosalyn asked, "Who's baby?"

"He's mine."

"No he's not."

"Ana tell her."

"It is."

"Whose else?"

Ana answered, "Paula."

"Paula?"

"Yes. Remember my friend from college?"

"Really? Isn't she older than you?"

"Yes, she has me for about two years."

"Where is she?"

"She couldn't make it. She has catching up to do with school."

"What about the baby?"

TJ interrupted, "He has me."

Rosalyn said, "I can't believe she's not here with her baby."

"Everyone has a choice. She's trying to better herself."

"What about you?"

"I am. I'm going to school at home this year and return next fall."

"It seems like you're the only one giving up something."

"That's cause you look at things the way everyone else does. You think that a mother is suppose to give up her life, because maybe somehow it's her fault that she got pregnant and it's ok if the guy goes about his business. He doesn't have any responsibility in any of this."

Rosalyn looked at TJ surprised. She couldn't believe that he was capable of being such a person. She admired him.

"I didn't mean to offend you."

"You didn't. I apologize."

"No, don't. You are right. So I was never in bad company."

TJ looked at her curiously. He gave her a sly smirk and then excused himself. Tommy Jay had fallen asleep. TJ took him upstairs and put him to bed. Soon after TJ heard a knock on the door.

"Come in."

Rosalyn came into the room. She walked over to the crib. She looked at the baby while he sleep.

"He is beautiful."

"Thank you."

"If you don't mind me asking, what happened?"

"I don't know what you're asking."

"Why her?"

TJ looked at Rosalyn in a questioning manner.

"I mean let your guard down."

TJ thought about the question. He looked at Rosalyn. He recalled their moment in time.

"I don't think I ever thought when I was with Paula." Rosalyn looked confused. "Paula was different than any girl I ever met. She was free spirited. She knew she had sexual desires and didn't hold back."

"So she did things."

Without realizing it TJ smiled.

"Yes, she did things." Rosalyn showed jealousy. TJ continued, disregarding Rosalyn's expression. "I loved her. It didn't start out that way. As Paula said often, we were just having fun."

"Why didn't you use protection?"

"Paula said not to worry. I know it was foolish, but like I said I didn't think when it came to her."

"Were you angry when you found out that she was pregnant?"

Before he answered TJ thought about the question.

"No. I wasn't really shock either. When Paula told me that she was pregnant I accepted the responsibility. Rosalyn I asked her to marry me."

Rosalyn looked at him, not believing what he was telling her. Although they had decided to be friends something inside hurt. Rosalyn's eyes became glassy.

"She said no." Relief showed in her face.

"Why?"

"She said that she couldn't ask me to give up everything. She felt like I had given up so much. I don't think that I have. She thought of giving the baby up for adoption."

"You didn't consider it?"

"No. I don't want my child not knowing who I am. Look at him. I would miss this."

"You could have more."

"Knowing my child is growing up not knowing his true family, no amount of children would be able to replace him."

Rosalyn looked at TJ. She was impressed.

"TJ you are a catch."

"I know. That's what I kept telling you."

Rosalyn smiled. "I know. I think this is better."

"Are you sure?"

"I think you have enough on your hands."

Ana came up to TJ's room.

"Hey what's going on?"

"I came up to talk to my friend."

Ana sat on the bed.

"He's gotten bigger since I left. I'll be back."

Ana left the room. She rushed down the hall. Ana was only gone a short while. When she returned Ana was carrying a camera. As soon as Ana walked in the room she took a picture of TJ. Then she walked over to Tommy Jay's crib and took his picture.

"What are you doing?"

"I'm going to make a book for you and Paula. When I'm at school you take pictures of everything my nephew does and when I come home on break I'll arrange them."

Karen came upstairs. As she was walking pass TJ's room she noticed them in the room.

"There you are. What I wasn't invited to the party."

Ana said, "I didn't mean to stay up here. I came up to tell you that mom ordered pizza."

"Ok I'll be down in a little while."

The girls left TJ's room….

TJ enjoyed Ana's visit. He was surprised how close Ana was to Tommy Jay. Tommy Jay also seemed to love his aunt. When she left to return to school TJ handed Ana a letter with some pictures of the baby in it….

Chapter 5

WHEN ANA RETURNED TO HER apartment Paula was there studying. Ana gave her the letter and pictures from TJ. Paula looked at the pictures. Paula smoothed her fingers down the pictures.

"Isn't he beautiful?"

"Yes he is. He's getting big."

"Yeah I couldn't believe it when I saw him."

"How's TJ doing?"

"He's taking such good care of Tommy Jay. He barely let anyone help. I took Tommy Jay one day and we spent the day together. He is such a good baby. TJ has him on a schedule for eating, naps and bedtime. I'm so proud of my bother."

"He's a good guy."

"Paula why don't you go back with me when I go home for Christmas break?"

"My parents called while you were gone. I told them about the baby. They want me to come home for Christmas."

"So you won't be able to see your son?"

"Ana right now I'm trying to take care of me. I haven't spoken to my parents since I got pregnant. While you were gone I happen to call them. I told them about the baby and what was decided. They invited me to come home for Christmas."

"Did they say anything about Tommy Jay?"

"No. They were happy I was still in school."

"Well I guess it's good that they at least want to see you."

"You're not mad are you?"

"Paula you don't have to worry about me."

"What does that mean?"

"Nothing really. If you're willing to give up watching your child grow up that's on you. My brother has been very responsible and is devoted to his son. I'm confident that Tommy Jay will be healthy. I plan to make you a book of his accomplishments and we will tell him his mother loves him."

"Ana I do love Tommy Jay and I'm sorry if I'm being selfish, but I have to succeed."

"I guess it's a price you pay for wanting success."

"Maybe so. Ana let me go. I have to study."

"Ok. I'll see you in the morning."

Paula went into her room and sat on her bed. She opened the letter that TJ sent her.

> *"Hi Paula,*
>
> *It seems like a long time since I held you in my arms. I miss our late nights. I wonder if I'll ever feel the way you made me feel. I hope all is well with you. I'm staying out of school this year. I'm going to school at home. I'm returning next year. It'll be my senior year. Well I don't have to worry about prom night, you know getting anyone pregnant. I know it's not funny, but it is amusing.*
>
> *Paula our son is growing big so fast. I can't believe it. He smiles so much and when I talk about you he acts like he's talking."*

Paula thought to herself, "Yeah he's probably asking where is that horrible lady."

> *"I know what you told me, but I hope you change your mind about getting to know him. I know he's young, but he is smart. I changed my room. I'm in the room that you slept in. Wish you were here. I'm going to end this letter now. I'll give our son a kiss from his mother.*
> *Love you TJ."*

Paula kissed the letter and then closed it. She placed it along with the baby pictures in her dresser. Paula went back to studying. She thought about TJ's letter a few minutes and then scolded herself. Paula decided to go to bed. She laid there a few minutes wondering what TJ was doing, wondering if he was thinking of her. Paula finally drifted off to sleep….

As time past Paula and Ana spent much of their time studying for examines. After her last exam Ana packed. She said goodbye to Paula….

After Ana left Paula called her parents to make sure she was still welcomed. Her mother answered the phone. They talked a few minutes and then hung up. Paula gathered her things. She called a cab. When the cab arrived Paula was waiting outside. She got into the cab. Paula was excited to be returning home. She wanted her parents to be proud of her. When the cab pulled up in front of her parent's house Paula quickly gathered her things. She paid the cab driver and exited the car. As Paula walked up to her parent's home she wondered if she should ring the door bell or use her key. Once she got to the door Paula chose to ring the door bell. After a few minutes the door opened. Paula's mother hugged her. Paula felt good knowing that she had been missed. Her mother told her to come in and put her things in her room. Paula walked to her room. When Paula opened the door, she noticed that her room had remained the same. Paula went into her room. She sat on her bed. Paula was happy to be back in her room. Her mother did not come into the room. When her father came home Paula was called for dinner. They sat down for dinner. While they ate the three of them discussed school. Paula was proud to say that she was on the dean's list. Tommy Jay was not mentioned…..

After the group finished their meal, before they got up Paula's father told her that she could return home. Paula jumped up, briskly walked over to her father and hugged him. When she went into her room Paula laid across her bed. She was very happy. Paula dialed TJ's number. He answered on the second ring.

"Hello."

"Hi TJ."

"Hi you. How are you?"

It made Paula feel good that TJ didn't sound angry that she didn't come for Christmas recess.

"I'm doing alright. I'm home with my parents."

"Really?"

"Yes. My father told me I can come home."

TJ was quiet for a little while.

"That's good. So everything's working out to your satisfaction?"

"Yes. I made the Dean's list."

"That's great. I did rather well myself."

"I'm happy for you. I got your letter."

"Good."

"What are you doing?"

"I was just laying here."

"Me too and I thought of you. I wanted to share my good news with you."

"I'm glad you did. What do you have planned for the holidays?"

"Nothing. I'm going to just enjoy my family. Could you do me a favor?"

"What's that?"

"Tell your mother I said thank you for her help. Also can you tell Ana that I appreciate her friendship. Tell her that I'm staying home, that I won't need a space for the next school year."

"Why don't you tell her? I'm sure she'll be happy to hear from you."

"I don't know. She's mad with me."

"Why?"

"Because I've chosen to go after my career."

"Believe me she understands. That's why she doesn't date. She doesn't want anything preventing her from obtaining her dream."

"You really think so?"

"I know so. Don't let your friendship go."

"Ok you better be right."

"I am." TJ noticed Tommy Jay getting fidgety.

"Paula it was nice hearing from you. I have to go right now. If I don't hear from you before Christmas, have a Merry Christmas and Happy New Year."

"Merry Christmas TJ and I wish you and your family a great new year."

Both individuals wanted to say I love you, but didn't want to make the other feel obligated to return the sentiment or feel bad, so they just hung up the phone....

The holidays were over and Ana returned to school. She on occasion ran into Paula. Their conversations were brief and related only to school....

Tommy Jay was growing quickly. He had turned one year old. Ana tried to make up for Paula's absence by returning home whenever there was a recess at school. Ana felt partially responsible because she had brought Paula home.

TJ returned to school. Tommy Jay was put in daycare. TJ realized that he had missed school. When he got out of school he picked his son up. Margaret watched as TJ tried to juggle school, his son and a job. Margaret stepped in when she saw him tiring. She split up some of TJ's schedule. She would pick Tommy Jay up three times a week. Margaret enjoyed her grandson. She watched the baby on the nights that TJ had to work....

Tommy Jay was getting older. Margaret suggested that TJ turn the guest room into a bedroom for Tommy Jay. TJ moved his things back into his old room and began fixing his son's room up. Margaret helped TJ decorate the room. She took joy in helping TJ fix up her grandson's bedroom.

As the holidays quickly past Spring was approaching. He was now in the twelfth grade. The prom was coming up. TJ debated whether to go. A few girls had asked him. After talking it over with his parents TJ decided to attend. He did not accept any of the girl's invitations. Instead TJ asked Stacy Lawson. She accepted. She was eighteen years old. Stacy was quiet and stayed to herself. She was a pretty girl, not flashy. TJ knew that she was attracted to him. He often caught her staring at him. He would smile at her and she would look bashfully away.

Prior to the prom TJ was invited to Stacy's home to meet her family. Her parents were actually impressed with TJ. TJ did not divulge having a child. Actually no one other than Rosalyn knew about Tommy Jay....

The evening of the prom Margaret took lots of pictures. Ana wasn't able to come up so she instructed Margaret to make sure she took pictures of TJ with Tommy Jay. After Margaret had taken what seemed to TJ a thousand pictures he left in the limo. The limo driver drove him to pick up Stacy. When they pulled up in front of Stacy's house the limo driver parked and then got out of the car. He went around to TJ's door and opened it. He remained standing there. TJ walked up to Stacy's home and rang her door bell. Shortly after Stacy opened the door. TJ stared at her. After realizing that he was staring TJ spoke.

"You look beautiful."

Shyly Stacy responded, "Thank you."

Stacy's parents came to the door. Stacy's father shook TJ's hand and said, "Take care of my daughter."

"I will sir."

Stacy's parents took pictures of the two. Stacy's parents continued taking pictures until the limo drove away.

After they got into the limo and the door was closed TJ took a closer look at Stacy. He thought, "This girl is beautiful." Although the other girls who asked him to the prom were very pretty Stacy had a charm about her. She was shy which TJ thought was a turn on. She was pure, for Stacy was still a virgin. While this was a turn on for TJ it wasn't a requirement. It was just something about Stacy that was attractive about her. TJ started up a conversation to relax her. They talked a while and Stacy seemed to relax. TJ could tell she had never gone out on a date. He asked Stacy about it and she admitted it. While TJ talked to Stacy she either looked down or out the window.

Forty-five minutes later they had arrived at the banquet hall. The driver parked. He got out of the limo and opened the door for them. After exiting the car TJ put his arm out and Stacy took it. They walked into the hall. Stacy looked around in awe of it's beauty.

"I would love to have my reception in this place."

TJ looked at her.

"Are you planning to get married anytime soon?"

"No. I have my career to think about. Besides I don't even have a boyfriend."

"Have you ever?"

"No."

"Why not?"

"No one ever asked me."

"Really?"

"Yeah. You ask that like you're surprised."

"I am. You're beautiful." Stacy blushed. "Are you blushing? You are. What you've never been told how beautiful you are?"

"No. No one ever noticed me. Not even you."

"I noticed you. I asked you to go to the prom didn't I?"

"Yes, but you never noticed me before. By the way why did you ask me?"

"I noticed you. I didn't say anything the first time that I saw you because of my age. I was younger. I didn't know how the older girls felt about this young guy coming on to them. Then I had some things going on and then I worked on graduating early."

"I would have talked to you. I didn't realize you are younger."

"Yes. You have a problem with that?"

"No."

Stacy and TJ found their table. They spoke to the couples who had arrived before them. There was soft music playing. The couples mingled while they waited to be served dinner. After an hour the servers began going to each table bringing the appetizers, the salad and then the main course.

Soon after everyone were done eating desert was brought out, which consist of cake decorated with the schools color and ice cream. Stacy and TJ had eaten a small amount when the DJ picked up the pace of the music. TJ stood up and held his hand out to Stacy.

"Would you like to dance?"

Stacy stood up and took TJ's hand. They walked onto the dance floor. TJ spend Stacy around and then began dancing. The couple danced throughout the night, only resting to toast once.

The last song that the DJ played was a slow song. TJ took Stacy into his arms. Stacy told TJ she never danced slow before. He told her not to worry. TJ guided her. She rest her head on TJ's shoulder....

When the song was over the DJ said good night and the lights were turned up. The students began leaving. The limo driver was standing with the door open. Stacy got into the car and TJ followed. After they got into the car the driver closed the door.

Stacy took this opportunity to do what she had wanted TJ to do all night. She reached over and kissed him with a closed mouth. TJ looked at her surprised.

"What was that?"

"I didn't think that you would kiss me."

TJ was quiet for a minute. He thought about what Stacy said, then he moved closer to her. He put his hand under her chin. He kissed her lips. He continued to kiss her until Stacy parted her lips. Stacy put her arms around TJ's neck. The driver interrupted them. He asked where did they want him to take them. TJ asked Stacy was she ready to go or expected home right away. Stacy told him no. TJ asked the driver to take them to New York and drive around. The driver pulled off.

"That was nice. Where did you learn to kiss like that?"

"This is my first time kissing a guy."

"Really? I wonder what else you do great for the first time."

Stacy blushed and looked away. TJ put his arm around Stacy. He lifted her head up. TJ moved in and kissed Stacy again. They kissed for a while and then TJ pulled back.

"We better stop this."

"Why? I like it."

"I like it too and that's why we better stop."

"TJ I don't want to stop. I like you."

"I like you too, but I don't want to start something that we can't finish."

"Why can't we finish?"

"Why can't we finish?" TJ looked at Stacy. "Do you know what you're saying?"

"I'm saying yes."

"Are you sure?"

"TJ I like you. I always have and I want you to be my first."

"I feel honored, but this is a big step. What about waiting for marriage?"

"There's no promise of that."

TJ cupped Stacy's face.

"A beautiful girl like you shouldn't have a problem." He kissed her again.

"TJ I've never been kissed by a boy. You say that I'm beautiful, but no one ever approached me. No one ever noticed me. Why is that?"

"I don't know."

"So what are we going to do?"

"Are you absolutely sure?"

"Yes."

"So you want to do this?"

"Yes."

TJ turned his attention to the driver.

"Jerry."

"Yes."

"Take us to the Airport Hilton."

The driver looked in the back of the limo through the rear view mirror. He wasn't far from the airport. A few minutes later they pulled in front of the hotel. The driver got out and opened their door. TJ got out first and then held his hand out to Stacy. She took his hand. As they walked past the driver he put something in TJ's hand and whispered in his ear. TJ looked in his hand and smiled at the driver.

The driver had given TJ several condoms and whispered that he had two hours. TJ and Stacy went into the hotel. TJ was able to get a room. After obtaining a swipe card for the room the two walked off. TJ took Stacy's hand. They entered the elevator. TJ looked at Stacy. She looked nervous. As they walked down the corridor to the room, TJ continued to hold her hand until they reached the room. TJ put his swipe card in. The door opened. TJ held his hand out to direct Stacy. She walked into the room. TJ followed. TJ wanted to take his time with Stacy. He knew this was her first time and wanted her to remember this night with good thoughts. TJ took his jacket off. He went over to the radio and turned it on. He searched the stations. After a few minutes TJ found a station playing a slow song that he liked. He stood up straight.

"Come here."

Stacy walked over to him. TJ took her arms and put them around his neck. He smoothed his hands down her arms and body until he rested them on her waist. He began to dance, directing her body to move with his. After moving together for a few minutes TJ bent down and kissed Stacy on the lips. She returned his kiss. As the kiss became more passionate TJ stopped moving and held her closer. They remained where they were standing. As the kiss got more intense TJ moved his hands up to the back of Stacy's neck. He ran his fingers through her hair and held it. He took the hair pins out, making her hair fall. It fell over her shoulders. TJ stopped and looked at her. He thought she looked even prettier with it down. He was use to seeing it in a pony tale.

"What are you looking at?"

"How you look even more beautiful than before. You should where your hair this way."

"Really?"

"Yes. You really don't realize how beautiful you are."

TJ kissed her lightly on her lips. Then he turned her around. He asked, "May I?" Stacy nodded. TJ unzipped Stacy's dress. He eased it off her shoulders. TJ let it fall to the floor. TJ held his hand out and Stacy took it. She stepped out of the dress. Although her lingerie wasn't fancy they turned him on. He looked at every curve of her body. When TJ looked up into her face Stacy was blushing. "You look appetizing." Stacy didn't understand what TJ meant. TJ kissed her chest above Stacy's breast. He ran his tongue down the middle of her breast. Stacy stood still, not knowing what to do. TJ unhooked her bra and then took it off. He threw it where her dress lay. Stacy subconsciously placed her arms to cover her breast. TJ moved her hands to her side. "Don't cover them. They're perfect." He kissed her breast and caressed them. TJ moved down her body. Stacy trembled under his touch. "Are you cold?"

"No."

TJ smiled. TJ continued his pursuit. TJ stopped only for a brief moment to remove his clothes. He guided Stacy to the bed. He prepared himself and then laid next to her. He gave her instructions wanting her to enjoy her first time. When TJ felt Stacy's body was ready he joined hers. TJ laid back bringing Stacy to him. He kissed her and told Stacy that she was beautiful. They laid there together holding onto each other, quiet, while their bodies relaxed. TJ closed his eyes. Stacy looked down at him. She couldn't believe how handsome he looked. She kissed him lightly on the lips. His hands held her tighter and they were lost. Afterwards the two got up. They took turns showering and got dressed. They left the room. TJ put his arm around Stacy's shoulder. They walked to the elevator. Once inside the elevator Stacy put her arms around TJ. She leaned her head on him. The two remained in this position throughout the ride. They did not speak. When the elevator opened TJ's arm remained around Stacy's shoulder. She left one arm around his back. When the limo driver saw them he got out of the car and opened the door. The driver smiled as he saw them arm in arm. Stacy and TJ got into the car. They remained quiet. Stacy laid her head on TJ's chest. TJ sat back with his arm around her. He laid his head back and closed his eyes. TJ thought of their night. He had not expected to have sexual intercourse with Stacy. It had been over a year since he had sex. He wondered if it was right or wise to have sex with Stacy and take her virginity. He held her tighter wanting to make sure she didn't regret what they did. TJ and Stacy drifted off to sleep....

When the driver pulled up to Stacy's home he cleared his throat. TJ opened his eyes.

The driver announced that they had arrived. TJ softly called Stacy's name. She looked up at him.

"We're here beautiful."

Stacy sat up quickly. She tried to fix her hair. The driver got out of the car, walked around the car and opened the door for them. Stacy got out of the car. TJ followed. He walked Stacy to her door. When they reached the door they just stood there quiet.

Finally Stacy broke the silence and said, "I had a great time."

"I'm glad."

They were quiet again. Stacy looked at TJ. TJ saw sadness in her eyes. He lightly kissed her on the lips.

"I guess I'll see you in school."

"Yes you will."

"Soon we'll be out of school and then we won't see each other."

"Do you want to see more of me?"

Stacy looked down. She waited a few minutes before answering.

"TJ I know this was just for a day. It was wonderful. Are you going away to college?"

"No."

"Really?"

"Yes. Are you going out of State?"

"No. I'm going to Rutgers, New Brunswick Campus."

"I'm going to Rutgers as well."

"Are you staying on campus?"

"No. Are you?"

"Yes. I wanted to get away, even if it's not that far. Maybe you can visit me between classes."

"Maybe I will. Well I better go."

"Ok. Thank you for taking me."

"Thank you for doing me the honors."

TJ waited on the steps until Stacy closed the door. After she closed the door TJ turned and walked back to the limo. He got in and the driver closed the door. The driver got into the car and pulled off.

"So did you have a good time?"

"Yeah."

"She's a looker. She's your girlfriend?"

"No."

"Wow girls aren't like they use to be."

"They surprise me too."

TJ leaned his head back. He thought about the night. TJ remembered the prom. He smiled thinking of how they danced all night. Then TJ thought about after the prom. He smiled to himself of how he thought they would go to the prom and go right home. He wondered if Stacy really liked him or if what they did was a type of prom ritual. When he got home TJ said thank you to the driver and then tipped him. TJ went in his home and went upstairs. He looked in on his son. Tommy Jay was sound asleep. TJ lightly kissed his son on the forehead, fixed his covers and then left the room. TJ went into his room. He slowly took off his clothes, tired from the nights events. When he had taken his suit off TJ layed back. He was exhausted. TJ quickly fell asleep.

The next morning he heard a faint knock on the door. TJ forced himself to get up. When he opened the door TJ was surprised that it was Tommy Jay.

"Daddy."

"Hey man. What are you doing out of your bed?"

Tommy Jay smiled. TJ picked him up. Tommy Jay hugged him. "Let's wash you up." TJ took Tommy Jay to the bathroom and gave him a bath. He then took him down to the kitchen and fed him. TJ took him outside. TJ's cell phone rang.

"Hello."

"Hi, it's Stacy."

"Hi, what's up?"

"I was just thinking about you, so I thought I would call."

"That's fine. Excuse me. Come back here. Sorry I'm back."

"That's ok. So what are you doing?"

"Stacy I have to tell you something."

"What, you don't want me calling you?"

"No it's not that. What I'm going to tell you may change your mind about me."

"I don't think so."

"Stacy I have a nineteen month old son." Stacy was quiet. "Did you hear me?"

"Yes. So you have a girlfriend?"

"No. It's not like that."

"So do you visit with him?"

"No."

Stacy was quiet for a few minutes.

"So you don't see your son?"

"I'm raising him."

"You're raising him?"

"Yes. His mother couldn't raise him."

"Really? Why?"

"She's in college. She has dreams and a baby right now wasn't in it."

"So she just broke up with you?"

"No. We never dated." Stacy was quiet again. TJ picked Tommy Jay up and took him into the house. He took him up to his room and sat him in his play pin. Tommy Jay played alone. TJ sat in the rocking chair. He decided to tell Stacy about his relationship with Paula. Stacy remained quiet as he spoke. When he was done they both were quiet for a while.….

Tommy Jay began to cry. "Stacy my baby needs to take a nap. I'm going to have to get off the phone."

"Ok."

"Talk to you later."

"Ok."

The two hung up the phone. TJ smoothed his hand over Tommy Jay's back the way his mother taught him. Tommy Jay soon fell asleep. TJ got up and took Tommy Jay up to his room. After laying him down he left the room. TJ returned to his own room. He left his door crack so he could hear if Tommy Jay woke up. TJ laid down and fell asleep.……

Stacy did not call TJ again. He figured maybe it was for the best. He already had a lot on his plate. He didn't need a relationship on top of taking care of his son and doing well in college.……

Graduation came. TJ and his family was excited. It seemed as if Tommy Jay was aware. TJ dressed. He went up to the school to graduation practice. When he walked in he spotted Stacy. She saw him as well and walked over to him. He bent down and lightly kissed her on her cheek.

TJ said, "Hi."

"Hi." Stacy slightly smiled.

"How have you been?"

"Fine."

"So we finally made it. Are you excited about college?"

"Yes. I'll finally be able to do what I want and come and go whenever I want."

"My sister said that there's a curfew."

"Yeah, but it won't be like my parents."

Everyone began lining up.

"Well I guess we better get in line."

Stacy touched his arm. TJ stopped and looked at her.

"I'm alright with what you told me. I would like to meet him. I hope we can study together."

TJ gave her an approving look and smiled.

"I hope so. Maybe we can get together this Summer and you can meet."

TJ walked over to the side of the field that he was suppose to be on. He got in line. The group practiced for a while. As it got closer to the event the graduates lined up. The graduates chatted as the families filled the stadium. The graduates looked around in an attempt to find their families. TJ spotted his family. His father was holding Tommy Jay. When his father saw him he pointed toward TJ so that Tommy Jay would see him. Thomas took Tommy Jay's arm and waved at TJ. TJ smiled and waved back. Stacy happened to notice the scene. She looked over at TJ. TJ noticed Stacy looking. Stacy gave him a questioning look. TJ knew what she was asking. He shook his head yes. She formed the word cute. He formed the words thank you.

The ceremony began. Each graduate was called. When TJ stood to get his diploma his family cheered him on. When he was handed his diploma TJ felt proud. He looked out at his family and saw their smiling faces. He knew that this was the first step of many accomplishments.

After the graduation TJ met up with his family. They all hugged him. Ana told him that she was proud of him. TJ took Tommy Jay from his father. Tommy Jay wrapped his arms around TJ's neck. Just then Stacy and her parents walked over to speak to TJ. Stacy hugged TJ. They said congratulations to each other.

TJ said, "This is Tommy Jay."

Stacy touched Tommy Jay's hand.

"Hi cutie."

TJ said tell the pretty lady hi.

Tommy Jay said, "Hi."

Stacy's parents spoke to the Gibsons. After a few pleasantries the families parted.

Stacy's mother asked, "TJ's mother waited a long time before she had another child."

"That not his parent's child."

"They're raising their daughter's child. I can't believe she's going away to school. If she's going to get herself in trouble at least she could have stayed at home to help raise her child."

"Mom the baby isn't Ana's."

"Well whose baby is it?"

"That baby is TJ's."

Her mother and father stopped. They looked at Stacy. Stacy's mother said, "Why didn't you tell us TJ had a child? We wouldn't have let you go to the prom with him."

"Well it's a good thing I didn't know."

"You didn't know?"

"No I found out the next day after the prom. We were talking on the phone and then he decided to tell me."

"Well that's it. You're not talking to him. He has a child. Is he being responsible?"

"Yes he takes care of the baby himself with the help of his family."

"Where's the baby's mother?"

"She didn't want the baby. She lives and goes to school in the south."

"She just left her baby?"

"She wanted a career."

"Well you make sure you stay focus on school and don't get yourself into trouble. And leave that boy alone."

Stacy and her parents began walking again. Stacy was taken to a nearby restaurant. When they arrived at the restaurant the family had to wait to be seated.

After thirty minutes the family was seated. Stacy noticed TJ and his family seated a few tables away. Stacy glanced over to his table a few times. She watched how attentive TJ was with his son. Stacy admired the way TJ cared for his son.

Shortly after TJ and his family left the restaurant Stacy was ready to leave. After Stacy and her parents were served she told them that she was tired... Her father paid the check and the family left the restaurant.....

Once they returned home Stacy went into her room. She laid across her bed and thought about TJ. She found herself falling in love with TJ. Tears came into her eyes. She thought, "How can I be in love with this boy. He probably only felt sorry for me, so he took me to the prom. But what about our love making? How could he have been so gentle and the fact that he took me to a hotel rather than us doing it in the limo? I must be a sadist and the most desperate girl in the world. How can I be in love with a boy who only communication was during prom? But I am"....

During the Summer TJ worked full time during the day and cared for his son at night. On their weekends off TJ and Ana would take the baby to the park. Ana and TJ had become closer than they ever had been. As the Summer came to a close TJ and Ana readied themselves for college. At the end of August Ana gathered her things. She said her goodbyes to TJ and Tommy Jay. Margaret and Thomas drove Ana back to school.

After leaving Ana they decided to spend some time alone. They decided to ride up to Martha Vineyards. Thomas called and reserved a room......

When they arrived there Margaret commented, "This place is so beautiful."

"You are so beautiful."

"Thomas stop."

"Stop what? You are a beautiful woman." Thomas placed his arms around Margaret's waist. "You know we haven't been alone in a long time."

"I know. It feels strange."

"No it feels good. Are you hungry?"

"Yes."

"Well lets go somewhere and get something to eat."

Margaret and Thomas left their room and headed down the street. Coming into town Thomas had noticed a restaurant. When they arrived at the restaurant the two were quickly seated. They ordered right away. As they sipped on their drinks the couple looked out onto the ocean. They watched the people in the water. As Margaret watched a family with a boy and girl she remembered Ana and TJ. Margaret thought it would have been nice to have had more children, but after getting sick a short time after TJ was born she was told that she could not have any more children. Margaret was too afraid to try so she got a hysterectomy. Although she wasn't happy with TJ having a child at such a young age Margaret loved her grandson. She often thought of her mother and knew she would have gotten a kick out of a great grandson. She smiled to herself and thought, "Boy her mothers would have loved to meet their great grandson." Tommy Jay reminded her of TJ when he was a baby, so smart and well mannered. Thomas called Margaret's name, bringing her back. Dinner had been brought to the table. Margaret sampled hers.

"This is good."

Margaret took a fork, gathered some of her dish and fed it to Thomas.

"That is good. Taste mine."

Thomas fed Margaret some of his meal.

"Hmmh."

They finished their dinner and then left. The couple visited a few shops. Margaret couldn't resist purchasing a few items. After walking around a while Margaret and Thomas returned to their room.

"This feels nice." Thomas pulled Margaret to him.....

The next day the couple woke up early. They headed out to the restaurant for breakfast. After spending several hours there Margaret and Thomas left and headed to the boardwalk. They walked hand in hand, stopping at several shops. As it got late the couple headed home.....

Chapter 6

ANA GOT SETTLED IN SCHOOL. She took two extra classes so she would finish college with a double major....

As the school year progressed Ana struggled with two of her major courses. She went to see her guidance counselor. The counselor referred her to a tutor. Ana was hesitant about using a tutor, but knew if she didn't it's possibility that she would have to drop the classes. Ana called the number that she had been given. There wasn't any answer, so she left a message....

The next day the tutor named Marcus returned Ana's call. They scheduled to meet later that day.....

At two o'clock Ana left to meet Marcus at Starbucks. Marcus told her he would be wearing a grey and black jersey.

When Ana arrived there she looked around for him. Ana did not see anyone wearing the color shirt that Marcus described. Ana went to an open seat by a window. She wanted to see this Marcus before he came into the restaurant. Fifteen minutes lapsed. Ana knew that if Marcus was any good she needed his help. She went up to the counter and ordered coffee. When she returned to her table she noticed a handsome man standing in the doorway. She looked him over thinking how good looking he was. He looked her way. He was such an attractive man Ana couldn't help but smile. She quickly looked away. She pretended to study. The young man walked up to the counter and ordered coffee. After paying for it he walked over to Ana's table and stopped in front of it. Ana looked up into his big dark oval eyes. He wore a heavy blue sweatshirt and blue jeans that she was sure loved when he wore them.

Ana smiled at the thought and then put her head down, not wanting him to know what she was thinking.

He said, "Hi."

"Hi."

"May I sit?"

"Sorry I'm waiting for someone."

"You're waiting for me."

Ana became irritated, thinking, "How conceited."

The man saw her irritation.

"You're Ana right?"

Ana looked at him with confusion." I'm Marcus."

Ana looked at him in disbelief.

"You're late."

"I apologize. I was on my way and I spilled soda on my shirt." (Ana thought that explains the different color shirt) "I had to change."

"Since you're here I guess we should get started."

Marcus sat down. Ana opened her books.

"So what is it you're having problems with?"

Ana told Marcus. He took her pad and then a pen out of his pocket. As he wrote Marcus explained what he was writing. Two hours past and then Marcus asked Ana what she was drinking. Ana told him. Marcus got up and went up to the counter. He purchased two more large coffees. He brought them back to the table. Ana sipped hers. They began to study again. Two hours went by. Marcus looked at his watch.

"I'm starving. Would you like to go somewhere and get something to eat?"

"What did you have in mind?"

"I was thinking maybe go to Subway."

"That sounds alright."

"Don't worry we can study."

"So what are you driving?"

"Why?"

"I can follow you."

"Oh. We can take my car."

"No, that's alright."

"What's the problem?"

"I just think it would be easier and I don't want to put you out."

"You won't."

"Marcus we're wasting time. It's getting late."

"I guess you won't change your mind."

"No."

"Ok, let's go."

The two got up and walked out of Starbucks.

"This is me." Marcus was driving a late model blue BMW.

Ana thought "Wow." She tried to look unimpressed. She walked over to her car. Marcus got into his car. Ana watched as he pulled off and then followed him.

Twenty minutes later they pulled up in front of Subway. Ana turned off her car and began gathering her books. She heard a tap on the window. Ana looked up. She smiled and then opened the door. Marcus held his hand out and she took it. Marcus helped Ana out of her car. She reached in her car and got her books. When she stood up Marcus took the books. The two walked into the restaurant. They sat by a window. Ana liked the scenery.

The restaurant was a few feet from a small park area with a lake. In the park was a Gazebo with flowers surrounding it. Ana ordered a sandwich and soda. Marcus offered to pay for it, but she refused. After paying for her sandwich she went to sit down. He ordered his sandwich and pay for it. He then went over to the table that Ana was sitting at. Marcus noticed Ana looking out the window.

"Maybe we can go out there when it's warm. "

Ana looked at him curious. She didn't say anything. Ana opened her books. She looked over the pages that they had covered. Marcus took her lead and began where they left off. The two studied for an hour.

It began getting dark. Marcus asked Ana if she wanted to meet up again. She told him that he had been helpful and she would be fine. Marcus stood and put out his hand. Ana took it. She said thank you. Marcus walked Ana to her car. Ana got into it. Marcus handed her books through the window. Ana started her car. Marcus told her it was nice meeting her. Ana pulled off. She concentrated on what they had studied.....

When she arrived at her apartment Ana parked her car and went inside. She went into her room and sat on the bed. She opened her books. Ana read the books and then looked over her notes. She matched up the notes to the books. After several hours she laid back. She closed her eyes. Marcus' face came to her. She saw his smile clear as if he was actually standing in front of her. Ana noticed that Marcus had deep dimples in his cheeks and perfect teeth. She wondered if they were paid for or if he had been blessed with them. Ana felt a chill. She pulled the covers over her. Ana soon drifted off to sleep......

The next morning Ana awakened early. She took a quick shower and dressed. Her stomach was in knots. She arrived early to each class, which gave her enough time to go over her notes. Before the test began Ana closed her eyes and said a quick prayer. Ana began her test. During the test she remembered what Marcus told her.

After her last test Ana returned home. She was exhausted. All the studying and stress had gotten to her. She laid back and fell asleep. Ana did not awaken until the next morning. When she awakened Ana immediately turned her computer on. Ana went onto the school's website and looked to see if the grades had been posted. She saw that two of her classes had posted, but they weren't the ones that she was concerned with. Ana was happy that she had A's in both classes, but this did not bring her relief. Ana tried to watch TV for a while. She was restless. She called her friend Karen. Karen assured her that she had pass the test and everything would be fine. The two girls talked until Ana got sleepy. After getting off the phone Ana closed her eyes. She tossed and turned until finally falling asleep....

She awakened early the next morning. Although she was exhausted Ana dragged herself out of bed. She went to her laptop, opened it and turned it on. She went to the school's website. Waiting for the site to load seemed like an eternity. When the site was up Ana clicked onto the grades. Each class took equally as long to get her results. After seeing each grade Ana stared at them to make sure she was seeing correctly. After viewing the final grade tears filled Ana's eyes. Without thinking Ana dialed Marcus' cell phone. It rang three times. Just as she was about to hang up Ana heard a voice say hello.

"Hi. Did I wake you? It's Ana."

"Hi. Yeah, but that's ok. What's up?"

"I Aced all of my examines. Thank you so much."

"You're welcome, but I didn't do anything."

'I think you did. Do you have plans tonight?"

"I was going to that party at Beta House."

"That's what I was going to ask if you wanted to go there. I feel like celebrating."

"Great. Would you like to meet me there or do you want me to pick you up?"

"I can pick you up."

"Ana."

"I asked you out."

"Ok."

Marcus gave Ana his address. She arranged to pick him up at seven so they could get dinner before the party.

After hanging up the phone Ana looked in her closet, but did not fine anything that she thought was appropriate for the night. She dressed and then went to the mall. Ana searched a few stores and then found what she thought was perfect. Ana found a "Doobie" shop to get her hair done. After getting her hair done Ana went home. Ana ate some cereal to keep from being too hungry at dinner. She showered. Ana sprayed perfume over herself. She was excited. Ana had not gone out much while at school. She put her stockings on and then her dress. Ana took a look in the mirror. Ana looked at the time and then left. She hadn't realized that Marcus lived as far as he did. Ana looked at her watch and thought how she was still on time.

As she pulled in front of Marcus' apartment Ana dialed his cell phone. Marcus answered on the second ring. Ana told Marcus that she was outside. Marcus came out. Ana watched him as he walked to the passenger's side of her car. Ana unlocked the door. Marcus got in. They spoke and Ana pulled off. Marcus smiled showing his beautiful dimples and perfect white smile. He told her that he was happy to hear from her. He admitted that he was surprised and that no one ever called him back to say that they pass. Ana explained the importance of passing those classes and that she would be graduating in May. Marcus told her that he was happy that he was able to assist.

A few minutes later Ana pulled up in front of the restaurant. The two got out of the car and walked into the restaurant. They were seated right away. The waiter took their orders. While waiting for their food Marcus and Ana got to know each other better.

When they were finished eating their meal Ana insisted on paying for it. Marcus protested, but finally gave in with reservations. The two left the restaurant and headed to the fraternity house. Ana and Marcus sat in the car a few minutes before going into the house. They could hear the music. Finally the two exited the car and walked up to the house. The door was open. Marcus opened the screen and Ana walked into the house. Marcus walked in behind her. The house was full of people mingling and dancing. Marcus asked if Ana wanted to dance. She smiled and said yes. The two began to dance. They had to dance close because of the number of others dancing. Ana was having a good time. She looked up at Marcus and smiled.

Marcus said, "You have a beautiful smile."

"Thank you."

A female came up behind Ana and tapped her on the shoulder. Ana turned.

"Excuse me."

"Oh did I bump you?"

"No! You're dancing with my man."

"Oh. It's nothing."

"It didn't look like nothing. You looking up at him with dreamy eyes."

"I'm sorry if it looked that way. He did me a favor and I was just celebrating."

"Oh that's what they're calling it now?"

"No it's nothing like that. He tutored me."

"That's pathetic."

"Can you get your mind out of the gutter. He tutored me in a few courses and I passed so I thought it would be nice to celebrate."

"What, you don't have any friends."

"I apologize. I didn't mean any harm I just wanted Marcus to know that I pass."

"Well you thanked him, so be gone."

Ana looked at the lady. She started to say something, but decided against it. He wasn't her boyfriend, nor was she interested in getting involved. She would be leaving in a couple of months and will never see this guy again.

"Like I said I apologize for any harm I caused. Good night."

Ana left the house and walked over to her car. She got in, started it and drove off. As she drove to her apartment Ana thought of her dance with Marcus before his girlfriend showed up. Ana thought about their one dance all the way to her apartment. When she got into her apartment Ana undressed and went to bed. She closed her eyes. In it's darkness she saw Marcus' face. It was beautiful, strong and big brown eyes. After some time she soon drifted off to sleep....

The next few months Ana prepared to graduate and go home. She had been accepted at a medical school near her home in New Jersey. Ana had enjoyed her experience away from home, but decided that she would like to help her brother with his responsibility..... Graduation day had finally arrived. Ana's family flew down. She was semi-surprised and happy at the same time to see Steve, Shirley and Rosalyn there.

When Ana walked across the stage they all stood up and cheered. She looked out into the crowd and felt proud to be in the top ten. Ana was surprised when she saw Marcus. She wondered how she had never seen him before. She smiled at him. At first he looked surprised. He gave her one of his beautiful smiles and then winked at her. She blushed and then took her seat.....

When the ceremony was over Ana's family rushed over to her. They hugged and congratulated her. Some how Marcus made his way over to them. With all of the excitement and everyone hugging Ana had not noticed or realized Marcus had taken her into his arms and was hugging her. When he pulled away she realized it and looked at him surprised. He congratulated her. She told him the same. Margaret, Thomas and TJ were surprised to witness this exchange. When Ana noticed them watching she introduced Marcus to everyone. She explained that he had tutored her. TJ and her parents were equally surprised that Ana and this stranger seem to have something going on between them. They didn't press knowing that this was new to Ana and she seemed unaware of the connection. They moved away from Ana and Marcus to give them some privacy.

"Well I guess this is goodbye. Thank you again for helping me."

"It was my pleasure. So you're leaving tonight?"

"In the morning."

"So what are your plans now?"

"I'm returning to New Jersey. I've been accepted at a graduate school there."

"Really? That's good."

"Yes. Well it was nice to have met you, I better go."

Without thinking Ana reached up and kissed Marcus on the side of his face. "It was nice meeting you."

As she walked away Marcus called out "You too."

Ana and her family went to dinner. Her parents tried to get information about Marcus, but Ana was closed lip. She insisted that there wasn't anything going on.

The next day they loaded up Ana's car and the family were on their way back home. Rosalyn and TJ road with Ana. They drilled Ana about Marcus. Her family thought that she was holding out, but Ana had not thought much of her feelings, she didn't even realize that there were any feelings. She turned the questioning towards TJ. She asked him about college and Tommy Jay. TJ told her excitedly about his first year of college. Rosalyn also shared her college experience with them. After several hours of driving Margaret called Ana. She told her to stop at the hotel that was coming up. Ana did as she was told. Her parents got two rooms and Steve got a room for he and his wife. Ana, TJ and Rosalyn shared a room. The young people talked into the night until they finally drifted off to sleep....

The next morning Margaret called Ana to wake her. The group got ready, ate breakfast at the hotel's restaurant and were on their way.....

Several hours later the group arrived in Jersey. Ana made herself comfortable in her room. She laid in her bed and thought of her years away home. It was nothing extraordinary. She didn't allow herself to get caught up with the college scene. Ana had plans and so far she had not deferred from them. Ana's mind wondered to her night out with Marcus. She couldn't believe how easy it had been to talk to him. She wondered how it would be to date him, what kind of person he was and if he thought about her. Ana heard a knock on the door.

"Come in."

It was Margaret.

"Hi Baby."

"Hi mom."

"So are you happy to be home?"

"Yes. It was interesting being away. I enjoyed being on my own, but home is nice."

"Good. We miss you around here. Ana."

"Nothing mom."

"I didn't ask anything."

"You were going to ask about Marcus. He just helped me study. That's it."

"It didn't look that way."

"What?"

"The way he looked at you."

"What look?"

"The way he looked at you. Even you should have noticed."

"I don't know what you're talking about."

"Ana he likes you and you like him."

"Well that doesn't matter now. He's not here."

"Don't you have his number?"

"Yes, but we're too far away to even think of trying to have a relationship. Besides he has a girlfriend."

"Really? I wouldn't suspect that."

"I met her at a party we went to."

"You went to a party?"

"I was celebrating passing my classes. I called and told him. Then I asked him out to dinner and a fraternity party."

"You?"

"Yes. We had a good time at dinner and we danced once at the party. Then this girl came up and said he was cheating on her."

"What did he say?"

"I left."

"So you don't know for sure."

"It doesn't matter. Nothing could have happened. I came back home."

"Oh baby. Your first, what would you call it?"

"Nothing, because it was nothing."

Margaret hugged Ana.

"I love you baby."

"I love you too."

The next night Ana went out to a club with Karen. Karen noticed the change in her friend. Ana seemed to come out of her shell. She danced more and didn't have to be coached. She even accepted offers from two different guys to dance. Karen watched her friend and was happy that Ana was finally enjoying life....

Ana's family also noticed the change. Margaret wondered what had brought it out, but decided not to pry. Ana worked hard at the hospital and when she was not working went out with her friends.

At the end of Summer Ana seemed to turn back into the serious student she had been her entire life. She prepared herself for medical school.

Her first year was difficult. She didn't mingle much because Ana wanted to make sure that her grades remained as they always were. Ana didn't make many friends and she got through her first year and did well......

Ana was in her second year of medical school. One day she was walking to her last class. Someone tapped her on the shoulder. Ana turned. She smiled.

"What are you doing here?"

"Same as you."

"You attend school here?"

"Yes. Why are you so surprised?"

"I just am. You never mentioned that you were going to attend school here.

"It wasn't in my original plans." Ana looked at him curiously.

"So is this your first year?"

"No. I registered late last year."

"I'm surprised that I didn't run into you before now."

"I saw you a couple of times."

"Why didn't you speak?"

"You were a distance away and I figured I'd let you get your bearings."

"I wished you had. Well I have to go. I have a class."

"Yes I know." Ana gave him a suspicious look. "I'm in your class."

"Are you serious?"

"Yes."

"Why didn't you say something?"

"I just didn't."

"I can't believe that I didn't see you."

"You see your mind is too occupied for me."

"What do you mean?"

"You are all about school. There isn't any room for anything or anybody else."

"How do you know?"

"I am very observant."

"What do you have in mind?"

It was Marcus' turn to look surprised.

"I would like to date you."

"What happened to getting to know each other? How do you know you want to date me?"

"I think I know enough. Remember we spent some time together already."

Ana stopped walking and it was a disturbing look on her face.

"Are you sure you are free to date?"

Marcus looked confused.

"Of course. Why do you ask that?"

"Because the night that we went to that party."

Marcus thought about it. He looked as if a light went off in his head.

"Oh. I talked to Lisa for a month, things didn't work out. As you can see she has issues. It was never anything serious. I apologize for you having to go through that."

Ana began walking again.

"So why didn't you say anything?"

They made it to class. Ana sat in her usual seat. Marcus decided to sit in his usual seat as well. Ana couldn't resist. She looked back. Ana wanted to know how she didn't see Marcus. When she first looked, Ana didn't see him. She scanned the room and then as if by magic there he was. He was looking at her, with his beautiful smile. Ana looked at him a few seconds before turning around. She could feel the warmth of his look. She tried to focus on her notes. Once the professor entered the room and began Ana's mind automatically focused on him.

After the class was over Ana got up and walked out the door. Marcus caught up with her. He lightly touched her arm.

"Hey. You're trying to leave me?"

"No."

"So where were we?"

"I asked why didn't you explain your situation with that girl?"

"I was amazed and impressed at how you handled it. I thought about coming after you, but then I thought you wouldn't believe me at the time."

"Why wouldn't I believe you?"

"I thought that you needed to think it over. I knew Lisa wouldn't have let us talk, so I let you go. I thought of calling you, but then I thought of you leaving anyway. Can we start now?"

"Yes."

"What do you have planned now? Do you have another class?"

"What, I thought you knew my every move."

"No. I'm not a stalker."

"I apologize."

"No need. No harm done. So do you have any plans right now?"

"No."

"Are you hungry?"

"Not really, but I could eat something."

"Do you know Tony's?"

"Yes."

"Would you like to go there and talk a bit?"

"Sure."

As they walked Marcus resisted putting his arm around her shoulders. He knew with Ana he would have to take it slow....

For the next three months Marcus and Ana had a meal every day after leaving their last class. They would study together in-between classes. A couple of nights a week they would talk on the phone.

In November Ana decided to invite Marcus over to Thanksgiving. He accepted.

As it got closer to Thanksgiving Ana told her mother. Margaret was surprised. She told Thomas. Thomas went to talk to Ana. He knocked on her room door. Ana told him to come in. When he entered Thomas asked if he could they talk. Ana said sure. Thomas drilled her about Marcus. He was surprised that Ana knew as much as she did about Marcus. He noticed her face light up while talking about him....

Thanksgiving Day came. Ana was nervous. She had never had a boyfriend over. She wondered how her family would act.

At three o'clock the door bell rang. Ana stayed in her room. She listened to hear if it was Marcus. A few minutes later Rosalyn came up to her room. They talked a few minutes and then Ana told her the news. Rosalyn sat with a shock expression on her face. Ana asked, "Why are you looking at me like that?"

"Are you kidding me? You never bring any one around. Have you ever dated before?"

"No."

"So you are?"

"Yes."

"Seriously?"

"Yes. I never met anyone that was important. I had studying to do."

"Have you ever kiss a guy?" Ana put her head down. "Are you serious? Oh my gosh."

"Don't say it like that."

"I don't mean anything negative. That's really special. Do you think this guy will be your first?"

"I like him a lot."

"Wow. This is exciting."

The door bell rang. Ana sat still. Rosalyn watched Ana. She was amazed at how Ana lit up when her mother called up to her that she had a guest. Ana got up, looked in the mirror, fixed her hair and then left the room. Rosalyn followed close behind. Ana walked slowly down the stairs acting as if there wasn't anything to rush to. Ana made it down the stairs and entered the living room. When she entered Marcus stood up. He spoke. Ana returned the greeting. Once she noticed Rosalyn standing there Ana introduced them. Marcus held his hand out to Rosalyn and she shook it. Rosalyn sat quiet looking from Ana to Marcus. Tommy Jay ran into the room. Ana coax him to her. He ran up to Ana. She picked him up. Marcus looked at them curiously.

"He's cute."

"Thank you."

Rosalyn noticed Marcus' expression. Ana played with Tommy Jay a few minutes. She was happy for the distraction. A few minutes later TJ entered the room. Tommy Jay left Ana and ran to his father yelling daddy. Rosalyn noticed the relief that came over Marcus' face. Rosalyn smiled. Ana noticed. She looked at Rosalyn as to ask what. Rosalyn said, "Later."

Margaret came into the living room. She announced dinner was ready. Everyone got up and went into the dinning room. The group sat down. Margaret said grace. The food was pass around. Margaret noticed the occasional looks that Ana and Marcus shared between each other. After everyone was finished eating the group casually sat around the house. Thomas made his way to Marcus and Ana while they were alone. Ana was nervous listening to her father drill Marcus. A half hour later Ana had survived it. She and Marcus went down to the basement. Ana challenged him to a game of pool. They played a few games and Ana won each one. They sat and talked a while. Ana couldn't believe how much she was enjoying Marcus' company. TJ and Rosalyn came down and the two teamed up and challenged Marcus and Ana to a game. They ended up playing several games. As it got late the group sat and talked. Ana was impressed by Marcus' comfort with her sibling. Eventually Rosalyn excused herself and a few minutes later TJ followed. He walked over to Marcus and shook his hand. TJ then went over to his sister. He kissed her on the side of the face and said, "Don't be too long." After he was gone Marcus sat next to Ana. He placed his arm around her.

"We're finally alone." Marcus placed his hand under Ana's chin. "You are so beautiful." Ana had never been told this before. She didn't know what to say. She was nervous. Ana had never been this close to a guy before. She remained silent. "Are you cold?" Ana shook her head no. She trembled. "Are you nervous?" Ana didn't want Marcus to know that she had never been touched. "Would you like me to move?"

"No."

Marcus smiled. "So tell me what do you have planned this weekend?"

"Nothing."

"I would like us to spend some time together. Not studying, just enjoying each other."

"What do you have in mind?"

"I have heard about some historical sites in Philadelphia. I would like to take you there."

"I'd love to."

"Great. How about tomorrow?"

"Ok. What time?"

"How about ten and then later we can get dinner."

"I'd like that."

"Then it's a date. I should go. It's getting late." Marcus looked into Ana's eyes. She thought he would kiss her, but he smiled at her and then took her hands. He pulled her up to him. He held her hand as they walked upstairs. She walked him to the front door. Marcus said good night. Ana closed the door behind him and then ran up to her room. When Ana went into her room Rosalyn was waiting up for her.

"So what happened? Did you kiss him?"

"Nothing happened. We talked."

"You didn't kiss him?"

"No. I don't do that."

"He didn't try to kiss you?"

"No."

"Really?"

"We're taking it slow."

"How long have you known him?"

"I've known him over a year, but we just started talking. It takes time."

"To kiss? I don't know where you've been, but you kiss on the first date, even before you're a couple."

"I don't."

Rosalyn smiled.

"I had sex and I didn't even date the guy."

Ana looked at her.

"What was it like?"

"It was great, but that's because the guy knew what he was doing and he took his time. He wanted to make me feel good."

"I wonder if my first time will be that great."

"I'm sure it will. So when are you going see him again?"

"Tomorrow. We're going to Philly."

"Really? Where?"

"He wants to go to some historical sites and then to dinner."

"That sounds nice. So do you think you're let him kiss you?"

"I don't know. I may if he wants to kiss me."

Rosalyn got a concerned look on her face.

"Do you think you're his first?"

"Definitely not."

"Why not? No one would suspect you've never done it. Maybe I should retract that. If they didn't know you."

"You didn't know, but trust me I won't be his first anything."

"Ooh, you've thought about having sex with him."

Ana put her face in the pillow. The young women talked a little while longer and then went to sleep....

Ana got up early, showered and quickly dressed. She went downstairs. Margaret had cooked breakfast. Margaret told Ana that she had to go into work. She ask Ana what she had planned. Ana told her about going into Philadelphia. Margaret looked at her daughter. She was so proud of her. She was happy that Ana had found a young man that she liked, but was concerned because she knew this young man was her first boyfriend.

"Ana can I ask you something?"

"What?"

"Have you had?"

"Mom, no. I just started dating him. We haven't even kissed."

"Really?"

"Why is that so shocking to everyone. If you must know I have never done anything with any boy. Am I a freak?" Margaret looked at Ana with a surprised look. "I didn't have time. I was studying remember?"

"Yes I know. Don't get me wrong. I am overwhelm with happiness. That time is special and should only be shared with someone you really care about."

"You really think so?"

"Yes."

Margaret walked over to Ana and hugged her.

"Your grandmother would be so impressed with you."

"I wish that she was still here."

"Me too."

Thomas came downstairs.

"What's going on?"

Margaret said, "Just female stuff."

"Is everything alright?"

"Everything is fine." She kissed Ana on the forehead. I have to go. Have a good time."

"Thanks mom."

Margaret kissed Thomas and left. Thomas fixed him a plate and then sat down. Ana valued her father's opinion. She wanted his input, but didn't know how to ask him without him becoming suspicious.

"So what do you have planned while you're on break?"

"I have a date with Marcus today?"

"I take it you like this young man."

"Yes daddy. Do you like him?"

"He seems to be respectful."

"Do you think he likes me?"

Thomas looked at Ana.

"Of course he likes you. He wouldn't have transferred up here to be closer to you if he didn't."

"He told you that?"

"Yeah. I had a talk with him."

"What did you say to him?"

"That's between your father and potential boyfriend. It's something that fathers do."

The doorbell rang. Ana got up. She went into the foyer and opened the door. Marcus smiled."

"Good morning."

"Good morning. Would you like to come in, my mother made breakfast."

"No. I think we should get on our way."

"Ok. Let me get my coat."

Ana reached behind the door and got her jacket. She yelled bye to her father. Marcus opened the car door for Ana. After getting into the car Marcus pulled off. As Marcus drove Ana looked out the window. She thought about her conversations with her family. She looked over at Marcus. Ana wondered how it would be to kiss him. She scolded herself. Ana didn't want to complicate things. She just wanted them to enjoy themselves.

"Marcus."

"Yes."

"My father told me that you transferred here for me."

"I wanted to get to know you."

"Isn't that a bit extreme?"

"It could be viewed that way. Ana in just that brief time I knew that I wanted to get to know you. You were leaving and you live too far and long distance relationships are difficult. The school you were registered at is as good as the school I was going to attend."

"I can't believe you did that."

"Why not? When you care about someone that is what you do, besides I had applied here as well and had been accepted."

"You care about me?"

"What do you think?"

"How, Why?"

"I just do. Love just happens."

Ana looked at Marcus.

"Love?"

"I'm just saying. I'm here to find out."

"I've never met anyone like you."

"Is that a good or bad thing?"

"It's a good thing."

They were quiet for a while. When they arrived in Philadelphia Ana became chattery. She had never been to Philly. Marcus pulled up to a house that Ana thought looked normal, nothing special. The two exited the car. They walked up to the house. When they walked into the house Ana was amazed at the beauty. It had cathedral ceilings. She thought the original owners must have loved art, for the ceiling in the foyer had a mural on it. There were build in shelves throughout the house. The woodwork was extraordinary. The bedrooms were huge. There were three. Each room had high ceilings. The master suite had a canopy bed. It was old style. Drapes enclosed the bed. The room was decorated with French décor. The rest of the house was much of the same. Marcus and Ana viewed the other rooms. One of the rooms was obviously for the family. The furniture was all made of cherry wood, even the toys. The toys were scattered as if just left there.

"I love these old houses."

"Why?"

"Because they have character. The people cared about these houses. They weren't just trying to make money."

"You are so beautiful, inside and out."

They completed their tour. After leaving Marcus drove them to a nearby, restaurant. When they entered the restaurant Ana looked around. It was very eloquent. She knew that the food would be costly. The host greeted them and they were quickly seated. Ana looked around the restaurant. Shortly after being seated a waiter came over to them. Ana ordered soda. Marcus ordered wine. The waiter left to get their drinks. While looking through the menu Ana and Marcus talked about the historical site. The waiter returned with their drinks. Ana informed him that she was ready to order. The waiter took their orders and left. The couple talked about their families. When the waiter returned with their food the couple began to eat. Ana caught Marcus a few times watching her eat.

"How's your food?"

"It's good thank you." All of a sudden she became nervous. Ana wasn't use to the attention Marcus was giving her.

"What's wrong?"

"Nothing."

Marcus took a bite of his food. He watched Ana . She seemed almost like a school girl. She was bright, intellectual, but there was something that made her seem younger. As if a light came on. He thought, "Could it be?"

Although he wanted to ask Marcus thought better of it. After they finished their meal Marcus asked if Ana wanted dessert. She declined. They left the restaurant and headed to New Jersey. The two were quiet during their drive to Jersey. When they arrived in Jersey Ana came alive. There were trees and houses showing signs of the Christmas season. Marcus noticed. He watched her face light up whenever she saw a house decorated.

"I take it you like the Christmas season."

"I love it. People act different this time of year. Everything is so beautiful. Do you like this time of year?"

"It's fine."

Ana continued to watch the trees and houses as they speed past them.

"Ana it's still early. Are you ready to go home?"

"What do you have in mind?"

"There's a movie that I wanted to see? Are you up for a movie?"

"Sure."

"There's one a few miles from here."

"How do you know?"

"I noticed it on the way down."

Marcus drove a few miles. He saw the theater. Marcus drove into the parking lot. He parked and they got out of the car. As they walked to the lot Marcus took Ana's hand. She liked the feel of his hand. He had never touched her before. He had moved close, but never had actually touched her. His hand was warm and strong. She wondered how it would feel for him to hold her. When they got into the movie Marcus showed her the movie that he wanted to see. It was a horror film. Marcus paid for two tickets. They went in. After they sat down Marcus put his arm around Ana's shoulders. She moved closer to him. Ana couldn't believe that she did that. It felt good to her.

Ana clutched Marcus' coat as the movie played. On occasion she put her face in his chest. After the movie they left the theater and headed to Ana's home. As Marcus drove the couple talked about the movie. They laughed about Ana's reaction.

When they arrived at her house it was eleven o'clock. She asked Marcus in. He asked if it was alright. She told him it was alright. Ana didn't think anything of it. She took him down to the basement. They played a couple of games of pool. Then they sat and talked. The two didn't sit far from each other. Marcus gave Ana a serious look. He put his hand under her chin. He moved in close. Ana didn't know if she should move away. She had never kissed a male before. She wondered if she would be clumsy. She looked into Marcus' eyes. She saw confidence. Ana thought, "He had probably kissed many women. I wonder if he's had many women."

Chapter 7

MARCUS LIGHTLY KISSED ANA ON the lips. He continued to look at her. He then closed his eyes and leaned in closer. Marcus kissed her gently. Ana couldn't believe she was kissing him back and as far as she knew doing it correctly. She placed her arms around his shoulders. She liked kissing him. Marcus placed his hands on each side of her face. She could tell that he wanted her. She felt the same. Ana felt tingles and sparks throughout her body. She had fallen in love with this man and she wanted him. She stopped kissing him and hugged him. Marcus kissed her neck and the side of her face. He caressed her hair and smoothed his hand over her breast. She allowed him to caress her breast through her blouse. Marcus found her lips and kissed her. She returned his affection. They kissed and Marcus held her to him. The two remained kissing for some time until Marcus pulled away. Ana looked at him in a questioning way. Marcus smiled slightly.

"I better go."

"Why?"

"I feel myself wanting you."

"Do you?"

"Yes."

They sat quiet for a few minutes. Ana moved up to him. She placed her hands on both sides of his face. She kissed him lightly. He pulled her close to him, kissing her with more passion. He leaned her back moving his hand over the top part of her body. After a while Marcus stopped. He sat up and pulled her to him.

"We can't do this?"

"Why not?"

"This isn't the place. It's not the way for you." Ana looked at him curiously. "You're special."

"What do you mean?"

"Can I ask you something without you getting offended?"

"What is it?"

"Ana have you ever had sexual intercourse?"

"Why do you ask that? Am I being too forward?"

"You haven't done anything wrong. I just had a feeling that you were a virgin." Ana was quiet. "You don't have to answer."

She remained quiet for a few minutes.

"Yes." Marcus looked at her as if surprised. Although he had thought as much he was still amazed at her admitting it. He didn't think that there were any their age. He smoothed his hand down the side of her face.

"Don't look like that. It's great that you have been strong enough to not give into someone's desires."

"Marcus that's not it."

Marcus looked at her.

"Then what is it?"

"Marcus, tonight is, you're the first."

Marcus stared at her trying to figure out what she was saying. Then as a light went off it came to him.

"You've never kissed before?" She shook her head no. Marcus put his hand under her chin and kissed her. "I feel honored. But why."

"I've never dated before." Marcus sat back. He couldn't believe this beautiful woman had never been approached. "I had my books and everyone knew it. Growing up and until this point studying was all I thought about. I had plans and at the time it didn't include men. I went to parties with my friends. I danced with guys, but that was as far as it went."

"So I should feel special. What made you let me kiss you?"

Ana teased. "Maybe I thought it was time."

"I don't think that's it."

"I like you."

"Why?"

"I just do."

"Well in any case I think I should go. It's late. I don't want your parents to get the wrong impression of me. Can I see you later today?"

"Sure. Come over. We can hang out here."

Marcus took Ana by the hand and they walked upstairs. When they got to the front door Marcus pulled Ana's hand behind his back. He kissed her on her forehead.

"I'll see you later."

Ana locked the door behind and then ran up to her room. When she opened her room door Rosalyn was up watching TV.

"What are you doing here?"

"I decided to hang out with TJ and wait to hear about your date. So how was it? What did you do?"

Ana told Rosalyn about the historical house and dinner. Rosalyn asked about the rest of the night. Ana told her about the movies. Rosalyn said, "I know you didn't send him home without kissing him. Please tell me you didn't."

"I didn't."

Rosalyn sat with a smile across her face.

"So how was it?"

Ana smiled.

"It was nice. Rosalyn he knew."

Rosalyn frowned up her face.

"Knew what?"

"What I am."

"What?" Then Rosalyn realized what she was talking about. "How?"

"I don't know. He just did."

"Well how did he feel about that?"

"He was fine with it."

"Well I guess so. You're a jewel."

"What do you mean?"

"There's not many of you, at least, at your age."

"I'm tired."

"Ok, I'll let you rest, but you got to tell me about your kiss."

"I'm sure it was just like your first."

"No, it's got to be different, you're in love."

"I didn't say that."

"You didn't have to."

Rosalyn laid her head on the pillow and began watching television again. Ana removed her clothes and got into bed. She closed her eyes. Before falling asleep Ana thought of her time with Marcus. She got a warm feeling. She remembered his arm around her shoulders. Although she was nervous it excited her. Ana thought of the feeling she got when Marcus kissed her and then when he touched her breast she was ready to give herself right then. Ana was happy that she hadn't; thinking it would be nice if her first time was romantic. Ana drifted off to sleep.....

The next couple of days Ana and Marcus spent most of their time together.

Margaret noticed the change in her daughter. She preyed that this young man would be good to her daughter.

When the couple returned to school Ana returned to the dedicated student she had always been. The times that she was with Marcus they spent studying. Marcus saw the change from their few days after Thanksgiving. While he adored her commitment to her calling, he missed the innocent girl he had the pleasure of meeting one fall day. Marcus had asked Ana out on a date several times, she declined saying that she needed to study.

A week before Christmas finals were over. Ana and Marcus hard work had paid off. With no more studying for a few weeks. Ana reverted back to that girl he met just a month before. Marcus hung out at Ana's house. They played pool and watched movies at her home. Marcus ate dinner with Ana and her family several nights a week. He decided to stay in New Jersey for Christmas.

Christmas Eve, after several games of pool, once they had sat down and were relaxed Marcus got on one knee. Ana looked at him.

"Ana will you do me the honor of becoming my wife?"

Marcus pulled out a diamond ring. Ana looked at Marcus and then the ring. She touched it, wondering if she should accept it.

"Marcus."

"What's wrong?"

"Nothing's wrong, but."

"But what?"

"I still have a ways to go with school."

"We can be married and finish school."

"It would be a distraction."

"How? Don't we study well together?"

"Say, but if we get married, you or we would then want to have children."

"Some day, but you wouldn't have to get pregnant right away. We could wait until we finish our residency."

"You would do that?"

"Ana I love you. I don't want to do anything to cause any distraction."

"Marcus."

"You don't love me?"

"I didn't' say that."

"You've never said that you love me and you still haven't said it. I guess you can't love me because you have another love." Ana gave him a puzzled look. "Your career." Ana remained silent. "I have to go."

"I'm sorry."

Marcus closed the box with the ring still in it. He walked up the stairs without looking back.

Christmas morning Ana heard the laughter of Tommy Jay. She got up and went downstairs. Everyone was already up and had opened their gifts. The only things left were Ana's gifts. She was encouraged to open them. Ana tried to act excited, but it was noticeable that something was going on. Everyone asked her, what was wrong. She told them everything was fine. She stayed in her room most of the day.

Ana got through dinner. After everyone had gone home Margaret went up to Ana's room. She knocked on the door. Ana told her to come in. Margaret opened the door. Margaret sat in Ana's lounge chair. Margaret asked Ana where was Marcus. Ana told her that he decided not to come over and that she shouldn't expect to see him around. Margaret looked at Ana with sadness in her eyes. She asked Ana what happened. Ana told her mother about Marcus proposing to her Christmas Eve. For a moment Margaret was quiet. Then she asked Ana what was her answer. Ana told her that she did not answer him. She told her mother about the discussion she and Marcus had. Margaret sat listening intensely to her daughter. Margaret remained quiet, trying to take in all that her daughter was telling her.

When Ana finished telling her, Margaret sat back. She looked at her daughter with compassion. Margaret felt bad for her daughter. She really didn't know what to say. Then she asked Ana how she felt about Marcus. She could see that Ana had no clue as to what she could be potentially giving up. Margaret asked Ana again. Ana shrugged her shoulders. Margaret was confused about her daughters' answer. She pried further.

"Ana how do you feel about Marcus?"

Ana shrugged her shoulders again. Margaret walked over to her daughter and placed her hand on her shoulders.

"Ana what's going on?"

"Nothing."

"I thought you liked this guy."

"I do mom, but."

"But what?"

"I have always wanted to be a doctor, but when I'm with Marcus I find myself thinking of only being with him."

"What's wrong with that?"

"I find myself thinking that he is the only thing important. I am a different person when I am with him. I can't concentrate."

"Baby that only means that you're in love."

"But I have always wanted to be a doctor."

"You can have both."

"I don't see that."

"Baby are you sure you want to give up on love?"

Tears streamed Ana's face. Margaret placed her arms around her daughter. Ana laid her head on Margaret's chest.

"I love you baby. Things will work itself out."

Margaret held her daughter in her arms until she fell asleep. Margaret placed Ana's wet face on her pillow. Margaret got up and left Ana's room. When Margaret came into her bedroom Thomas asked her if everything was alright. Margaret explained about Ana. Thomas laid awake feeling bad for his daughter. He thought how much Ana reminded him of himself.

The next day when Ana came down for breakfast she looked like she had cried all night. Ana spoke when she came into the kitchen. Thomas allowed her to get her breakfast. When Ana sat down Thomas began to talk to her. Thomas told Ana about his college days and that he dated a lady in college. He told her how he was too engrossed with school and his career to make it work. He told Ana that if she had stronger feelings for Marcus and if it was making her feel bad she should try to work something out. Thomas asked Ana if she was in love with Marcus. She didn't answer him, instead tears filled her eyes. Thomas stood up and walked over to Ana. He took her into his arms....

Spring classes began. Ana's focus was back on school. On occasion she ran into Marcus. They only spoke. Marcus wanted to try things Ana's way, but he was afraid of rejection. After their third year was over Marcus decided to move on.

The next year Ana happened to see Marcus with his new girlfriend. She felt as if someone had staved her in the chest. She threw herself into her studies. Once Marcus was by himself, Ana began to approach him, but fear got the better of her and she remained quiet. Throughout the year Ana tried to avoid any places that she thought she might run into Marcus. She was unable to avoid him totally. He was in one of her classes. On several occasions Ana felt eyes on her, but thought that she was probably imagining it. Ana found that while school certainly kept her occupied her heart mourned for it's lost.

The last few days of the school year several of the students threw a party and invited Ana. She didn't want to go by herself so she asked TJ. TJ hadn't been out too often so he was thrilled to escort her. The day of the party Margaret and Thomas baby-sat Tommy Jay. When the two arrived at the party music was playing and some of the guest were dancing. TJ asked Ana if she wanted to dance. She declined. A few of the students came over and talked to Ana. TJ saw an attractive young woman and excused himself. TJ talked with the woman and after some time began dancing with her. TJ noticed Marcus at the party. He looked over at Ana. It didn't appear as if she noticed or was moved by him so TJ stayed with the young woman.

Marcus noticed Ana with the group. He walked over. Marcus congratulated Ana. He smiled as only Marcus could. For a brief moment their eyes locked. It was as if they were the only ones in the room. He touched her hand lightly, sending electrical sparks throughout her. The moment was broken when a young attractive woman came up behind Marcus. She placed her arms around his waist. Marcus let go of Ana's hand. The young woman spoke to Ana. Ana spoke back, looking her over. Ana felt a little jealous, but tried to be neutral. The girl pulled on Marcus to dance with her. Marcus excused himself and then obliged the young woman. Ana couldn't help watching them dance. The girl was a good dancer. She danced up on Marcus causing Ana to turn her head. TJ seeing this excused himself from the young woman that he was entertaining and went over to rescue his sister. He took Ana by the hand and led her onto the dance floor.

After a few minutes of TJ dancing and encouraging Ana she began to dance. Marcus noticed her and watched Ana transform from the serious unapproachable student to a beautiful fun young woman. He watched as she spun around and danced with TJ. Marcus wanted to go over and hold her. He watched intensely until the young woman who he was dancing with kissed him. Marcus looked at the young woman. He took her by the hand, thanked the host and left. He took the young woman back to his room. He kissed her, not wanting to think of his sadness. The woman was more than willing to take him away. As he kissed the woman he thought of Ana. He kissed the woman more intense. As he removed her clothes he kissed her body. The young woman moaned at his touch. Marcus' cell phone went off. He stopped and looked at the number on the phone. He answered it.

"Hello."

"Hi. Were you sleeping?"

"No. Could you hold on?"

Marcus put the phone on mute. He walked over to the young woman and told her that he needed to be alone. The girl dressed. She kissed Marcus. He returned the kiss, but the earlier emotion had gone. He walked the woman to the door. She opened it. He watched as she walked across the street to her apartment. After she entered her place Marcus closed his door. He walked over to his bed and laid down. Marcus picked his cell phone up and said hello.

"Did I take you away from something?"

"Ana I'm going to be honest. I was with someone."

Ana was quiet a few minutes.

"I thought as much. Marcus I would like to be with you."

It was Marcus' turn to be stun. It was a few minutes before Marcus spoke.

"I'm not sure I heard you correctly."

"Marcus I miss you, let me come over."

"Are you sure?"

"I wouldn't be calling if I wasn't. Give me your address."

Marcus gave Ana his address. After he got off the phone he cleaned his apartment. He changed his sheets and took a shower. He looked over his apartment to make sure there wasn't anything to upset Ana.

Forty-five minutes later he heard a knock on his door. Marcus walked over to the door and opened it. He couldn't resist reaching over and kissing Ana on the side of her face. He took her by the hand. Ana walked into his apartment. She glanced at his apartment.

"This is nice."

"It's ok. Thank you. Come over here."

He pointed to his couch. They sat down. They were quiet for a while. Ana looked at Marcus. Ana sat back. She stared at Marcus. He allowed the quiet. Marcus didn't want to appear impatient. He wondered what was going through her mind and what made her call him. As if she read his mind Ana took Marcus' hand.

"I missed you."

"Did you?"

"Of course. Why do you sound surprised?"

"I didn't mean to."

"But you are."

"I guess I am. It's been a long time."

"I know."

"What made you call."

"Because I knew you wouldn't."

"Why now?"

"Because I need you."

Marcus looked at Ana in disbelief.

"What do you mean?"

"I miss you."

"Is that it?" Ana put her head down. "Ana are you in love with me? Ana's head remained down. Marcus put his hand under her chin. "I know you feel something. Why can't you tell me?" Tears filled Ana's eyes and streamed down her face. "Why is this so difficult for you?" Marcus still didn't get an answer. He put his arms around Ana and held her. Marcus leaned back taking Ana with him. He laid his head on the back of the couch and closed his eyes. He caressed her hair. It felt good holding her. He had given up hope on their relationship. Marcus dosed off.

Two hours later Marcus awakened. He looked around at first wondering why he was on his couch. Then he looked down. Ana was nestled in his arms. She had fallen asleep. He kissed the top of her head.

"Ana." At first she didn't move. "Ana." She sat up. He could tell she was trying to figure out where she was. She looked up at him with such a smile that his heart skipped a beat. "Ana it's late. Shouldn't you be getting home?"

"I told TJ where I was going. I don't want to leave."

"What about your parents?"

"I'm an adult, besides if they look for me he will know what to tell them."

"I know this is not comfortable."

"As long as I'm with you I'm fine."

Marcus stood up. He held out his hand. Ana took it. He led her into his bedroom. When they got into the room Marcus sat on the bed. He pulled Ana to him. Marcus placed his arms around her waist and held her. Ana placed her hands on his head. Marcus took her hand off of his head and brought them to his lips. He kissed them. Marcus moved further onto the bed bringing Ana with him. He held her. She snuggled onto his chest. Although Marcus wanted to make love to Ana he restrained himself. He didn't want to scare her off. Marcus caressed Ana's hair until he fell asleep. Ana laid there in his arms, not wanting this moment to past. Ana thought about her life up until now. How up until this moment nothing was more important than her career. Now this man had come into her life and he had changed the way she was thinking. It felt good to be in this man's arms. Ana wanted to be with Marcus, but she was afraid. Ana was afraid to tell or even think of how she felt. Ana remembered how she felt when her father rejected her. It was as fresh today as when it happened. Tears filled her eyes again. Ana tried to push them back. She sniffled. She tried to gain comfort by holding Marcus tighter. Through sleep he felt her and held her tighter. Ana drifted off to sleep.

After Ana had been asleep for three hours she was awakened by the doorbell. Marcus didn't stir. Ana knew she shouldn't answer a man's door. She called out Marcus' name. He still didn't stir. Ana nudged him. Marcus awakened. He looked at Ana through droggy eyes. He smiled at her. The person at the door began knocking again. Marcus looked more serious. He got up. He closed his bedroom door as he walked out. Ana sat up. Marcus opened the door. The woman seemed irritated.

"Marcus whose car is this?" She pointed at Ana's car. "This is why you put me out so abruptly? Who is she?"

"Calm down."

"Calm down? We have been together for a year. We made love and now you sleep with someone else. You put me out. I thought you loved me."

"I'm sorry if I led you on. I didn't mean to. I didn't mean to hurt you."

"You breaking up with me? She means that much to you?"

"I love her."

"So why were you with me? Where has she been? What I was just something to pass the time?"

"No. It wasn't like that. We kind of."

"Kind of. What is that?"

"I asked her to marry me and she chose her career over me."

"So you're going to dump me for someone who doesn't want to even marry you? I would have married you. I wouldn't have put anything or anyone before you."

"It's not like that. I see now that she needed more time. I love her and I see now, I have to give her the time."

"How do you know that she loves you? She didn't even want to marry you."

Marcus was quiet. He just stared at the woman. Marcus heard his room door open. He looked towards the room. The woman watched as Ana came out of the room.

"So you're the one trying to break us up?"

Ana defensively said, "I didn't mean to cause anyone harm."

"Sure you did. Marcus and I had a good thing. He never mentioned you."

"That's alright."

"Why are you here?"

"I know you think I don't care about Marcus, but I do. I'm sorry about you being hurt."

"You're sorry. You're not sorry about me. You're just sorry that you have to see the person you hurt."

Ana turned to Marcus.

"If you want or need me to leave I will."

"I don't want you to leave, but I think I have to take care of this."

"I understand." Ana put her shoes on and picked up her jacket. She looked back at the young woman. "I truly am sorry."

Marcus said, "I'll call you."

Ana got into her car. She turned the car on. Ana sat a few minutes and then pulled off. As she drove home Ana thought of her situation. She began to think about her conversation with Marcus' friend. Again Ana thought of her childhood. She recalled the day she met Thomas. He was very nice, but she was afraid he would take her mother from her the way Shirley had taken her father. When Thomas asked if she wanted him to be her father she jumped at the idea because she needed that male figure, but she didn't realize that her biological father would no longer be in her life. Through time Ana learned to deal with her life by being an excellent student. Ana avoided relationships with males because she was afraid they would reject her like her father. She refused to love another male. Now she was facing loosing another man in her life. Tears streamed Ana's eyes. She wanted to be with Marcus, but couldn't bring herself to say the words that he wanted, needed to hear.

Marcus asked his friend to sit down. He explained his relationship with Ana. Marcus apologized and told his friend that this was something he had to see through. He told the woman that he had made up his mind, that he would be patient and wait for Ana. The young woman tried to reason with Marcus and then attempted to kiss him. Marcus stopped the young woman and told her that it was no use. After she left Marcus tried to keep busy. He cleaned his apartment. He wanted to give Ana some time.

Ana arrived home. Thomas was sitting in the den. Ana heard the television. She went into the room. He saw that she was upset. He held his arms out to her. She went into them. She began to cry.

"What's wrong?"

"Something is wrong with me."

"Nothing is wrong with you. You're my perfect girl."

"Daddy why can't I tell Marcus how I feel about him. I can't even think it."

"Can you tell me?"

"No I can't."

"What are you afraid of?"

"I don't know."

"Are you sure?" Thomas put his hand under her chin and looked into her eyes.

"I'm afraid he won't love me back."

"Do you love Marcus?" Ana sat still. "If he asked you to marry him then he loves you. A man doesn't ask you to marry him without truly meaning it. Do you think he's just trying to sleep with you?"

"No. He's never tried."

Thomas was relieved.

"Then what is keeping you from saying this four letter word?"

"My father."

Thomas looked deeper into Ana's eyes as if to try to figure out what was lying beneath. Then it dawn on him. She was referring to her biological father. Thomas sat back. He was quiet for a few minutes.

"Ana do you think that your father didn't love you?" She remained quiet. "I know your father loves you."

"He left me. He didn't want me."

"He did love you and he did want you. The day that he signed your adoption papers, before he signed them he made me promise that I would love you as my own and that I would take care and protect you. I promised that I would. His hand shook as he signed the papers. After he signed the papers he told me why. He said that he signed the papers not that he had a new family, he wanted you to be a part of it, but it was that he had not given you the attention that he knew you needed. He didn't want you to hurt and with him having a baby he didn't want you to feel you had to fight for his affection. He thought you would be jealous and think that he loved your sibling more and he added that would never be." Thomas smoothed his hand over Ana's face. "He truly loves you. You have two fathers who worship the ground you walk on.

Ana looked at Thomas. She hugged him. She wiped her eyes, but remained in his arms. They sat there for a while, quiet holding each other. Ana was tired from her night out. She had not gotten much sleep. Ana relaxed and soon drifted off to sleep. Thomas held his daughter while she slept. Thomas recalled holding Ana when she was a small girl, while she cried, because she thought her father didn't want her. He held her when she fell down and when she had her first crush. Thomas smiled. He wanted to go shake the little boy for not returning his daughter's feelings.

Hours had past when Margaret came home. She heard the television and came into the room. Margaret was shocked when she saw the two. She walked over and kissed Thomas. Margaret gave Thomas a questioning look. He whispered his conversation with Ana. When Thomas had finished telling Margaret about his afternoon she got up and went up to their room. Margaret showered and dressed. She returned downstairs and went into the kitchen and started cooking. A couple of times she checked on Ana. She was still asleep. When she was finished cooking Margaret went and shook Ana. Ana looked up. She sat for a few minutes to figure out her surroundings. "Hi mom." She looked down at her clothes. I need to change clothes. Ana got up. She kissed her father, thanked him and went up to her room. Ana got into the shower and turned it on. As the water ran down her body she thought of Marcus. She thought how it would feel for him to touch her. She washed her body and then dried off. Ana felt like a weight had been lift off of her. After she got dressed Ana got her cell phone and dialed Marcus' cell phone. Marcus answered it.

"Hello."

"Hi Marcus. It's Ana."

Marcus heart skipped a beat.

"Hi. How are you?"

"I'm fine. We need to talk."

"Ok. Where do you want to talk?"

"Can I come over?"

"Are you sure that you want to come here?"

"Yes."

"When would you like to come over?"

"How about in two hours?"

"I'll be here."

"Ok. I'll see you soon."

Ana placed her cell phone in her pocket. She got her car keys and jacket. Ana placed the keys in her jacket pocket. She laid the jacket on the chair in the foyer. Ana went into the kitchen where her parents were eating. She fixed her plate and sat down. While they ate her parents talked about Ana's childhood and told her that they were proud of her. Margaret handed Ana a letter. Ana looked at it and cautiously opened it. Ana read the letter. A smile formed on her face. Tears were in her eyes. Margaret's face looked concerned. Ana yelled, "I got in." Her parents jumped up and hugged Ana. Her parents said they have to celebrate. Ana informed them that she had plans to talk to Marcus. Although Ana was no longer a child her parents had the urge to tell her to be careful. They also knew that Ana had always been careful and realized at that moment that Ana had grown into a beautiful, intelligent and responsible young woman. They were proud of their daughter. They conveyed this to Ana. A short while later Ana kissed her parents and told them that she would see them later. Ana left her home. She got into her car. Ana looked at her parents' home. As she pulled off Ana knew that she was no longer the little girl who grew up in her grandmother's home. Ana turned on music and sang as she drove to Marcus' apartment....

When Ana arrived at Marcus' apartment she parked. Ana dialed his cell phone. He answered. Ana told him that she was outside and asked if it was alright to come in. Marcus went to the door and opened it. Ana got out of her car and walked up his few steps. When she reached the top step Marcus moved aside. She walked into the apartment. Ana sat on his love seat. Ana tap the side of the chair next to her. Marcus sat next to Ana.

"Marcus I apologized for all that you have gone through because of me. I didn't mean to cause you or anyone else harm."

"Don't worry about it."

"Marcus I need to tell you something about me."

Marcus sat back. Ana told him about being adopted. Marcus remained silent. He listened intensely. She explained why she had a problem with what he asked of her. She then smoothed her hand down the side of Marcus' face.

"Marcus I love you with all of my heart. If you decide you don't want to be with me, know that I will never love anyone as much as I love you."

Marcus looked at Ana in disbelief. He was speechless. He just sat next to her seeming to be frozen. Ana looked at Marcus going over his body. He was so handsome. She missed him. Ana moved closer to him. She kissed Marcus. He remained still. Ana took this as a rejection. Marcus noticed and reached out to her. Marcus took Ana into his arms and kissed her passionately. Ana melted into his arms. Marcus picked Ana up. He carried her into his bedroom. Marcus still kissing Ana gently laid her onto the bed. He stopped only for a moment. He looked into Ana's eyes. He smiled at what he saw. Marcus returned to kissing Ana. She placed her arms around his shoulders. She loved the way he felt. His arms were strong and muscular. He smelt so good. She ran her hands down them. Marcus caressed her body. It felt like nothing she ever knew. Marcus kissed her neck. He ran his tongue down her neck. He nibbled her ear. As he began to undress Ana, Marcus ran his tongue down her body. Marcus sampled each inch of Ana's body. Ana couldn't believe how Marcus was making her feel. He stopped only momentarily to remove his clothes. Ana watched. He had a beautiful body. His muscles were well defined. As he removed his pants and then his underwear Ana could see his arousal. Ana became nervous as to whether making the connection with him would be very painful. Marcus noticed the expression. As Marcus laid next to Ana he gently kissed the side of her face. He whispered in her ear not to worry. Marcus began caressing Ana's body again. Her mind reeled from such pleasure. When Ana called out Marcus name he joined her. Their minds and bodies took a journey where only pleasure existed.......

The next day Ana awakened. She found herself still in Marcus' arms. She smiled thinking of their love making. Although she was still sore Ana wanted to feel the pleasure that Marcus brought to her a few hours earlier. Ana kissed Marcus' chest. She then moved up to his lips. Ana kissed Marcus until he awakened and returned her affections. Marcus pulled her onto him. He looked up at her, revealing his beautiful smile. His eyes showed desire. Marcus caressed her body until it called out to him. Ana held onto Marcus, never wanting to let him go. In the heat of passion Ana called out Marcus' name and told him that she loved him. Marcus held Ana tighter and kissed her passionately.

Afterwards the two lay basting in the essence of their love making. Both holding onto each other, not wanting this moment to end.

"Ana." Marcus got up. He walked over to his dresser. Marcus took something out of the draw. He walked over to the side of the bed Ana was laying on. He kneeled on one knee. Ana watched him, still mesmerized. "Ana I'm not sure if this is the right moment, but I feel compel to ask. " Marcus handed her a small box. She looked down at it. "Ana will you marry me?"

Ana looked at the box. She took the box and opened it. Ana thought the ring was beautiful. She held her hand out in a gesture for him to put the ring on her finger. With tears in her eyes Ana said yes. Marcus shakily placed the ring on Ana's finger. After placing it on her finger Marcus kissed her hand. Ana smoothed her free hand down the side of Marcus' face. He got up and pulled her up to him. He held Ana.

"Marcus I need to go home. Can I use your bathroom to take a shower?"

"What's mine is yours. Can I join you?"

Ana took Marcus by the hand and then walked into his bathroom. They took turns washing each other. When they were done Marcus dried Ana off and then himself. Ana dressed. She picked up her purse. Ana opened it to get her keys. As she took her keys out a letter fell out. She picked it up. Ana looked at it and smiled. Marcus noticed.

"What's that?"

"Oh. I got in." Ana handed the letter to Marcus. Marcus looked at Ana and then the letter. He read the letter. He smiled. Marcus hugged her.

"Congratulations."

"Thank you. Have you applied?"

"Yes, but I haven't heard anything."

"Did you have anyone to write a letter?"

"Yes."

"Maybe my mother can get one of the doctors to write you a letter."

"No baby. I can't do that. I want to get in on my own merit."

"You would be."

"Baby let it go."

"Well let me know if you change your mind."

Ana kissed Marcus and left.....

Chapter 8

ANA BEGAN AT THE HOSPITAL right away. Marcus finally heard from the hospital and was told that they would have an opening for him in two years. They commended him on his outstanding references and grades, but because of the extraordinarily high enrollment they did not have an opening. Marcus thought of returning home to his old job, but Ana asked him to remain in Jersey. Marcus looked for work, but was not fortunate enough to find one. Six months went by. Marcus informed Ana that he had to return home. Ana understood, but it didn't take away the hurt and once again she felt rejection. The night before Marcus was to leave Ana returned his ring. Marcus pleaded with her to keep it and he promised that he would return, but Ana insisted. Marcus kissed her on the forehead and left.

For several weeks Ana cried herself to sleep. She felt so bad that she took a week off school. When she didn't get any better Ana went to the doctor. Ana had never been sick. She thought maybe her illness was due to unhappiness. The doctor examined her. After his examination, urinalysis and blood work being done it was positive that Ana was six months pregnant. She sat there in disbelief. She could not believe this was true. They had taken precautions. Ana couldn't figure out how she could be pregnant. As she drove home Ana's mind went through every time she and Marcus had made love. They had used protection. Just as she pulled in front of her parents home a light came on in Ana's head. Ana figured out that she had gotten pregnant the very first night they made love. Ana couldn't believe it. She sat there in the car and began to laugh. Shortly afterwards she began to cry. Ana laid her head on the steering wheel. Time elapse. Ana heard taps on her window. She looked up. It was TJ smiling. He held Tommy Jay on his back. Ana wiped her eyes. She opened the car door. TJ held the door. Ana reached over and kissed her nephew.

"Hey sis, what's going on?"

"TJ I'm pregnant."

At first TJ stared at her in disbelief. He couldn't believe Ana was going down this road. He hugged Ana.

"Did you tell Marcus?"

"No. I just found out."

"So what are you going to do?"

"What is there to do?"

"What does that mean?"

"I'm going to have the baby and raise it like you're doing Tommy Jay."

"You're not going to tell Marcus?"

"No."

"Why not? I'm sure he would want to help you raise the baby."

"He has his life and things have been rough for him. I don't want to take him away from succeeding."

"Shouldn't it be his choice and what about you?"

"Oh I'm going to succeed. I'm going to make this work and in little over a year I'm going to be Dr. Ana Gibson."

"My big sister. You inspire me, but are you sure you want to do this alone?"

"I'm not alone. I have you, mom and dad right?"

"So when are you going to tell the parents?"

"I guess tonight. Help me make dinner."

"Oh you're going to try to soften the blow."

"I guess that's what you can call it."

Ana, TJ and Tommy Jay went into the house. Ana and TJ prepared dinner. When Margaret and Thomas came home they were surprised and suspected something was going on. When they sat down for dinner Margaret decided to say a prayer out loud. When she was done TJ looked at Ana knowing that their parents suspected him. They were quiet for a few minutes and then Ana not knowing how else to tell them blurted out that she was pregnant. At first Ana's parents just stared at her. Then as if in slow motion Margaret began to speak.

"Are you sure?"

"Yes I went to the doctor."

"So what are you going to do?"

"I'm going to have the baby."

"What about your career?"

"I can still finish school on time. I'm almost half way through now anyway. I can put the baby in day care."

Margaret looked at her daughter being strong. Ana had groan up to be a strong woman. She was proud of Ana for getting as far as she had and not falling apart right now. Margaret thought of her mother, of the stories of her life. At that moment she thought how much Ana reminded her of Ann.

"Ana what about Marcus?"

"What about him?"

"You're going to tell him right?"

"Mom he has his dreams."

"I remember at one time his dream was being your husband."

"That was only one dream. He has another. One that he had before he met me."

"Ana he deserves to know. He's a good man. Maybe he'll come back and you won't have to do this alone."

"That's the thing. He would give up what he needs to do."

"Ana I really think you should give him that opportunity to make that decision."

"Mom let it go."

"Alright, but I think you should put more thought into this. By the way you're not alone."

After dinner Ana and TJ cleaned up. Ana went up to her room afterwards. She took her cell phone out and scrolled through the numbers. Marcus' number came up. She stared at it and thought of calling it. She loved Marcus and knew that this moment should be with him. They were suppose to be married when she got pregnant. She felt something and then realized that the baby was moving. She got up and ran into her parent's room. Ana told Margaret about the movement. Margaret smoothed her hand over Ana's stomach. Thomas came and saw the women. He asked if everything was alright. Margaret explained what was happening. Thomas rubbed her stomach. Just then the baby moved. He was thrilled. It had been a long time since he'd felt a baby move still in it's mother's womb…..

It was Monday morning, before Ana began her rounds she went to discuss her situation with the director. The director assured Ana that as long as she complete the required hours she would graduate………

As Ana's pregnancy progressed many nights she layed awake thinking that she had made a mistake in not telling Marcus. Many nights she thought of calling him, but as quickly as the thought came up she would brush it away. To help get her not be so sad and overwhelmed Ana would talk to the baby. She would tell the baby about Marcus…….

Ana got up early Friday morning. She was tired and didn't feel well. Ana dressed and then left for the hospital. Once she arrived at the hospital Ana parked and walked slowly into the hospital. While Ana was talking to one of the doctors she had a strong contraction and then her water broke. The doctor notified the staff. Ana instructed them to call her parents. Ana was taken to the nearest room. When the doctor checked her he saw that the baby was coming. They had no time to take her into the birthing room. After the baby had been delivered Ana was taken to her room. Soon after Margaret and Thomas walked into the room. They hugged Ana and congratulated her.

A hour later the nurse brought the baby into Ana's room. The proud grandparents looked at their beautiful granddaughter. Margaret asked, "What are you going to name her?"

"Mary Ann Gibson-Stiles."

"Wow, she has a name to live up to."

"Do you like it?"

Margaret kissed Ana on her forehead.

"I love it."

The next day Ana was released. Ana had fixed her room up to fit her baby in it. Ana had divided the room to accommodate them until she graduated and obtained a job. Ana clinged to her baby girl.

On several occasions Ana thought of calling Marcus, but she wouldn't bring herself to do it.

As weeks past Ana questioned her determination to return to the hospital and put off finishing when Mary Ann would be older. Ana thought how her entire life had been centered on becoming a doctor. She was so close, there was no stopping. Margaret switched her hours so the baby would not have to go to day care.....

The first day Ana returned to work it seemed like time stood still. She missed her baby girl. Ana thought of her baby. Mary Ann's face came to her. It made her think of Marcus. Although her baby girl was small Ana noticed that she had her father's smile. She also had his eyes. When Ana looked into her baby girl's eyes she saw Marcus.....

As the days quickly past Mary Ann grew bigger. Each day looking at her daughter tempt Ana to call Marcus, but with determination to allow Marcus to have a chance to achieve his career it stopped her.....

A year had past. Ana threw a birthday party for Mary Ann. She invited her closes friends and family. Mary Ann enjoyed everyone fussing over her. When everyone left Ana went up to her room. Mary Ann was sleeping. Ana looked at her baby girl and wished that Marcus was with them.

The next Wednesday the family was celebrating Ana's graduation. When she was given her stethoscope tears streamed Ana and Margaret's face. She had finally achieved her life long dream. As her family stood and clapped Ana watched her baby girl waiving and clapping.

After graduation Ana and her family went out to dinner. TJ toast to his sister. He was so proud of her. He told her that she was his hero. TJ had also completed college. He had received a degree in accounting....

Ana landed a position at a hospital. She traveled to the hospital she trained in twice a week. Ana loved her job. Things were working out well. After six months Ana began looking for an apartment. Margaret helped her to decide. It was a sad moment when Ana packed Mary Ann and her things. Her parent's helped her move her things. Margaret helped Ana pick out furniture for her apartment and decorate it. It took some time for her to get use to living away from her parents. Mary Ann was also having a difficult time. Ana was trying to get Mary Ann to sleep in her room, but she was having no part of that.

Three months later Ana managed to get Mary Ann to stay in her room. Ana had become accustomed to going to her own place. She often thought of Marcus and how things would be if she had married Marcus....

When Mary Ann turned two Ana threw a party in her apartment. Her brother, nephew and parents all came. A few of Ana's friends came over as well and helped celebrate Mary Ann's birthday. Ana watched as her daughter played. Everyone raved about how beautiful Mary Ann was.

When the party ended everyone began to leave. Ana hated for them to leave. She felt lonely. Each year Mary Ann reminded Ana of Marcus. Ana thought by now she would have gotten over him, but each day that past her loneliness grew.

Mary Ann was getting use to their new place and now sleeping in her own room every night. Everyone had adjusted to the schedules created to keep Mary Ann out of daycare. Ana didn't want Mary Ann to go until she was three.....

Ana got up her usual time. She showered and then dressed. She woke up Mary Ann and then dressed her. Ana helped Mary Ann into her car seat and then got into the car. She drove to her mother's and dropped off Mary Ann. She kissed her daughter and then headed to the hospital. Ana saw several patients. For lunch she went to the cafeteria. The new class had began that week. She smiled thinking of her first day. Ana finished her lunch and got up to return her tray. Just then she stopped short. As if the temperature had dropped a chill went through her. Ana became dizzy and she felt sick. She had to sit down, but Ana knew she had to get out of there. Ana managed to pull herself together enough to get to the door. She left her tray on a nearby table. Ana made it to a rest room and to a toilet. She threw up. One of the nurses came into the restroom. When Ana came out of a stall the nurse asked her if she was alright. Ana told her that she was fine. Ana looked into the mirror and tried to make herself look alright. The rest of the day she was on pins and needles. When her shift was over Ana quickly left the hospital and got into her car. As she drove to her parent's home Ana contemplated her situation.....

When she arrived at her parent's home TJ was playing with Mary Ann. When he looked up TJ noticed that Ana looked stressed. TJ asked if anything was wrong. She sat down and told him what happened at work. TJ asked her what she was going to do. Ana said she didn't know. TJ told her that she should talk to their mother. Thomas was the first to arrive home. Ana told him what happened. Thomas advised her to tell

Marcus. He explained to her that he had a right to know. Ana explained that she was afraid of what his reaction would be. Thomas assured her that eventually the anger would go away. Ana didn't wait for Margaret to come home. When Ana arrived home she bathed Mary Ann and got her ready for bed. Ana was happy that she was not due at the hospital until the next week.

On the days Ana had to work at the hospital she avoided the cafeteria. Ana also tried to avoid the new class. This went on for several months.

One day Ana was finishing up at the hospital. She walked towards her car. Ana felt someone behind her. She turned. Ana felt dizzy. Marcus could see it in her face. He asked if she was alright. Ana told him that she needed to sit down. He helped Ana to her car. Ana got into her car. Marcus asked Ana if she was alright. Looking up at Marcus Ana knew she could no longer deny him the knowledge of his child. Ana unlocked the passenger's side door. She asked Marcus to get in. Marcus gave her a questioning look and then walked over to the passenger's side of the car. He opened the door and got in. Marcus asked her what was going on. Ana was quiet a few minutes and then slowly and clearly Ana told Marcus that they had a child. Marcus was silent. He stared at Ana as if to wait for her to say she was joking. When this did not happen Marcus asked how. Ana explained that it happened the first time. Marcus thought about it. He sat back in his seat. He did not say anything. The silence was unbearable. After fifteen minutes Marcus looked at Ana. She could see in his eyes the hurt and anger. Before he could ask, Ana explained why she hadn't told him. He listened to each word.

After she was done he asked what did she have. She told him that they had a daughter. Marcus continued to have an expression of disbelief on his face. Ana asked him if he would like to meet her. Still in shock he nodded his head. Ana asked him when did he want to meet her. Marcus told Ana that he could meet her at her parent's home. Ana told him that she had her own place. She gave him her address and directions. She told him that they would have more privacy there. Marcus looked at her with a surprised expression on his face. Marcus got out of the car. He watched as she drove off. Ana looked in her rearview mirror and saw that he was finally moving. Ana had mixed feelings. She was relieved that she didn't have anymore secrets between them. She was sad for keeping this from him.

As she drove to her parent's home Ana recalled the hurt in Marcus' eyes. She kept reminding herself that she did it in Marcus' best interest. When Ana arrived at her parents, she parked and went into the house. Ana gathered up Mary Ann and left. She did not want to tell her parents about her seeing Marcus right now. Mary Ann played with her doll. Ana glanced at her baby girl, wondering how she would respond to Marcus. Ana decided that she would not say who he was unless he authorized it.

As Ana pulled up in front of her apartment she noticed Marcus' car. Ana got out of her car. She went to the back of her car to help Mary Ann out. Mary Ann had taken the buckle off. Ana lifted her out of the car. Ana noticed Marcus standing nearby watching them. Mary Ann took Ana's hand. As they walked to her door Marcus walked up. Ana spoke to Marcus. She watched as he looked at Mary Ann. Mary Ann looked at him. Marcus spoke to her. Mary Ann held Ana's hand tighter and moved closer to her. Mary Ann spoke to Marcus. He seemed to be surprised at her speech. When they got into the house Marcus asked her age. Mary Ann gave her age and birth date and then ran into her room. Ana told him to have a seat. She offered him a drink and he accepted a bottle of water. They sat on her couch. Ana gave him a brief synopsis of what had been going on in her life. Marcus congratulated her on her becoming a doctor. Ana and Marcus was quiet for a few minutes and then Mary Ann came out of the room. She ran up to Ana and asked who Marcus was. Ana look at him in a questioning manner. Marcus told her to introduce him. She remained quiet. Marcus spoke the word father. Mary Ann looked up at her mother.

Ana said, "Mary Ann this is your daddy."

Mary Ann looked at Ana and then repeated the word daddy. Mary Ann leaned against her mother. Ana was surprised when Marcus put his hand out and said, "Hello baby girl."

Mary Ann put her finger in her mouth as if to contemplate what to do. Mary Ann cautiously walked over to Marcus. She took his hand. Marcus looked down at her hands. He thought of how tiny they were. He told Ana that she was beautiful. Mary Ann asked him if he wanted to see her room. She pulled his hand and led him into her room.

Marcus looked at Ana in amazement. Ana got up and followed them. She watched as her daughter showed Marcus all of her toys as if she had known him all of her life. Ana eventually asked Marcus if he would like to stay for dinner. Marcus accepted the invitation. After Ana began the meal she informed Marcus that Mary Ann studies her alphabets while she cooks. Marcus joined in the activity.

After dinner was done the three of them sat down to eat. Ana said grace and then they began to eat. As they ate Ana watched Mary Ann. She seemed so happy with her father. Mary Ann bounced back and forth as she ate her meal.

After they were done eating Ana explained that Mary Ann takes a bath and then she reads her a book. Marcus asked if he could read the story. Marcus watched a movie while Ana gave Mary Ann a bath. When they were done Ana tucked Mary Ann into bed and then went into the living room to get Marcus. Marcus was instructed what book to read. Ana sat back to give them time together. It felt comfortable watching them interact. She was happy that Marcus didn't seem angry. She wondered if this was a one time thing or would he take his fatherly roll.

When Marcus finished reading and talking to Mary Ann she laid back and he tuck her in. Ana stepped in and kissed Mary Ann. Mary Ann wrapped her arms around Ana's neck. After Ana stood up Mary Ann reached for Marcus. He bent down. Mary Ann hugged and kissed him. Marcus returned her affection. As he held his daughter for that brief moment he knew he wanted to be in her life. As he was leaving her room Mary Ann said good night daddy. Ana left the door cracked. Ana and Marcus went into the living room. Ana asked Marcus if he wanted to stay and talk. Marcus accepted her invitation.

They talked for several hours with Ana explaining her reasoning for not telling him. Ana was surprised at how well Marcus was taking everything and how he never questioned the paternity. When she asked him about it Marcus explained that he did the math and he knew that she was a virgin when they had their first sexual encounter. They sat quiet for a while. Ana realized that she had missed Marcus more than she thought. She missed his strong masculine voice.

Once it got late Marcus told Ana that he should go. Ana walked him to the door. He left. Ana got ready for bed. As she laid in bed Ana thought of her evening. She thought of how good Marcus was with Mary Ann. Ana wished she had married him. She could only hope that he sticks around to help raise their daughter.

The next day Ana woke up sluggish. She didn't sleep well because Ana kept thinking of her life if they had gotten married. Ana dressed and then woke up Mary Ann. She quickly dressed her. During their ride to her mother's Mary Ann slept. When Ana arrived at her parents her father was waiting to take the baby. She rolled her window down, Thomas kissed her on the side of the face and then took Mary Ann out of her seat. She was still sleeping. When they had made it into the house Ana pulled off. She tried to block her thoughts of Marcus by thinking of what she had to do at work. Ana was happy that she was not due at the hospital today. Ana kept herself busy and was happy when it was time to go home. She changed clothes and went to pick up Mary Ann.

When she arrived at her parents Ana parked the car and went inside. When she got inside Ana heard voices in the back of the house. Ana walked towards the family room. There she saw Margaret, Thomas and TJ sitting, back amused at the tales about her daddy. When they noticed Ana the group all looked at her in a questioning manner. Ana started out by saying, "I can explain." Ana remained standing. She went back to the first day that she saw Marcus. Her family listened intently. After she was finished talking Margaret asked what her plans were. Ana told her family that she didn't know what was going to happen now. She would just have to wait and see…

Several months went by without Ana hearing or seeing Marcus. She figured maybe it was too much for him. It was surprising because she thought he and Mary Ann had connected. On occasion when Mary Ann would see a show with a child and their father Mary Ann would ask about her father. Ana would tell Mary Ann that he love her, because she was sure he did, but was just very busy. Ana was happy that Mary Ann accepted the explanation and would move on to playing or whatever she was doing.

One day Ana had left work. She went to her parent's home and picked Mary Ann up. She didn't stay long. Ana told TJ that she was tired. She and Mary Ann left. When Ana arrived home she helped Mary Ann out of the car and then went into the house. After Ana put Mary Ann to bed the phone rang. She answered it. She was surprised that it was Marcus. He told her that he was outside and asked if he could come in. Ana went to the door and opened it. She hung up the phone. Marcus got out of his car and came in. Ana was happy to see him, but she tried not to show it. She asked him to have a seat.

After sitting Marcus began speaking. He apologized for not being in touch sooner, explaining that he had to make sense of everything. He told her that it was a lot to take in and for Mary Ann being two already, close to three and he not knowing was very difficult to take. Ana sympathized with everything he said. After he finished Ana apologized for keeping this from him. She also apologized for putting her career before their relationship. They both sat quiet for a little while. Then Ana asked Marcus his plans. He looked at her quiet for a while and then said that he wanted to be in his daughter's life. Although he wanted to add her to that statement he had decided that this time if they were to be together Ana would have to make that move. Ana told him that he could see Mary Ann anytime he liked. Marcus got up. He told Ana that it was time for him to go. Ana stood up and walked him to the door.

After he left Ana got ready for bed. Before falling asleep Ana laid in bed thinking about her conversation with Marcus. She was happy that Marcus wanted to be in his daughter's life. She wondered if he was still attracted to her. She asked herself, "Wouldn't he say so if he was and then it came to her, maybe he has moved on." Still she took comfort in him wanting to be in their daughter's life.

Ana was true to her word. Whenever Marcus came by Ana's house she welcomed him. Marcus and Mary Ann had become very close. When it was Mary Ann's birthday Marcus asked Ana to place his name on her birth certificate. Ana agreed. Ana and Marcus' relationship was closer than it had ever been. Many nights she laid awake wondering if he was interested in them getting back together. During their time together she always felt something, but he never said anything.

It was coming along Christmas time. Mary Ann was very excited. Ana invited Marcus to her parent's home. He accepted.

Marcus talked with Mary Ann, asking her what she wanted for Christmas. She just asked for dolls. Marcus talked to Ana about it and she explained to him that right now Mary Ann wasn't really a kid that ask for a lot. She explained that she was still young.

Two weeks before Christmas Ana and Marcus went shopping together for Mary Ann's gifts. The two looked through the age appropriate toys. They purchased some.

As they drove to Ana's apartment to hide the gifts Marcus asked about Mary Ann's likes and dislikes. Marcus wanted to know everything about his daughter. He wanted to catch up all the years that he missed.

When they arrived at Ana's apartment Marcus followed Ana into her bedroom. She opened her closet door and told him to put the gifts in there. Marcus took a quick look around her bedroom and wondered if he had been the only man in there. Then he laughed to himself, knowing Ana he was the only man. At that moment he wanted to pull her to him and make love to her.

Just that short time now seemed a century away. She was even more beautiful than the woman he had left. He wondered if maybe he should have stayed, where would their relationship have been. He thought better and knew Ana and although it hurt she understood. She knew the importance of following one's dream. She had done this her entire life and it paid off. He wondered what went through her mind when she discovered that she was pregnant. Had she ever thought of calling him. He wished she had. Here he had a baby growing inside the woman he loved and he did not know. He wondered how wonderful it was when that beautiful baby girl entered the world. He would have given everything up to see that. Ana tap him on the shoulder. He excused himself. Ana wondered what he was in deep thought about. She asked him if he wanted to have lunch before they go to pick Mary Ann up. Marcus accepted. He cherished every moment that they got alone hoping that Ana would show some sign that she wanted a relationship with him. Ana was happy that Marcus accepted her invitation. She enjoyed being with him. She only wished that he was equally interested in her as he was in being Mary Ann's father.

Ana went into the kitchen and prepared a chef salad for them.

As the two ate they discussed the days events. Ana inquired about Marcus' training. She told him about hers and offered her assistance. Ana noticed the expression on Marcus' face change to something she couldn't decipher. Then he asked about her training during pregnancy. She eased his mind telling Marcus how everyone had been so nice and helpful. She laughed saying how Mary Ann had already done her training, maybe she'll follow suit like her parents and become a doctor.

Marcus smiled. For a moment Ana was lost. He always blew her away with his smile. Marcus noticed that familiar look. He wanted to reach out and touch her hand, but he held back.

Ana stood up and began cleaning the table. Marcus got up to help. It felt like home to both of them standing side by side, she washing the dishes and he drying. Ana showed him where to place the dishes.

On their drive to Ana family's home the two were quiet. Marcus remained in the car while Ana went to get Mary Ann. She went into the house. Ana didn't tell anyone that Marcus was out in the car. For a little while she just wanted him to herself.

While Marcus waited he thought about their situation. He wondered if Ana was still in love with him. He went over the past weeks. He thought of how they had become friends. He knew their relationship was special. Here he shared a baby with his best friend. He examined their friendship. He thought wasn't it more than that, they had a bond. They had this beautiful little girl and he knew or at least felt there was more than that. Whenever they were together he could feel a closeness. When Marcus returned to New Jersey he made a promise to himself that he would wait for Ana to make the next move. He wondered even feared that she wouldn't. Marcus knew that Ana was not like other women. He smiled to himself. She was a virgin when he met her. She definitely had not been out there and maybe she didn't know how to make the move he needed. Marcus considered that even just a small gesture would do. Hadn't she made the move their first time. He resolved to be patient. He just hoped that he was making the right decision to wait on her.

Mary Ann and Ana came out of the house. When Mary Ann saw Marcus she ran over to the passenger side of the car. Marcus got out and Mary Ann jumped into his arms. He kissed his daughter and put her in her car seat. Mary Ann was very chattery. Ana could see a difference in her daughter since Marcus had come into her life. Not that she wasn't happy, but Mary Ann was a different child. Ana felt that she seemed happier.....

Christmas Eve Marcus came over to Ana's house. Ana cooked dinner. Marcus read Christmas stories to Mary Ann. When dinner was ready Marcus, Ana and Mary Ann sat at the dinning room table. Ana said grace and then they began to eat. While the three ate Ana thought how nice the past month had been with Marcus being there.

She thought how wonderful it would be if they were married. She looked at Marcus while he ate. Ana long for them to be together again. She had not felt strong arms around her since Marcus. She had not wanted any man since Marcus.

As Ana was swept away in thought of being with Marcus he glanced at her. He noticed that her mind was somewhere else and that she had a familiar look on her face. He knew this look. She had it when they first made love. He wondered if she was thinking about that. He could only wish that Ana wanted more from this relationship.

Marcus interrupted her thoughts by saying "Penny for your thoughts." Ana blushed wondering if he could guess what she was thinking about. At first Ana was quiet. She tried to think of how to ask Marcus if he was interested in their relationship becoming more. She was afraid of being rejected, but she knew that she couldn't go on like this, having these feelings and doing nothing about them.

When they were done eating Ana gave Mary Ann a bath. Ana helped Mary Ann put on her pajamas. Mary Ann called out to Marcus to come read to her. Marcus came into the room. Ana left to give them some time alone. She went into the kitchen and began cleaning up.

While cleaning the kitchen Ana thought how she always imagined she and her husband would be doctors, having children and he reading bedtime stories to their children. Ana felt complete.

Ana was still cleaning when Marcus came out of Mary Ann's room. He walked into the kitchen. Marcus asked if he could assist. Ana told him to relax because she was just about done. When Ana was done she joined Marcus in the living room. He was seated in the love seat. Ana sat next to him. Without seeming pushy Ana wanted to be close to him, even if it was just sitting next to him. At first Ana leaned back and closed her eyes. With her eyes still closed Ana told Marcus that he had won Mary Ann over. Marcus looked over at Ana. She still had her eyes closed. He thought of how beautiful she was. He went over her body with his eyes remembering how good she felt. Marcus noticed Ana shiver. He wondered if she had felt his gaze.

"Ana."

With her eyes still closed she answered, "Yes."

Marcus wondered if she was answering the question deep within him or just the call of her name.

"It's getting late. I think I better go."

Ana opened her eyes. She looked at Marcus with desire. She gazed at his lips, wanting to feel the taste, the warmth of them once more. When Ana noticed the questioning look on Marcus' face she adjusted her look.

"Why don't you stay here tonight?" He continued to have a questioning look on his face. "I mean, then you'll be here when Mary Ann wake up and opens her gifts. I have some covers and sheets you can sleep on the couch."

"Are you sure?"

"Yes."

"Ok."

Ana got up. She could feel Marcus watching. She walked into the bathroom and got a sheet and blanket. She made up the couch.

'Is it anything that you need?" For the first time she saw a look in Marcus eyes that gave her an answer, but then it was gone.

"No. I'm fine. Thank you."

As Ana walked to her room she wondered if she had imagined the look. She showered, not feeling at all tired. Here she had this gorgeous man in her living room and she so needed to be held. Ana put on a pair of short pajamas. It was always very warm in her apartment. She laid down. Ana toss and turned. After an hour of not getting any sleep Ana sat up. She saw the light still on in the living room. Ana got up. She went into the living room. Marcus was watching a movie. Ana sat next to him.

Ana asked, "You can't sleep?"

"No."

"Is the couch uncomfortable?"

"It's alright."

"If you want, my bed is big enough. We can share it." Marcus looked at her. "What I mean is you could sleep on one side and me on the other. You'll be comfortable."

"No I wouldn't."

"I'm telling you the mattress is very comfortable."

"Ana it would not be a good idea for me to get into your bed. I would not get any sleep."

"You're not getting any sleep out here either."

"That's cause I have a lot on my mind. What about you, what are you still doing up?"

"I saw your light on and came out to see if you were alright."

Ana sat back. They began to watch the movie. The two were quiet. Ana balled up and soon drifted off to sleep. Marcus shared his blanket with her. After the movie went off Marcus brought Ana closer to him so he could get comfortable. He laid back. He soon fell asleep......

The next morning Ana awakened first. She realized Marcus was holding her. She smoothed her face in his arms. Ana closed her eyes. She didn't want this moment to end. It felt so good being in Marcus' arms again, even if it's only while he slept. As she laid there Ana wondered when and how she ended up laying on him. He must care. Why else would he hold her next to him? With a mixture of courage and arousal Ana moved up Marcus' body. She smoothed her hand over the side of his face. Ana smoothed her hand over his lips. Marcus jumped. He opened his eyes. Marcus moved his head back. He looked at her confused.

"What's going on?"

"I found myself laying here."

Marcus thought about it.

"You were bald up in the corner of the chair. I thought you would be more comfortable stretched out. I didn't want to wake you."

"Well thank you." Ana reached up and lightly kissed him on the lips.

"What was that for?"

"Marcus, what are we doing?"

"What do you mean?"

"Marcus I've never done this. I'm afraid if I don't do something our lives are going to past us by and we won't be what we suppose to be."

"I'm still confused."

"Marcus I'm in love with you. I've never stopped. I know I hurt you before. I'm sorry about that. I realize that if I don't jump out on faith right now and take this chance we're going to miss out on a great relationship." Marcus looked at Ana curiously. "Yes I believe what we have inside for each other is something great. Can we begin again? Can we start right now?"

Marcus looked at Ana with such tenderness that her heart melted. Marcus pulled her to him.

"I've been waiting for this moment to come for a long time." He kissed her passionately. Ana returned the passion. Marcus held her closer, wanting to be one with her. It had been such a long time since either one had been with anyone. They held onto each other not wanting to let go. Marcus held Ana's face in both his hands. He whispered, "Can I make love to you?" The look in his eyes made her want to do anything he asked. She remembered Mary Ann in her room.

"Mary Ann."

"Can we go into your room?"

With everything in her soul Ana wanted to give Marcus what he asked for, but she knew that Mary Ann would be waking up soon.

"Mary Ann will be getting up soon."

"Well let's just go where I can at least hold you for a few minutes."

Ana got up. She held her hand out to Marcus. He got up, took her into his arms and carried her into the room. He closed the door behind them. Marcus began to kiss Ana. He continued to hold her. It felt so good being in his arms. Ana held on as Marcus kissed her neck while walking towards the bed. He returned to her lips and ever so gently laid Ana onto her bed. Marcus looked down at Ana. He gently sat down next to her. He lifted her to a sitting position. Marcus lifted Ana's top over her head exposing her breast. Marcus laid the top on the nearby chair. He ran the back of his hand down the middle of Ana's chest. "You are so beautiful." He kissed Ana passionately. Ana returned the passion. Marcus leaned Ana back. He caressed her body until Ana called out to him. Marcus joined Ana in a slow rhymic motion wanting to savor each delicious feeling. Ana called out Marcus' name again. He held her tighter. Ana whispered she loved him. Marcus laid there holding Ana. She felt at home in his arms. Ana wanted to stay in his arms, but knew Mary Ann should be awake and she didn't want her to come into the room and find them this way. She leaned over and kissed Marcus. She told him that she had to get dressed. He understood.

Ana got up and went into the bathroom. She took a quick shower. When Ana came out of the bathroom she threw a lounge shirt on. Marcus looked at her with desire in his eyes. Ana told him to get dressed. Marcus got up and went into the bathroom. He dressed. They decided it would be a great Christmas gift for Mary Ann to see her father when she awakened. When they walked into her room Mary Ann was awake.

She had been playing with her dolls. When she saw Marcus she jumped up and ran to him. Marcus picked her up, kissed her and said Merry Christmas. Mary Ann hugged Marcus around his neck. He carried her to the living room and then sat her down. Mary Ann excitedly opened her gifts. Ana watched on, not remembering Mary Ann being as happy. She thought maybe it was that Mary Ann was older. Ana watched how happy Marcus was. For a minute Ana felt a twinge of guilt. She tried to shake it. Marcus happened to look over at Ana and saw the uneasy look. He asked her if she was alright. Ana tried to tell Marcus what was wrong without Mary Ann knowing what they were talking about. Marcus told her that he wasn't holding it against her and not to worry herself about it. He went on to say that he was embracing this moment, not any that was lost. Ana smiled slightly, but still felt bad.

After Mary Ann finished opening her gifts she hugged both parents. A few minutes later Ana got up and fixed breakfast. After she was done they sat down to eat. Mary Ann excitedly talked about her toys. A few times Ana caught herself thinking about Marcus and how wonderful she felt in his arms. When they had finished eating Ana got up to clean the kitchen. While she was cleaning Marcus offered to get Mary Ann dressed. When she was dressed Marcus told Ana that he needed to go home and get changed for dinner at her parents. Marcus lightly kissed Ana on the side of her face. After he had gone Ana could still feel the heat from his lips.

After Marcus was gone Ana put the gifts she had purchased for the family in a bag. She went to her room and began to get dressed. Ana put on a navy blue velvet dress. She placed her grandmother's pearls on. She had given them to her before she past away. Margaret had kept them until she turned eighteen. Ana looked in the mirror and was pleased with what she saw. Mary Ann confirmed it when Ana came out of the room and she said, "Mommy you look pretty." Ana smiled at her daughter and returned the sentiment. Ana gathered the bags and took hold of Mary Ann's hand. They walked out the door to her car. Ana helped Mary Ann into the car and buckled her in. Ana put the bags in the trunk. She started the car and then drove away.

As they drove to her parents holiday music played on the radio. She and Mary Ann sang along. Ana was happier than she'd ever been. She couldn't help but wonder if this feeling would remain. Ana told herself that she would enjoy every moment she had with Marcus. When they arrived at her parents' Ana parked. Mary Ann had taken her seat belt off. Ana allowed Mary Ann to run up to the house and ring the doorbell. Ana got the bags out of the trunk. Tommy Jay opened the door. Mary Ann yelled Merry Christmas and hugged him. TJ came to the door. He saw Ana with the bags and helped her with them. They went into the house. TJ placed the gifts under the tree. Margaret was in the kitchen cooking. When Thomas heard the group he came downstairs. Mary Ann ran up to him. He picked his granddaughter up. He pointed to a gift under the tree. She ran over to get it. As she opened it Mary Ann told the family how her daddy had brought her lots of gifts and he was at her house when she opened them. Ana's family turned and looked at her. Ana facial expression was as if to ask what. The family continued to open their gifts…

Guest began to arrive at three o'clock. Everyone mingled. Marcus showed up at four. Margaret announced that dinner was ready. Everyone sat at the table. Margaret said the blessing. Everyone began to eat. Ana and Marcus gazed into each other's eyes throughout dinner.

After dinner when Marcus and Ana was alone he handed her a small box wrapped in a red velvet like paper with a small bow on top. Ana looked at him curiously. She shakily opened the box. Inside was her ring. Of course she remembered it. She had looked at it every night when he first gave it to her. She asked him what did it mean. He in turn asked her what did it mean before. Ana knew this was the best that he could do because of her rejection before, so she blurted out "Yes, I will marry you."

Marcus took Ana into his arms and kissed her. As they kissed Margaret walked into the room. She saw the two hugging. She asked what was going on. Ana looked at Marcus and told her that they were going to get married. Margaret hugged both of them. She asked if they had a date in mind. Marcus said as soon as possible. Ana felt the same. Looking at Marcus Ana said June……

A month went by. To save money Marcus moved in with Ana. Mary Ann was thrilled that her father was there everyday. Ana had never felt so complete. She and Marcus went to look at a few banquet halls. After visiting a few they finally agreed on one. Marcus made reservations for the limos and for their honeymoon. They decided to go to Hawaii......

Three months had past. Ana began feeling sluggish. She had been running a lot with working, taking care of Mary Ann and wedding planning. She had gone over her mother's to go over the guest list one more time and get them ready to be mailed out. Ana went to stand up and became dizzy. She sat back down. Margaret noticed and asked her if she was alright. Ana told her that she was just tired. Margaret gave her a suspicious look. She assured her mother that they used protection. Ana then thought of Christmas morning. As if a light came on Ana's expression changed. Margaret noticed it. She questioned Ana. Ana admitted about Christmas. Ana left her parent's house and went to the store. She purchased two pregnancy kits. Ana returned to her parents' home and went into her old bedroom. She waited as the test took it's course. When she read the results Ana couldn't believe her eyes. She took it downstairs to show her mother. Margaret looked at it and then asked what was she going to do. Ana told her she would let her know. Ana gathered up Mary Ann and the invitations. She stopped by the post office and mailed them off. Ana then drove home. She helped Mary Ann out of the car. They went into her apartment. Ana put the kit up an then got Mary Ann ready for bed. When Marcus came home Ana was asleep. He got ready for bed. When he got into bed Marcus put his arms around Ana and held her all night.....

The next morning Ana awakened earlier than usual. She eased out of bed. Ana went into the bathroom and pulled out the kit. As she waited for the results Ana thought back to the first time she was pregnant. Fear came over her. She felt irresponsible again. She thought "How could I be so irresponsible? What will Marcus think? Should she tell Marcus or begin her marriage in deceit?" She loved this man. He has been so understanding. A tap on the door made Ana jump. She looked at the stick. It revealed she was pregnant. Ana sat there, not knowing what to do. Another tap on the door made her stand. She walked over to the door and unlocked it. Marcus came in. Marcus asked if she was alright and then he saw it. The box on the tub. He walked over to it. Marcus picked it up and then saw the stick in Ana's hand. She couldn't speak. Ana was afraid that her words would end their relationship once again.

Marcus took the stick from her. He read it. Marcus saw the fear in her eyes. He took his free arm and put it around her. Marcus pulled her to him. He whispered, "So we did it again?" Ana looked at him with a surprised expression and then embarrassed one. He joked with her.

"You've got to be the most fertile woman I've ever met. It's a good thing that you never had sex before now, but I guess that's why you can get pregnant so easy." Ana gave a questioning look. "You've never had any birth control or abortion."

"Are you ok with this?"

"Well let's see, I missed out on my first, I am not going to miss out on any others."

Ana gave him a questioning look.

'Any more? Do you want to have more?"

"Yes. I've always wanted four children."

"Four?"

"Yes. I'm sorry."

"No. That's fine."

"Besides with you it should be a breeze."

Ana pushed him. What?"

"Don't tease."

"Baby it's a good thing. Don't you know there are women who can't get pregnant at all."

Ana thought about it. Then she thought of her mother. She was one of those women who was blessed with two children, wanted more, but wasn't able to have anymore. Ana thought she would give her mother those children through way of grandchildren. Ana smiled.

"You're right…."

Chapter 9

THE DAY CAME. ANA AWAKENED in her childhood bed. She was sluggish, but quickly became energized because today she would become Mrs. Marcus Stiles. Ana showered. She woke Mary Ann and they went downstairs to eat. The family ate and then began getting dressed….

The photography team arrived and began snapping pictures. When Ana finished dressing she opened the front door where a white Rolls Royce and white limo was waiting in front of her parent's home. Ana was escorted to the Rolls. Mary Ann sat next to her with a similar dress. Her bridesmaids Karen and Rosalyn road in the Rolls Royce with Ana. Her mother road in the limo with her father.

When the group arrived in front of the church tears formed in Margaret's eyes. Thomas put his arm around her shoulders.

After the cars parked the group exited the cars.

The ushers and grooms' men walked Margaret and the brides-maids into the church.

The music began to play. Although Tommy Jay was older than the usual ring bearer he carried the rings.

Mary Ann began her walk throwing rose petals as she walked to the front of the church. A soloist began to sing.

With her two fathers on each side Ana began her walk.

As she walked towards her groom Ana thought of how wonderful it was to have both of her fathers at her wedding. Ana watched Marcus as she walked to the front of the church. He was so handsome, inside and out. He was a good man, caring and understanding. She couldn't have asked for a better man. She felt blessed. Ana was caught in his gaze.

Marcus watched his bride as she walked towards him. He thought of how long it has taken for this moment to get here. When Ana made it up to Marcus he took her hand. They stood side by side.

As the minister talked about marriage Ana and Marcus gazed into each other's eyes. When the minister asked who gives this woman, both Thomas and Steve stood up and said "I do." Ana smiled. The minister told them to repeat after him and then he asked for the rings. Tommy Jay brought the rings to them. The minister blessed the rings and then handed them to Ana and Marcus. After the couple exchanged the rings the minister pronounced them husband and wife. Marcus took Ana into his arms and kissed her. Everyone stood up and the couple walked out of the church. They got into the Rolls and it drove away. The bridle party followed. When they arrived at the hall the photographers took pictures.

After the pictures the group was escorted to the banquet room. The hall doors were opened and the group was announced. Music began to play, everyone stood up. Marcus and Ana were announced. They walked to the middle of the dance floor and had their first dance. Marcus held her closer than he ever had. She felt at home, secure in her husband's arms. Ana rested her head on his chest. He twirled her a few times, but because of Ana's pregnancy Marcus was careful. No one except her family knew. Ana was not showing. The next dance was for the father of the bride. Ana and her father's had practiced a routine. Ana walked to the middle of the dance floor. Steve held his hand out. Ana took it. As the music played Steve and Ana danced a waltz. When the music changed over to a blues and jazzy tune Thomas walked over to them and tapped Steve on the shoulder. Steve graciously gave Ana's hand to Thomas. Because he knew she was pregnant Thomas tried not to over due it when they danced. When the dance was over Both fathers took Ana's hand and kissed it. As everyone watched they clapped and laughed at the routine....

Throughout the evening the couple mingled and danced often. During the toast one of Marcus' best friends and best man stood up. He began, *"Marcus I've known you all of your life. We had a lot of fun. Out of all of our friends I knew someone would eventually snagged you. You know why? It's because you have a big heart. Ana you have a good guy and I wish you all the happiness that you two deserve."*

Karen got up next.

"Ana I am truly surprised. I never thought that you would pull your head out of those books long enough to notice anyone. Marcus you have got to be a special and patient man. You two have to be destined to be together. I wish you the very best. I love you both."

Everyone stood up and clapped. Soon after the speeches the couple cut the cake.

The couple shared a piece of cake and then readied themselves to depart. They thanked everyone and left for their honeymoon.

While they drove to the airport Ana rested her head on Marcus' chest. She closed her eyes and thought about the wedding. Just as she drifted off to sleep Marcus kissed her on the forehead and told her they were there. They exited the car and checked in at the curb. The two hurried to their gate. The flight had started boarding. They got in line. When they finally boarded Ana leaned back and fell asleep. Marcus watched a movie. When they arrived in Hawaii a taxi was waiting for them. Marcus and Ana got into the cab. They were taken to a ship which took them to their island. Ana gazed out onto the ocean and thought what a paradise. When they pulled into port they gathered their things and got off the ship. A taxi was waiting. A mile down the road they arrived at their hotel. Ana stood at first looking at the hotel in awe. After checking in the couple was taken to their suite. Marcus picked Ana up and carried her into the room. After he put her down Ana looked around. She went out onto the terrace and laid on the lounge chair. She was mesmerized by the beautiful clear blue water. She couldn't believe how clear the sky was. Ana felt as if it was perfect because God was shinning down on this day. Marcus came out and sat in the other chair. He looked out onto the water and smiled.

"It's beautiful isn't it?"

"Yes. I take it you're be camped out here."

"When we're here."

"Are you hungry?"

"Starved."

"Good I ordered room service."

"Great. You think we can take the food onto the beach with us?"

"Sure. You want to go out?"

"Yes. It's too beautiful to stay inside. Let's get changed and when the food come take it with us. I want to experience everything."

Marcus just looked at Ana. He had never seen her so carefree. Ana got up, took Marcus by the hand and they walked into the room. Ana kissed Marcus. He put his arms around her waist. They embraced. Ana moved back. She smiled and then began taking off her clothes. Marcus stood still and just watched her. She had a beautiful body. There was no sign that she was pregnant or ever had been. When she was completely naked Ana walked closer to Marcus. She kissed him and began undressing him. Marcus was turned on by her seduction. When she had removed his clothes Ana led Marcus to the bathroom. She turned the shower on. Ana tested the water. She climbed in and then took Marcus' hand. He got in. Ana picked up the bath sponge and put gel on it. She then began to suds her body. She moved the sponge slowly in a seductive way. When her body was completely soaped up she began to soap up Marcus' body. He had never seen Ana this way. He stood quiet, still wanting to enjoy this side of his wife. Ana looked into Marcus' eyes and saw that he was turned on. She began kissing and continued caressing his body. Marcus leaned against the shower wall. He watched Ana as she brought him pleasure. She kissed him again and Marcus took over. He caressed her body and kissed Ana. Each place that he touched burned with desire. Marcus picked her up and she wrapped her legs around his waist. Ana wrapped her arms around Marcus' neck. Ana held onto Marcus feeling all of his passion. As tears rolled down her face Ana tightened her arms around him. Marcus felt Ana's body tighten. He held her tighter. They remained locked in each other's arms until the knock on the door interrupted them. Marcus kissed her passionately and then put her down. Ana let him go. He stepped out of the shower and wrapped himself with a towel. He went to answer the door. Marcus opened the door. Standing there was the delivery person. Marcus took the food, tipped the delivery person and then put the food on the dinning table. He returned to the bedroom. Ana had gotten out of the shower and was getting dressed. Marcus tried to persuade her to stay, but she insisted on going out. He took a quick shower and dressed. They gathered the food and left the room. The two walked down to the beach. Marcus laid a cloth on the sand. Ana sat down. Marcus followed her. They took the food out. As the two ate they watched the surfers, families and couples running in and out of the water. Ana got up and held her hand out to Marcus. He took it and she led him down to the water. They walked along the beach. The waves brushed along hitting their legs. Ana hung onto Marcus trying to catch her balance. Marcus picked her up and pretended to drop her into the ocean. She held on tightly to his neck.

"That's the way I like you to hold me." Ana laid her head on his shoulder. "You ready to go back?" Ana nodded her head yes. Marcus continued to hold Ana. He carried her to where they had been sitting. Marcus gently laid Ana down. He laid down next to her. He rubbed her stomach and began talking about the baby. Ana placed her hand on top of his. She closed her eyes.

After a few minutes Marcus noticed she had fallen asleep. He watched Ana and caressed her hair. He watched the families with their children and wondered how he and Ana would be with theirs. Marcus closed his eyes. When he felt himself drift off he sat up. After a few minutes Marcus packed up their things. He lifted Ana into his arms and picked up the basket. As he walked towards the hotel Ana awakened. She told him that she could walk, but Marcus insisted on carrying her. Ana laid her head back on his shoulder and enjoyed the ride......

When they got to the room Ana swiped the lock and Marcus pushed the door open. Marcus placed the basket on the table and carried Ana into the bedroom. He laid her down and got in beside her. Ana looked at Marcus with such love in her eyes that his heart melted. He pulled her onto him and kissed her. Ana put her arms around his neck as he kissed her neck. Marcus caressed Ana's body. She felt his arousal. Ana loved Marcus' touch and the way her made her feel. Ana and Marcus held onto each other, savoring each kiss, touch and wonderful way their bodies responded....

For the next two days the couple couldn't bare to share each other with the world. They stayed in, ordered food and made love throughout the days and nights.

Their forth day there the couple ventured out to tour the island. They went to a local club and took in the island's traditions.

On the seventh day Ana and Marcus prepared their luggage. A taxi arrived and took them to the ship. They took the ship to an awaiting taxi, that brought them to the airport.

When they arrived at the airport Ana called her mother to let her know that they were on their way back. When she talked to her mother Margaret's voice sounded strained. Ana asked her if Mary Ann was alright. Margaret assured her she was. Although Margaret told her Mary Ann was fine Ana was still concerned.

Throughout the ride back Ana tried to recall her conversation with Margaret. There was something in her voice. Ana mentioned it to Marcus. He tried to comfort her.

When they arrived in Newark Marcus gathered their things. A car was waiting for them. Ana asked Marcus if they could go straight to her parent's home. Marcus saw the concern. They were taken to Ana parent's home. They took their items out of the car and went up to the front door. Ana got her keys and opened the front door. They entered the house. Ana called out, but there wasn't any answer. Ana went into every room trying to find someone, but no one was there. She took out her cell phone and called her mother. Margaret answered after four rings. Ana told her that they were at her home and asked where was everyone. Margaret explained that everyone was at the hospital. Ana asked what was going on. Margaret explained that TJ and Tommy Jay had been in a car accident. She told Ana that Tommy Jay had a few bruises, but other wise fine. On the other hand TJ was in critical condition. Ana became dizzy. Marcus noticed and went to her assistance. He took the phone. Margaret told him what she had just said to Ana. He hung up the phone and lift Ana into his arms. He carried her into the den. He checked her pulse. Marcus held her close to him until she gained consciousness. When Ana came to she looked at Marcus and then around the room. Ana remembered. With pain in her eyes Ana sat up. She looked at Marcus and he confirmed what Ana believed she heard. Marcus put his arms around Ana. Ana stood to her feet. She walked into the kitchen, over to the key rack and saw Margaret's car keys hanging up. Ana took them and headed to the garage. Marcus followed. When Ana put the key in the lock to unlock the car door Marcus took it from her. He walked over to the passenger side of the car and held the door for Ana. He then walked over to the driver side. He got in and started it. After pulling off Marcus took Ana's hand and held it. Ana started to cry. Marcus squeezed her hand. Marcus and Ana was quiet throughout the ride.....

When they arrived at the hospital Marcus parked the car. He didn't want Ana to go in alone. He got out of the car and walked over to open her door. Marcus held his hand out. Ana took it. Marcus helped her out of the car. He held one of her hands and put his other arm around her. Marcus held Ana as close as he could. He wanted to comfort her.

When they got into the hospital Ana gave her brother's name. They allowed them to go up. Ana and Marcus took the elevator to the floor that TJ was on. They walked down the hall. Ana looked at the room numbers. When she spotted TJ's room Ana slowly walked in. As she saw the tubes in TJ's nose, mouth and arms tears streamed her face. Ana moved closer. She saw the bandage on the side of his face. Ana saw her mother holding TJs' hand and then she spotted the cast on both of his legs. Ana walked over to the bed. She touched her mother's hand. Margaret looked up. When she saw that it was Ana, Margaret stood up and hugged her. Ana asked her how was TJ. Margaret told her he was in a coma.

Margaret explained that TJ had been in a car accident and suffered third degree burns to his left arm. Both legs were broken and the side of his face had been cut. Ana walked out of the room. Marcus followed. She went to talk to the nurse. TJ's doctor happened to be present. As the doctor told TJ's prognosis Ana held back tears. Marcus placed his hand behind Ana's back to support her. When the doctor was finished Ana thanked him and returned to TJ's room. Ana asked the whereabouts of Mary Ann. She was told that Mary Ann was with Rosalyn. She then went to see Tommy Jay.

When she saw her nephew Ana walked over to him and hugged Tommy Jay. He had been spared any major trauma. He had bruising and his arm had been burned. Ana asked him if he remembered what happened. Tommy Jay told them that his father was driving on route 22. A car was chasing another and trying to ram it. When the one car hit the other it hit the guard rail. His father tried to avoid it and ended up spinning out and hitting it as well. He told Ana that a man and his little girl died from the accident. He went on to tell them that his father was pinned. The car caught on fire. Tommy Jay told them that he managed to crawl out of his window. He saw his father was unconscious. TJ said that he crawled back into the car and started pulling his father. The car caught on fire and his father began burning. He managed to get him out just in time before the car blew up. Someone else pulled the two of them out away to safety and put TJ out. Tommy Jay began to cry. Ana held him. Through tears Tommy Jay murmured that he thought his dad was dead. Ana rubbed his back.....

The next day Ana took a leave from work. Rosalyn agreed to watch Mary Ann when Marcus couldn't. Thomas, Ana and Margaret stayed with TJ and Tommy Jay around the clock......

A month later Tommy Jay was released. Margaret cut her visits short to be with Tommy Jay. Ana took turns to allow her mother to be at the hospital.

In the middle of the second month Margaret's doorbell rang. She went to open the door. Standing on the other side was Paula. Margaret hugged her. She told Margaret that the hospital had contact her after the accident. Paula explained that it had been difficult to get away because of work. Margaret escorted Paula up to see Tommy Jay. When Paula entered the room she exclaimed that Tommy Jay was the splitting image of his father. She stared at him. Paula talked to Tommy Jay about his father. After an hour of drilling him she told Tommy Jay that she had to go and would be back the next day. Margaret offered Paula a room, but she declined.

When Ana came over that night Margaret informed her of Paula's visit. Ana tried to call her cell phone, but her number had been changed. A few days had past and there wasn't any word from Paula.....

A week later two letters from the family court came in the mail, one for TJ and the other for Ana. Margaret opened TJ's letter. She was shocked to read that Paula had filed for custody of Tommy Jay. Margaret called Ana to tell her that she had mail at their house and that it was very important that she come by to pick it up. Ana had returned to work. Ana told Margaret that she would come by right after work.

When Ana got off she went straight to her parent's home. She called Marcus and asked him to pick Mary Ann up.

As Ana drove to her parent's home she wondered what was so important. Her mind went to her unborn baby when she felt it move. Ana rubbed her stomach. She had just started showing. She rubbed her stomach and began talking to the baby. The baby moved again. Ana thought of how things were not going the way she figured. Ana imagined she and Marcus coming home to their home, picking up Mary

Ann and preparing a room for their baby. She realized at that moment that she had forgotten her doctor's visit. It was too late to call and reschedule. Ana pulled up in front of her parent's home. She parked and got out of the car. Ana went into the house. She called out to Margaret. Ana knew something was wrong when she saw the expression on her mother's face. Ana asked what was wrong. Margaret handed Ana both letters. Ana opened her letter and read it. Without a word she read TJ's letter. Ana asked if she told Thomas about it. Margaret told Ana that she had and he called one of his partners to get on it. Margaret explained that he didn't want to handle the case himself because it was too close to home. Ana stayed a while at her mothers.....

It was dark when Ana arrived home. Marcus had put Mary Ana to bed. Ana went into her daughter's room. She walked over and kissed her daughter, careful not to wake her. Ana stood over her daughter a few minutes watching her sleep. Ana left Mary Ann's room and went into her bedroom. Marcus was laying in the bed watching television. When he saw her Marcus sat up. He saw that Ana looked tired. He asked if she had eaten. Ana thought about it and said no. Marcus got up and left the room. He returned shortly afterwards with a plate he had made earlier for Ana. She smiled. While Ana ate she undressed. When she was done Ana placed the plate on the dresser. She went into the bathroom and took a shower. After getting into the shower the door opened. Marcus asked if he could join her. It had been months since they had been together. Ana had been staying at the hospital with her brother and nephew. Marcus took the sponge put soap on it and began soaping Ana's body. Ana felt so relaxed. He turned her around and soaped her back. He bent down and kissed her shoulder. Ana's body responded. She placed her arm around the back of his neck. Marcus dropped the sponge and began caressing her body. Ana turned around and placed her arms around Marcus' neck. They began kissing. Marcus picked her up. Ana wrapped her legs around his body. The warmth of the water ran down their bodies. Ana held onto Marcus' muscular shoulders, feeling their strength. She kissed them, tasting salt and the sweetness of his body. Marcus held her tight enjoying the silkiness of her body. Their bodies mesh together as one.. .....

The next morning Ana awakened. She was happy that it was Saturday. She got out of bed, took a shower and dressed in lounging clothes. Ana went into the kitchen and started cooking breakfast. After she was done cooking Ana fixed herself and Marcus a plate, put it on a platter and took it into her bedroom. She bent down and kissed him. Marcus awakened. He saw the food and smiled. Marcus sat up.

"What's all this?"

"For you being so good to me."

"Wow. I could get use to this."

"Well you keep being a wonderful husband and you might just continue getting it."

Ana and Marcus enjoyed their food. Ana rubbed her stomach. Marcus asked what was wrong. She told him nothing was wrong that the baby had just moved. The baby moved again. Ana took Marcus' hand and placed it on her stomach. The baby moved again. Ana watched Marcus' expression as he felt the baby move around. He was amazed. Ana thought how nice it was sharing such an experience with him.

Ana remembered when she first felt Mary Ann move and how different it was not having Marcus to share the experience took away some of the pleasure of being pregnant. Marcus put his face to Ana's stomach and began to talk to the baby. A few minutes later Mary Ann came in. She asked what Marcus was doing. Ana explained that he was talking to her brother or sister. Mary Ann asked if she could talk to the baby. Ana told her sure. Mary Ann put her face to Ana's stomach and began to talk. The baby moved. Mary Ann felt it. Ana explained that the baby was stretching. Mary Ann announced that she was hungry. Ana got up. She picked up the tray and took Mary Ann into the kitchen. She warmed up the food and placed the plate down in front of Mary Ann. Mary Ann chatted while she ate. Marcus dressed and came into the kitchen. Mary Ann had finished eating and Ana was cleaning up the kitchen. Ana remembered about the letter her mother had given her. Ana told Marcus about the letter. Ana explained that she had joint custody of her nephew. Marcus noticed that Ana was upset. He tried to sooth her....

Later Ana called Thomas and asked him to watch Mary Ann while she and Marcus visit TJ. She dropped Mary Ann over her parent's home and headed to the hospital. Once there Ana held TJ's hand and talked to him. She asked him to come back to them and that his son needed him.......

Two weeks later Ana, her parents and Tommy Jay arrived at the court house. They waited to be called. While they waited Ana saw Paula. Ana nodded her head to speak to Paula. Ana had not spoken with Paula since she moved out of her apartment in undergraduate school. Ana showed Marcus who Paula was. When their case was called everyone got up and went into the court room. The judge asked everyone who they were and their interest in the minor. Paula testified that she was seeking custody because his father was in a coma and could not take care of him.

When Ana testified she informed the court that she had joint physical custody of her nephew and that her parents are also listed on the court order. Ana informed the court that in eleven years they have not heard from Paula. She informed the court that Paula has not sent a birthday, Christmas card or any other correspondence. Ana told the courts that if there was ever a time not to move a child this would be it.

The judge asked Tommy Jay into her chambers. She asked him what did he think about his mother asking for custody. Tommy Jay told the judge that his aunt gave him a picture of his mother. He admitted that he always wanted to know her, but he didn't want to live with the woman out there. The judge looked at him curiously. He told the judge that he didn't know that person out there and his home was with his father, grandparents and aunt.

The judge returned to her bench. She left custody with TJ and his family. She ordered a psychological evaluation and weekend visits with his mother. They were ordered to return to court for the judge's decision.

For the first month Paula came up on the weekends. She would come over and pick up Tommy Jay to take him to the movies and eat out. On occasion Paula would spend the day with Tommy Jay at Margaret's home in the basement. She sometimes shared stories of her childhood with Tommy Jay. The rest of the time Paula asked about his father.

During Tommy Jay's visits with the psychologist he talked about his accident and concern about his father. When asked about his mother Tommy Jay told her that his mother didn't really seem committed. He told her that he didn't think that she really cared about him. When the psychologist asked why did he think that Tommy Jay said that he didn't feel what he felt when he was with his aunt and grandmother.

During the second month Paula didn't come over as much. Tommy Jay was okay with it because he felt the meetings were strained. The psychologist met with Paula alone and then with Paula with Tommy Jay. She also met with Margaret, Thomas, Ana and her family.

When the two months had ended the group returned to court. The judge had already read the psychologist's report. She again spoke with Tommy Jay privately. The judge was ready to rule. Ana sat quiet and still trying to ignore the pain from her contractions. The sheriff officer called the family into the court room. When Ana went to stand her water broke. She told Marcus. They informed the officer. Ana didn't want to leave, but Marcus convinced her that she would have the baby in an unsanitary environment if she stayed any longer. Margaret and Thomas hugged Ana and assured her that they would let her know what happened as soon as they could....

Marcus helped Ana walk to the car. He helped her in and then ran to the driver's side. He began driving to the hospital. Marcus told Ana to practice her breathing. Ana informed Marcus that they weren't going to make it to the hospital. He looked at her thinking that she was panicking. Ana told him to pull over. He did as she asked. Ana instructed him to help her into the back seat. Ana laid back. Marcus pulled her pants and underwear down. When Ana put her legs up Marcus saw the baby's head crowning. Marcus looked up at Ana. Marcus carried extra white surgical coats in the back seat in a bag. He went into his medical bag and took two out. He placed one under Ana and held the other one to wrap the baby in. He instructed Ana to push. She did as her husband instructed. After several pushes the baby was out. Marcus cleaned the baby's airways and then wrapped his son in his jacket. He looked at his beautiful son and then handed him to his mother. Marcus cleaned Ana and went into his trunk. He took out a blanket. Marcus placed the blanket over Ana and the baby. He kissed Ana lightly and then got back behind the wheel. He proceeded to drive to the hospital. Marcus called Ana's doctor and explained that he was on his way and Ana had the baby.

When they got to the hospital Ana was taken to a private room and the doctor examined her. He told them that they did an excellent job and congratulated them. He then left them alone. The baby was taken to be examined. Marcus hugged his wife and thanked her for his son. Ana drifted off to sleep. Marcus went outside of the room and called Margaret. They were out of court and on their way to the hospital. Margaret put him on speaker phone. Marcus told them what happened. Margaret asked if Ana and the baby were alright. Marcus assured her that they were. Margaret told Marcus that they would be at the hospital shortly.

As Marcus was walking down to the nursery a nurse was bringing his baby to the room. Marcus walked back to the room with the nurse. The nurse checked Ana's wrist to make sure the baby was in the right place. After she left Marcus picked up his son. Marcus couldn't believe how small he was. Marcus talked to his son. Ana woke up. She watched Marcus with his son. It warmed her heart. Marcus turned and saw that Ana was awake. He walked over to her. He handed Ana the baby. Ana kissed him. The baby got fidgety. Marcus said, "I think he's getting hungry. Ana opened her top and began feeding the baby. Marcus pulled a chair close to Ana's bed and looked on. A half hour later Margaret and Thomas entered the room. They came over and kissed Ana who was still holding the baby. Thomas and Margaret took turns holding the baby. Margaret asked what they had decided to name him. Ana looked at Marcus and said that he is Jr. Marcus smiled with pride. Then Ana thought about TJ. She asked her parents what happened in court. Margaret said that the judge left custody as it was. She told Ana that the judge told Paula that she felt that she was looking for a payday and that she wanted to be there when it came. Ana was hoping that the judge saw through Paula, but she didn't think of the money angle....

A year went by. TJ was released from the hospital and brought home. Ana and Marcus decided to purchase a home. Ana didn't want to move far from her parents. She wanted to continue to be close so she could be there for TJ and Tommy Jay.....

Six months went by. Ana and her family found a home large enough for a growing family. Ana was pregnant again.

The day they moved in Margaret called Ana. She asked Ana to come by. Ana told Marcus. Ana left and drove to her parent's home. Soon Ana pulled up in her parent's driveway. Ana let herself in. She called out to her mother. Margaret didn't answer. Ana became concerned. She went up to TJ's room. Ana didn't believe her eyes. She walked slowly to his bed. TJ had come out of his coma. Margaret was holding his hand and crying. Thomas and Tommy Jay had tears in their eyes. Ana put her arms around TJ, laid her head on his chest and cried. TJ was too weak to move her. He took his free arm and put it around her.

After a half hour Margaret began to tell TJ what happened. TJ looked at his son. He was older. Thomas explained that he had been gone for a while.

The door bell rang. Tommy Jay went down to answer it. It was TJ's doctor. He followed Tommy Jay to TJ's room and examined him. The doctor told the family that TJ's prognosis looked good......

For the next four months TJ went through therapy. Ana and Margaret took turns taking TJ. On one of Ana's turns she went into labor. Ana drove TJ to his session. Ana did not let on that she was in labor. After dropping him off, she tried to get through it and get him back home, but her water broke in the waiting room. She called her doctor and then Marcus. He worked in a nearby hospital.

On his way from work Marcus talked to Ana. Marcus couldn't believe that he was stuck in traffic. A half hour later Marcus was running down the hall of the center. They went to let TJ know. He cut his therapy short to go with them. Once again Marcus found himself pulling over to the side of the road and delivering his second son. TJ was amazed.

When they arrived at the hospital Ana's doctor joked about them trying to get a discount. The doctor checked Ana. Ana was taken to her room. Marcus called Margaret. Margaret thought he was joking, but then believed him when he asked her to pick up their children.

The next day Ana and baby Steven were released from the hospital......

TJ began driving himself to therapy. He was becoming independent. TJ received a substantial settlement and decided to purchase a home for he and his son. Ana gave TJ her realtor's number. TJ called Tracy. Tracy was a few years older than TJ. She graduated two years before Ana. When he meet Tracy he looked her over. Tracy was fare skinned, long hair and had a beautiful complexion. She was just a few inches shorter that TJ. When TJ met her he thought she could have easily been a model. When she smiled Tracy's teeth sparkled. During TJ's search for his home, Tracy and TJ got to know each other and became friends. They went out to dinner a few times after looking at houses. TJ finally found a house. He decided to have a house warming. He invited Tracy. Tracy asked if she could bring someone. TJ told her she could. Ana and Margaret helped TJ decorate his house and get it ready for his party.

TJ went to get dressed. Ana and Margaret let the guest in. The people mingled. TJ came into the living room where a few of his friends were talking. They noticed him and all greeted TJ with a hug. TJ was happy to see them. He had not seen many of them since high school. As time past TJ wondered if Tracy had decided not to come.

The door bell rang. Ana went to open it. It was Tracy. Ana hugged her. Ana spoke to the two women that Tracy brought. Tracy introduced them to Ana. Ana told them to come in. The women came in and Ana escorted them into the living room.

When they entered the room TJ noticed and immediately walked over. He kissed Tracy on the side of her face. Tracy introduced her friend Michelle and sister Francis. When she introduced Francis TJ looked at her in disbelief. Francis smiled. She had often thought about TJ. She hugged him. Francis felt good in his arms. TJ thought she felt like home. They had not realized that they were still hugging until Tracy cleared her throat. TJ looked embarrassed. TJ explained that he met Francis years ago on a cruise. Tracy smiled and asked Francis if this was the guy she was talking about. Francis looked away saying yes. TJ smiled at the idea Francis had talked about him. Francis heard music playing. She took TJ's hand. She asked him if he could still dance. TJ told her that he had not danced in a very long time and he was literally just learning to walk again. Francis looked at him in disbelief. She wondered if he was joking. TJ asked if they could sit instead and catch up. Francis realized that he was leaning against the wall. She wondered if he was in pain. Francis took TJ by the hand. TJ led her to an empty room. When they were seated Francis asked TJ what happened. TJ told her about the accident. When he was done TJ asked Francis' about her life. As she told TJ all about her life he listened intently. TJ looked at her, taking in every word. He thought how she had become more beautiful then he remembered.

Francis had grown up. She wore her hair long. She had a head band around it and a few long curls in front. Francis was golden brown with large brown eyes. Her eye brows were arched and had long eye lashes. Her nose was narrow and lips he thought were perfect for kissing. TJ watched them as she talked. TJ looked over her body. It was no longer the young girl's body he remembered. It had grown to be a woman's body. She was not much shorter then he. Her breast were full, small waist and perfect hips. Her body was perfect and it looked like she worked out. At one point Francis asked him if he was with her. When Francis had finished catching him up on her life. TJ told her about his son. Francis couldn't believe that he had a child. She asked TJ if she could meet him. Just then Tommy Jay walked into the room. As TJ introduced his son Francis looked at Tommy Jay. She told Tommy Jay that he was handsome and was the splitting image of his father. Tommy Jay smiled as he looked at his father. He thanked Francis for her complement and then told his father that Tracy was looking for him. TJ got up. He held his hand out to Francis. Francis took it. He felt guilty that he had left Tracy.

The three went into the living room. When he walked into the room Rosalyn walked up to him. She hugged him. TJ return her hug. Rosalyn kissed TJ lightly on the lips. TJ looked at her curiously and then shrugged it off. He walked over to Tracy. She joked with him saying, "So you've traded me in for a younger model." She then asked him to go with her somewhere private to talk.

They went out on the deck. It was late spring. It was not very cold. Tracy told TJ that it would be alright if he was interested in her sister. She explained to him that nothing could come between them. He looked at her in a questioning manner. Then he understood. His questioning look turned into disbelief.

He thought here was a beautiful woman that would have her pick of any man and she's not interested. He felt relieved that he could get to know Francis. Tracy and TJ talked a little while. Her friend found them and joined in the conversation. TJ looked at Tracy's friend. He thought she was equally as beautiful as Tracy. She was a little taller and kind of muscular. They sat for a while talking and than Francis came in. She sat by TJ. TJ felt something familiar that he had not felt in a long time. He tried to ignore it. He continued to mingle with the rest of his guest to share himself with all of them.

Although TJ was enjoying himself he was getting tired. It had been a long day and his health was still not a hundred percent. As it got later the guest began to leave. After the last guest left Ana and Margaret cleaned up for TJ. He stayed up until they were done. After they left TJ went into his room. He went straight to bed. The day had proved to be tiring. Before drifting off to sleep TJ thought of the evening. TJ recalled Rosalyn's expression when she saw him talking to Francis. He said to himself he would have to have a conversation about it. TJ thought of how amazing Francis looked and found it remarkable that she could still be interested in him. He had found out that Francis didn't live far from him. Thinking of her he became aroused. He tried to think of something else. TJ had not been with a woman since his prom. It had been a long time since he had been so bothered. He had concentrated for so long on his son and career that there wasn't any room for a relationship. TJ tossed and turned throughout the night.

The next day TJ awakened tired. He got up and showered. TJ turned more cold water on then hot. TJ couldn't believe how he was feeling. He had a therapy session. TJ dressed. He looked in on Tommy Jay. Tommy Jay was still asleep. TJ told him to get up. Tommy Jay quickly dressed. TJ dropped him off at his parent's home. TJ drove to the center. As TJ did his exercises he thought of the first time he met Francis. He thought she was attractive. TJ smiled when he remembered the time that he spent with her. TJ managed to get through the session. When TJ got into his car he decided to call Francis. She did not answer her cell phone. He decided not to leave a message. TJ began driving to his parents. His cell phone went off. He answered it.

"Hello."

"Hi."

"Did I take you away from anything?"

"No. I didn't hear the phone. What's going on?"

"You." Francis smiled to herself. "Do you have anything planned tonight?"

"No. Why, what do you have in mind?"

"I couldn't get you off my mind."

Francis couldn't believe her ears. She really liked TJ and had wondered if he was interested.

"Really?"

"Really. How about coming over and I order something to be delivered?"

"What time?"

"Six o'clock. If that's alright?"

"That's fine. I'll see you then."

The two hung up. TJ pulled up in front of his parent's house. He got out of the car. When he entered his parent's home Tommy Jay was in the basement. TJ yelled down to let him know that he was there. Tommy Jay stayed a little while before coming upstairs. TJ went into the family room. Thomas was there. TJ sat down. He told his father about Francis coming over. Thomas suggested that Tommy Jay stay the night there. TJ was happy that his father had suggested it. TJ hung out with his father a little while longer. An hour later TJ got ready to leave. TJ yelled downstairs that he was leaving. Tommy Jay ran up the stairs. TJ told him that he could stay the night. Tommy Jay was happy that he could finish his game. He told his father fine. Tommy Jay said bye to his father and ran back downstairs.

TJ left the house and got into his car. TJ called a restaurant and ordered. He drove to the restaurant to pick it up. When he got home TJ put the food on the stove. He then went to his room and got clothes to change into. TJ took a quick shower. He put a pair of slacks and dress shirt on. TJ went into the dinning room, set the table and then went into the kitchen to get the food. He sat the food out. The door bell rang. TJ looked at the table to make sure everything looked alright. He went to open the door. When he opened the door standing there was a beautiful woman. He held his hand out and she took it. TJ leaned and kissed her on the side of the face. TJ told her to come in. He led her to the dinning room. He pulled her chair out. TJ sat down. He asked Francis what she wanted to eat and then proceeded to fix her plate. TJ poured sparkling cider in their glasses. TJ said grace and they began to eat. TJ and Francis talked about their jobs. Francis confided in TJ that she was surprised when he called.

When they were done eating TJ and Francis cleared the dishes out of the dinning room. TJ told her that he would cleaned them later. He didn't want to waist time cleaning dishes. They went into the living room. TJ sat on the couch across from Francis. They both felt something. TJ resisted touching her. While Francis talked about growing up TJ watched her lips. He thought they were perfectly shaped. They had been colored with scented lip stick that had a glow to it. He looked at her neck wondering what part could he touch to send shivers throughout her body. TJ then looked at her body. He saw what he thought was a perfect body. TJ long to taste, caress and feel the softness that he once knew. He knew it would be different now. Her body had matured. At one point Francis stopped talking.

After a few minutes TJ realized that Francis had caught him checking her out. Francis smiled knowing that she felt what she saw in his eyes. Francis tried to ease some of the tension by asking TJ about Tommy Jay's mother. TJ went back to the beginning, from the first time Paula came into his room. He told Francis everything including Paula's most recent action. Francis was surprised to notice that there wasn't any anger when he spoke of her. TJ told Francis that he asked Paula to marry him. He admitted that although Paula was not his first it was as if she was. He confided that he liked how free she was when it came to love making. TJ changed the subject. He asked Francis did she have anyone in her life. She told him that she had been in a committed relationship a few years back, but it didn't work. Francis told him that she had not dated in five years. TJ looked at her unbelieving that such a beautiful woman would not have men breaking down her door. Francis explained that she was tired of men with a one track mind. She wasn't interested in short term relationships. Francis asked him how long had it been since he had been in a relationship.

TJ admitted that he had not thought of dating and had not had sex with Paula, since she delivered Tommy Jay. Francis looked at him in disbelief. It began getting late. TJ asked Francis if she wanted to stay the night. She looked at him. TJ told her that it was an innocent question. He told her that it had been a long time and that he would just like some company. TJ said that he could put in a movie. Francis agreed to stay. They went into the media room. TJ turned the television on. He put in a movie. TJ and Francis sat close. Although he wanted to put his arm around her he resisted. Francis felt their closeness. She wanted to touch his hand, but resisted. They tried to concentrate on the movie, but found it difficult. Half way through the movie TJ asked Francis if she was available the next weekend. She told him that she had to work. TJ focus on the movie again. When the movie was over TJ got up. He turned the television off. He walked over to Francis. TJ held his hand out. Francis took it. TJ and Francis walked hand in hand to one of TJ's guest rooms. When he got to the door, he paused. TJ placed both hands on either sides of her face. He looked into her eyes, wanting to take her into his arms. He bent down and kissed Francis on the side of her face, leaving a warm scent of his cologne on her face. He said good night and walked down the hall. TJ undressed and then took a shower. He put on a pair of pajama bottoms and got into bed. TJ laid there thinking of how just a few feet away was a gorgeous woman. He laid there wondering how she would be. He remembered their first time together and how inexperienced she had been. He thought of how young they both were. TJ toss and turned throughout the night.

Francis laid in bed wondering what TJ would think of her if she came into his room and asked him to make love to her.

Francis sat up. She wondered if she should look for TJ's room, but she didn't want him to get the wrong impression of her. Francis wanted to have a relationship with TJ. She could see herself for the rest of her life with this man. Francis laid back down and after some time fell asleep......

The next morning TJ woke up at his usual six o'clock. He got dressed. At eight o'clock TJ ordered breakfast. He left out to pick it up. When TJ got back he sat the food out on the table. He then went to wake Francis. TJ knocked on the door. Francis was still asleep. When Francis didn't answer. TJ knock again. Francis finally awakened. She looked around. When she realized where she was, Francis jumped up. She went to the door. She peeped out the door. TJ said good morning and told Francis that he ordered breakfast. Francis told him to give her a few minutes. She looked in her purse and took out a tooth brush and tooth paste. She then went into the bathroom, brushed her teeth and took a shower. Francis felt self conscious putting on the same clothes. She put on her clothes and shoes and then went into the kitchen. TJ was seated at the table. When he saw her come in TJ got up and pulled a chair out. Francis thanked him. She liked this man. He was a gentleman. Francis recalled her previous relationship. Although he was a nice guy he wasn't as attentive as TJ, or as good looking. TJ and Francis fixed their plates. He asked Francis if she slept well. Francis confided that she had a difficult time, getting to sleep. TJ told her that he too had a difficult time falling asleep. He joked saying that he wasn't use to a gorgeous woman sleeping in his house. Francis blushed.

After eating Francis helped TJ clear the table. She told him that she needed to get home. Francis told him that she didn't feel comfortable wearing the same clothes. TJ understood, but he hated her to leave.

After Francis left TJ thought about his life. He realized that his life was incomplete. He wanted more. TJ cleaned his kitchen and then left his home to pick Tommy Jay up. When he got to his parent's home TJ sat and talked with his mother. He told her about Francis. She suggested he invite her to Thanksgiving dinner. Tommy Jay came downstairs. TJ hug his mother and kissed her. He and Tommy Jay said bye and they left.

When he got home TJ called Francis. She did not answer. TJ left her a message......

TJ did not hear from Francis for a week. TJ recalled Francis mentioning that she was going away, so he figured that she was busy...

At the end of the next week TJ received a text from Francis saying that things had run over. She accepted his invitation to dinner.......

TJ thought about his career. He decided not to return to work. He decided to work independently. TJ began reaching out to friends and family for potential clients.....

TJ and Francis schedules were hectic so they didn't get a chance to see each other when she got back. Occasionally TJ would send her a text saying that he was thinking of her.

On Thanksgiving TJ arrived at his parent's home early. Ana and her family arrived early as well. She helped her mother prepare the meal. The men sat in the family room watching sports. At three o'clock the guest began arriving. Shortly after everyone was there Francis arrived. TJ left the men in the family room and took Francis into his parents' office. TJ had not seen her in several weeks and wanted to have some time alone with her. He pulled the desk chair out for her. TJ leaned against the desk. He wanted to be as close to her without invading her space. TJ thanked her for coming and asked if she wanted anything to drink. Francis declined. TJ asked her about work. She told him that things had calmed down at the hospital. She explained that because of her position in administration things sometimes become hectic and everything falls on her. TJ asked if they could spend some time together....

Margaret announced dinner was ready. Francis and TJ left the office and joined everyone in the dinning room. Francis sat next to TJ. During dinner Margaret noticed how they looked at each other. She knew that look. Margaret thought back to TJ growing up. She had never seen that expression on his face before. The only time he had come close to infatuation was with Paula and she figured that was more he wanting to do the right thing because she was pregnant. Margaret looked at her son. She was proud of the man he had become.......

When everyone was through eating they left the dinning room and went into various rooms in the house. TJ went off with the men to watch the game. Ana, Margaret and Francis and the other women went into the living room. Ana and Margaret wanted to get to know TJ's new love interest. They talked a while. When the game was over TJ came into the living room. Ana and Margaret excused themselves. TJ sat next to Francis. He took her hand. TJ lift her hand to his lips and kissed it.

"Have I told you how beautiful you look?"

"No."

"Forgive me. Do you mind?" He looked at his hand holding hers.

Francis looked down and said, "No."

"I want us to spend some time together. I want to get to know you. I really think we could have something here."

Francis looked at TJ. No man had ever told her that before. Sure she had dated a few guys for a little while, but they had never verbalized anything long term. It was refreshing to find a guy who was honest and didn't play games.

"I would like that."

"Francis would you mind if I kissed you?"

Francis shook her head no. As TJ leaned closer, he continued holding her hand. TJ placed his free hand under her chin. He leaned in closer. As they kissed Francis thought how she had been waiting for this moment. TJ felt himself getting turned on. He pulled back.

"I think I better stop. I might get into trouble."

Francis knew what he meant. She was turned on as well.

The guest began leaving. They could hear them.

"TJ I think I should be leaving as well."

"How about going to a movie tomorrow?"

"Tomorrow is Black Friday. Me and my sister go out. We have lunch and hang out. Can we make it Saturday?"

"I have plans. I'll call you."

They got up. TJ walked her to the front door. He walked Francis out to her car. He opened her car door. When she was seated inside TJ bent down and kissed her lightly on the lips. TJ watched as she drove away.

Chapter 10

THE NEXT WEEK WAS BUSY. TJ and Francis couldn't get together. Instead they text each other.

Friday TJ called Francis. She answered. TJ asked if she was busy. She told TJ no. He asked her to go out with him dancing. Francis accepted his invitation. He asked if he could come by at seven and take her out to dinner first. She told him that would be fine. After hanging up Francis looked in her closets. She found a black dress that was mid length. She pulled out her strap up shoes a choker and earrings to match. She showered. When she came out of the shower Francis sprayed perfume over her body. Francis put on silk stocking and then her dress. She put her choker and earrings on. Francis usually wear her hair up, but decided to wear it down this time. At seven her door bell rang. Francis got her short fur. She went to answer the door. When she opened it the look on TJ's face gave her the answer of how she looked. She stepped out of the house. TJ leaned over and lightly kissed Francis on the lips. He opened the door to the car. TJ got into the car and drove off.

When they arrived at the restaurant TJ parked. After entering the restaurant they were seated quickly. The waiter took their order. While they ate TJ told Francis about his venture. Francis thought it daring and told TJ as much.....

After they finished eating the couple left the restaurant and headed to the club. When they arrived at the club TJ parked. He got out of the car and then opened Francis' door. He held his hand out. Francis took it. They walked to the club door. The door man let them in. They found a seat. TJ and Francis talked a little while. TJ hadn't danced in a long time. As they sat the two watched others dance. TJ remembered that Francis liked to dance. TJ leaned over and asked her if she wanted to dance. Francis asked him if it was alright. TJ stood up. He held his hand out. Francis took it. They walked through a crowd of people. Before making it to the dance floor TJ noticed Rosalyn. She saw him as well. Rosalyn walked over to him and hugged TJ. He returned her embrace. She asked him what he was doing there. TJ pulled Francis up to him. Rosalyn spoke, but Francis could tell Rosalyn didn't care for her. TJ excused himself. When they made it onto the dance floor TJ twirled Francis around and then began dancing. Francis told him that he still had the moves. They danced to two songs and then Rosalyn walked over and tap Francis on the shoulder. Francis turned around. Rosalyn asked if she could have a dance with TJ. Francis said sure. TJ stopped her and asked if it was okay. Francis turned to Rosalyn and said to TJ I'll be back. TJ danced with Rosalyn for two songs and then thanked her. TJ walked over to where Francis was seated. He asked her if she was alright. Francis told him that she was fine. She told him that Rosalyn seem to have a thing for him. Francis asked if they had a thing before. TJ told her that he tried to date her once, but she declined. TJ explained their relationship. He stood up and held his hand out. She took his hand. For the rest of the night they danced. When the club closed TJ took Francis home. He walked her to the door. He told her that he had a good time. Francis took a chance. She asked him if he was ready for the night to end. TJ told her that he would like it to continue. She opened her door and walked in. Still standing in the doorway Francis held her hand out. TJ took it. She told him to come in. Francis closed her door and led him to the living room. She told him to have a seat. Francis took her coat off. She then sat next to TJ.

"TJ I don't want to seem forward. I really like you and I don't want to see anyone else. I would like this to go somewhere. I guess what I'm trying to say is that I want to be in a committed relationship with you."

TJ was quiet for a few minutes. He thought about what Francis said. He felt the same way. He thought to himself, "I guess I was moving too slow." TJ put his hand behind Francis' neck, pulling her gently towards him. TJ kissed her lightly. He teased her lips. The kiss became passionate. He moved to her neck. Francis put her hand on the back of his head. He sat back on the couch and turned her to lean across him. He began kissing her again. TJ caressed her body sending sparks throughout it. Francis' body burned with desire. TJ continued until Francis whispered stop. She stood up. Francis held her hand out. TJ took it. Francis led him to her bed room. When they entered Francis placed her arms around TJ's neck and began kissing him. TJ placed his hands on her waist. As they stood there kissing TJ pulled Francis closer and tightened his hands on her waist. Francis began unbuttoning his shirt. TJ turned Francis around. As he kissed her neck, TJ unzipped her dress. He eased it off her shoulders. He kissed her back. TJ placed his arms around her. He kissed her neck and nibbled her ear. She could feel his arousal. Francis let her dress fall to the floor and then stepped out of it. TJ smoothed his hand over her curves. As they kissed the two moved towards her bed. They laid down. TJ looked at Francis' body. He told her that she had a nice body. Francis told him that he did too. TJ kissed and caressed Francis' body. His touch sent sparks throughout her body. Francis caressed TJ's body. He stopped her. Francis held TJ's face and kissed him. TJ pulled her close to him and then stopped. Francis asked what was wrong. TJ told her that he didn't have any condoms. Francis sat up. TJ saw desire in her eyes. He wanted so much to make love to this woman, but he was older now and wanted to be responsible. Francis got up. TJ watched her walk over to the desk. She opened a draw and pulled two items out. Francis brought it over to TJ. She handed him a slip of paper. TJ read it. It was a form showing a current HIV test. It showed a negative result. Then Francis showed a prescription that showed she was on birth control. TJ handed it back. TJ pulled out his wallet. He pulled out a form that he carried from his accident. It showed that he was negative for HIV.

Francis said, "So everything is alright?"

TJ cupped her face and brought her close. He kissed her. TJ pulled her to him. Francis loved his touch. His hands seemed to know her body well. TJ took his time. It had been so long and he wanted to enjoy every second. When neither one could stand being apart any longer TJ made them one. He moved slow, kissing and caressing her body. Francis remembered the boy she once met on a cruise and had her first sexual experience with. Since then she had been with a few other guys. They had done the job, but nothing mind blowing. Although her first time had been with a boy, TJ was still better than any man she had been with. Maybe because he cared how she felt. She thought "Maybe that's why Rosalyn was still interested. Francis kissed TJ's shoulder. He made her feel unbelievable. TJ took her to a place where all she could think of was pleasure........

The next morning TJ awakened. He was in pain. TJ got up and went into the living room. He began to stretch. TJ tried to do some of the exercises taught to him.

Francis awakened. She looked over and saw that TJ was not laying next to her. She got up and walked out of her bedroom. Francis heard something. She followed the sound. She saw TJ laying on her living room floor naked. She smiled and then saw the strain in his face. She left the living room and went back into her bedroom and into her bathroom. Francis turned on the tub water. When it was half full she returned to the living room. TJ was still stretching. Francis held her hand out and told him to come with her. TJ got up and took her hand. He followed her into the bathroom. He smiled thinking of how thoughtful she was. TJ got into the tub. He turned the water off. When Francis turned to leave TJ asked her to join him. Francis took her robe off and stepped into the tub. She leaned back on him. They sat relaxing and talking. Francis rubbed TJ's legs hoping it would help. TJ kissed the back of her neck. She placed her hand behind his head. She could feel him get arouse. TJ began caressing Francis' breast, arousing her. He kissed her neck and nibbled on her ear. TJ stood up. He stepped out of the tub. TJ grabbed a towel and held it out. Francis got up. He patted her dry and then himself. TJ lifted Francis up into his arms and carried her into the bedroom. He gently laid Francis onto the bed. As he made love to her Francis cried out that she loved him. TJ looked at Francis. She had her eyes closed. He kissed her with so much passion that Francis held him tighter. They laid in each others' arms. Francis caressed TJ's chest. He liked the way her hands felt on him. TJ couldn't think of a future without Francis. He recalled her telling him that she loved him. He questioned , "Could it be that she is really in love with him or was it said in the heat of passion?"

TJ held her tighter. Francis felt sparks each time TJ touched her. Francis wondered if he heard her say that she loved him. Francis wondered if TJ felt what she felt and if he heard her would he stop seeing her. She wondered what he felt.

TJ took a chance. In a low tone, "Francis."

"Yes."

"Did you mean what you said, or was it in the heat of the moment?"

Francis sat up and turned to look at TJ. He looked so handsome laying there.

"I meant it and it wasn't the moment. I mean the moment helped. You have always made me feel better than anyone else. I have always felt something. I'm not trying to rush things and I don't expect you to say it back right now."

TJ sat up. TJ took Francis into his arms. He kissed her passionately.

"I love you too."

"Are you serious? You don't have to say it just to keep from hurting my feeling."

"I would never tell anyone that if I didn't mean it. That's something too serious to just say."

"Really?"

"Really. So what are we going to do about these feelings?"

"What do you mean?" TJ got down on one knee. "What are you doing?"

TJ took her hand.

"Francis will you marry me?"

Francis looked at TJ in disbelief.

"TJ."

"Ok, I can't stay in this position too long."

"Are you sure?"

"I wouldn't ask you if I didn't mean it. Lady will you be my wife?"

Francis got down on the floor with him. She put her arms around his neck, said yes and then kissed him. No more words were spoken.

TJ awakened. He looked at the time. TJ picked up his cell phone and went into the bathroom. TJ called his parents. Margaret picked up the phone. He explained that he had just awakened and that he didn't realize the time had gotten away from him. Margaret told him not to worry. She insisted he leave Tommy Jay with them and pick him up on

Sunday. TJ thanked his mother and hung up. He took a shower and then returned to Francis' bed. Still asleep she snuggled up to TJ. He caressed her shoulder. TJ thought about what had happened between them. He wondered if they were rushing. Then he thought how they had known each other many years ago. He thought how this hadn't been either one of their first time and that they had relationships with other people. TJ began getting hungry. He squeezed Francis' arm. She opened her eyes. He kissed her on the nose and asked if she was hungry. Still mesmerized she just laid in his arms. He repeated himself. Francis sat up. She told him that she would cook him something to eat. TJ accepted.

TJ thought to himself how he would see what kind of cook this women would provide. Francis got up and walked into the bathroom. TJ got up and dressed. He went into the kitchen. TJ looked into the cabinets and refrigerator. He was impressed that she had food. He took out a few things for her to prepare. TJ looked for her cookware. Just as he found it Francis came into the kitchen. She told TJ to sit down. He did as he was told.

As Francis prepared the meal she asked TJ how long could he stay. He explained that his parents volunteered to keep Tommy Jay with them until Sunday. Francis tried not to show her excitement. She asked him to stay with her the rest of the weekend. TJ accepted. When Francis was finished cooking they sat at the kitchen table. TJ picked up a fork full of the food and put it in his mouth. He smiled saying that it taste good. Francis was happy that he enjoyed the meal. After the meal TJ helped Francis clean up the kitchen. She took something out to cook for dinner. Francis and TJ went into the living room. Francis turned on the stereo. TJ sat on the couch. He put his arms out. Francis went into them. TJ placed his arms around her and she layed back on his chest. They listened to music. For the rest of the weekend the couple discussed their future and made plans for their wedding. The two agreed on a June wedding. Francis wanted a big wedding. TJ wanted to give her anything she asked.

On Sunday they awakened. They had decided TJ would go home and change clothes. He and Francis would then go to his parents' home and break the news. Francis dressed. She and TJ went to his home. He quickly changed and then they started on their way to his parents' home. As they drove to TJ parents' home the two were quiet. They were both nervous.

When they arrived the two sat in the car a few minutes before getting out. TJ mustered up enough courage and opened his door. He got out of the car and walked over to the passengers' side where Francis had already opened the door. TJ held his hand out. Francis took it and they walked up to the house. TJ opened the door and they walked in. TJ called out to his family. Margaret and Thomas came downstairs. TJ noticed a surprised expression on Margaret's face when she saw the two of them. She greeted them both. TJ excused himself and went to the basement door. He called out to Tommy Jay. TJ heard music playing. He called out to his son again. Tommy Jay finally answered. TJ told him to come upstairs. Tommy Jay protested, but came up. TJ asked them to sit. He took Francis hand and they sat on the love seat. TJ started out by saying that he wanted them to be opened minded. Everyone remained quiet. TJ still holding Francis' hand brought it to his chest. He watched their expressions. Still they remained quiet. TJ began with "Tommy Jay, mom, dad I have asked Francis to marry me and she has accepted."

Tommy Jay was the first to speak. He asked Francis if she loved his father. Francis still holding TJ's hand told Tommy Jay that she loved his father with all her heart. Then Margaret spoke. She asked them if they thought that they were rushing.

TJ responded, "Mom there is no time limit on how long it should take two people to fall in love. I didn't just meet Francis. I'm in love with her and I want her to be a part of my family."

Francis asked if she could speak. Be began,   "From   the moment I first met TJ I liked him. I know we were children then, but it doesn't take away form my feelings. When I saw him again those feelings were still there. I can't explain how much I love him, but I will show you how much." Francis looked over at Tommy Jay. "Tommy Jay I will not try to be your mother, but I will care for you as if you were my own. I hope we can become friends."

Margaret invited them to stay over for dinner. Tommy Jay asked to be excused. He was permitted to return to the basement. The couple stayed in the living room and Thomas kept them company while Margaret prepared dinner. On occasion she would come into the living room and joined in the conversation.

When dinner was ready the group moved into the dinning room. During dinner TJ informed his family that he and Francis were getting married June 17th. Margaret offered her assistance…..

The next couple of weeks Margaret prepared for their engagement dinner. Ana was blown away when she heard about the engagement.

The day of the engagement dinner Francis was very nervous. She knew some people thought it was too soon. TJ continuously assured her that they were doing the right thing. TJ came by her place and picked Francis up. Tommy Jay moved out of the front seat and got in the back. Tommy Jay spoke to Francis, but didn't carry on a conversation with her. Francis liked Tommy Jay. She thought he was a respectful kid. Francis wanted them to have a good relationship.

When they arrived at the house Tommy Jay got out of the car and went into the house. TJ got out and walked over to the passenger's side. He helped Francis out. They walked in holding hands. Ana was there. When she saw her brother Ana walked over to him. She hugged and congratulated him. She did the same to Francis. Francis felt better after Ana's greeting.

When people began arriving they congratulated TJ and Francis. Everyone mingled until dinner. When Margaret announced dinner was ready TJ and Francis sat next to each other. Ana toast the couple. One of TJ's close friends also toast the couple. Francis' sister stood and wished the couple well. TJ noticed that Tommy Jay was very quiet and seemed to be withdrawn since his announcement.

After dinner TJ went down to the rec room where Tommy Jay was. No one else was down there. TJ was happy about this. He sat on the recliner and began talking to Tommy Jay. The two discussed the future with TJ having a wife and Tommy Jay possibly having sibling. TJ told Tommy Jay about Ana and they having different fathers and explained how much he loved his sister. TJ told his son to talk to his aunt about her feelings when her mother got married to someone other than her parent and then having a child. Tommy Jay told TJ that he would talk to his aunt. TJ told him that he was returning to the party. When TJ returned to the party the guest began leaving.

After everyone had left TJ and Francis were ready as well. Tommy Jay asked if he could spend the weekend with his grandparents. TJ had mixed feelings. Then he thought it would be good for Tommy Jay to talk to his grandparents and maybe it would help him deal with his decision to marry.

TJ hugged his son and said goodbye.

Margaret walked TJ and Francis out to the car. TJ confided his concern that Tommy Jay may not want to live with them. Margaret assured TJ that Tommy Jay would adjust and everything would be fine.

TJ and Francis got into the car. Francis asked TJ if everything was alright. He told her that everything would be fine. He put his arm around Francis shoulders and she moved closer to TJ. Once they got on their way TJ asked her to spend the weekend at his home. Francis accepted his invitation. She figured she might as well get use to the house.....

An hour later TJ pulled up to his home. He pulled into the drive way. TJ got out of the car and walked over to the passenger's side. Francis had already opened the door. TJ put his hand out. Francis took it. She loved how strong his hands were and the feel of them holding hers. They walked into the house. TJ led her to the den. He turned on the television and put a movie. He sat down and held his hand for Francis to sit next to him. Francis walked over to him and sat down. Francis walked over to him and sat close. TJ placed his arm around her shoulders. Francis laid her head on his shoulders and then TJ started the movie.

After a few minutes TJ put his free hand under her chin. He moved closer to Francis and kissed her. She returned his kiss. As their kiss became more passionate TJ picked Francis up. He carried her into his bedroom. He laid her down. TJ slowly removed her clothes. As he removed his clothes TJ kissed her body. He sent chills throughout her body. After all of her clothes had been removed TJ looked down at her. He smoothed his hand over her body and then got up. He finished undressing. TJ returned to the bed and laid down beside Francis. He looked into her eyes and told Francis that he loved her. She returned the sentiment. She smoothed her hand over his face. TJ pulled Francis close and kissed her. He smoothed his hand down the middle of her breast. He loved how soft her skin was. He kissed her stomach and asked if she ever thought of having children. Francis told him that she had been pregnant once, but was forced to abort it. He looked up at her and saw the pain in her eyes. He apologized for brining up sad memories. She told him that it was alright. Francis sat up. She told him that it was alright. She took his hand. Her eyes became glossy. They filled up with tears. TJ sat up. He put his arm around her shoulders.

"TJ promise me you won't get mad."

TJ moved so he could see her face.

"Why would I be mad at you?"

"Promise me."

"Francis I can't get mad at something that happened to you in the past."

"TJ the baby was yours."

TJ looked at Francis in disbelief."

"I don't understand."

"Remember the first time we met? We were young. I wasn't prepared, correction, we weren't prepared for what we did. When I got home, after a month my menstruation didn't come. I didn't know what was wrong. My mother knew that I hadn't gotten it. She asked me was I hiding it for some reason, because she didn't see any pads in the garbage. I told her that I was sick and maybe it was coming, but just hadn't shown. She took me to the doctor. My mother asked me who did I let touch me. I told her about you, but I said that I didn't know where you lived and I didn't have a contact for you." TJ continued to look at Francis with an expression of disbelief." TJ she made me get an abortion. The doctor did it right then. My mother didn't give me a chance to do anything. When we left the doctor's office my mother told me that we were never to talk about it. I went home. Things happened so fast that at first I didn't feel anything. A week went by. My menstruation came and all of a sudden it hit me. I cried everyday for a month. I felt so bad. Even though we just had that one week I really liked you and the way you made me feel I thought about it throughout my life. Tell you the truth I've always compared the guys I dated to you. I didn't do it intentional. It didn't even occur to me that I was doing it. I figured it out five years ago after my last boyfriend."

TJ took her into his arms. Tears streamed down her checks. She held TJ. TJ told Francis that he was sorry for her pain and for putting her through that. Francis kissed TJ. Her kiss was wet with tears. TJ took her face in his hands. He kissed Francis wet eyes. He wanted to kiss away all of the hurt; all of the tears.

"My mother had me get the birth control that last five years. After I met my last boyfriend I thought maybe we would get married and try to have a child, but things didn't work out. This is the end of my fifth year. I know you have a son. Have you ever thought of having more children?"

TJ smoothed his hand over her face.

"I would love to have babies with you."

"I'm not trying to rush you, but when do you want to start? I'm asking because if you want to start right away I have to stop taking my birth control. It will take a while for me to conceive."

"Do you want to?"

"I want to have your baby."

No more words were spoken....

The months went by quickly. Everyone was busy with the wedding plans. Francis gave her apartment up a month before the wedding. She moved into TJ's home. Her relationship had gotten better with Tommy Jay. Tommy Jay had taken his father's advise and talked to Ana. It was a big change for Tommy Jay. Sometimes when Tommy Jay watched his father with Francis he felt as if he was loosing his father. He had never had to share his father with anyone other then Ana and his grandparents. His conversation with Ana was helping him work through things.......

The night before the wedding Francis stayed with her sister Tracy. Tracy threw her a bridal shower. Ana and Margaret were invited. The guest played games and the married women gave advise. After the party Francis went to bed. She laid awake hours thinking about how her new life would be. After hours of no sleep Francis finally drifted off.....

The next morning Francis awakened to a busy and loud house. Francis thought of what the day was and got up. Francis went into the bathroom. She showered and brushed her teeth. When Francis came out of the bathroom she smoothed fragrance lotion on her body and then sprayed her favorite perfume on. Francis started putting on her stockings. She clipped them to her guarder. Someone knocked on the room door. Francis told them to come in. It was Francis' mother coming in to check on her. Then her sister, cousin and two friends.

The doorbell rang. Tracy went to open the door. It was Ana and her two older children. When Francis saw the children she thought of how beautiful they were. She placed her hand on her stomach hoping that she will be able to give TJ babies. Her mother jolted her to the activities. Francis stood up. Her mother and sister helped with putting her slip on and then her dress. Tears filled Francis mother's eyes. Francis told her that she was going to make her cry. Ana gave Francis a Kleenex. Francis dab at her eyes. The make up artist made up Francis' face first. When she was finished the rest of the women faces were done. Francis looked in the full length mirror. As Francis looked into the mirror she saw another woman looking back at her. This woman was beautiful. She was expecting happiness and fulfillment. She was finally going to be with the one man she had fallen in love with so long ago. Francis jumped when her mother touched her shoulders. She told Francis that it was time to leave. They walked to the front door where the photographers were waiting. They snapped pictures. Francis was escorted to the limo. She and her bridesmaids, ring bearer, flower girl and mother were helped into the limo. As they drove to the church Francis looked out of the windows. Francis recalled the first time that she saw TJ. She thought how cute he was. Francis remembered her first dance was with him. The first time she had intercourse it was with him. She remembered coming to his house warming party and seeing him again for the first time in so many years. Francis remembered how he felt when they greeted. She wanted him to continue holding her. Francis remembered the first night she spent at his home and how she wanted to go to him. Francis recalled making love to him as an adult. She remembered how he felt. How gentle he was. She remembered how he touched her body as if it was a treasure. Francis couldn't believe how just thinking about TJ's touch could make her feel sparks….. Francis' mother touched her hand. She asked Francis if she was alright. Francis said that she was and asked why. Her mother told her that she was flushed. Francis told her that she was thinking about something. Tracy chimed in saying, "What the wedding night?" Francis said surprisingly no. She was thinking about the past. Tracy said, "Wow, I can't believe I let him get by, but then again he's not my flavor."

The limo pulled up to the church. The driver got out. He walked to the back of the car and opened the door. The wedding party exited the car. They got into place. The usher opened the church door. The flower girl and ring bearer entered the church and began walking down the aisle. When they got to the middle of the church the bridesmaids and groomsmen entered the church. They began their walk down the aisle. After everyone had made it to the front of the church they begun singing the song that Francis and TJ chose. Francis took her father's arm. They began walking into the church. Francis held onto her father's arm. As they walked down the aisle Francis watched TJ. She thought of how handsome he was. She was so in love with this man and has been her entire life. Francis looked briefly up to the sky, thanking God for sending TJ back to her.

Francis prayed that they would have a long beautiful life together. She thought of how so many years had past between them. How they had grown up away from each other. Francis thought of how wonderful life works out sometimes. Here she was getting ready to marry the man that she had done most of her first with.

As she got closer to the front of the church Francis could see the love in TJ's eyes. He watched her. TJ thought of how she looked more beautiful then ever. As Francis got closer TJ met her. Francis' father kissed her on the side of her face and then gave her hand to TJ. With Francis' hand in his they walked the rest of the way to the front of the church and stood in front of the minister. The ceremony began......

Throughout the ceremony TJ and Francis stared into each other's eyes. It was as if no one existed, except the two of them. The two mechanically said their vows. TJ placed a wedding ring on Francis' finger and then she placed one on his. The minister blessed them in their new journey. He pronounced them husband and wife. The minister told TJ that he may kiss his bride. TJ took Francis into his arms and they kissed....

After a few minutes Francis stopped kissing TJ and reminded him that they were in church. TJ kissed her on the neck and with his arm around her waist faced their guest. Everyone stood up and clapped. TJ and his bride walked out of the church.

Before getting into the limo the guest hugged and congratulated them. TJ and Francis got into the limo. Once the door was closed TJ took Francis into his arms and kissed her passionately. The driver got into the vehicle and drove off. Although TJ had stopped kissing Francis she could still feel the heat he had imprinted on her lips.

As they traveled to the reception the newly weds stayed locked in each other's arms. TJ whispered how much he loved Francis in her ear and what he wanted to do to her. Francis snuggled into TJ. She rested her head on his chest. Together they sat quiet until arriving at the hall.

Once arriving at the hall the couple exited the limo and was escorted to the holding room. The wedding party had been taken to their holding area. After a few minutes in the room the wedding party, the bride and groom were escorted to the reception hall.

Music began to play.

As the DJ announced each name of the wedding party the couples came in dancing.

When it was time for the bride and groom to be announced the music changed. The DJ played jazzy and blues love ballet. TJ took Francis' hand and they began to dance. Everyone remained standing as they danced to the middle of the floor. The guest clapped and marveled at the couples' dance. When the music stopped TJ twirled Francis one last time, dipped her and bent down to kiss her. They kissed a few seconds and then TJ brought her up. Everyone clapped and then the couple went to their table. Dinner music began to be played. A buffet style dinner was set up. A plate was made for TJ and Francis. The minister said a prayer over the food. The couple began to eat. The guest gathered their meal and began to eat....

On occasion during the meal different guest tap their glasses. TJ and Francis would lightly kiss.....

After the meal TJ and Francis mingled with the guest and thanked them for sharing their day with them. The DJ interrupted the guest for TJ and Francis to cut the cake. After cutting the cake the couple danced with their parents.....

After the parents danced the floor was opened to the other guest. TJ took Francis by the hand and they began to dance. They danced to a few songs and then sat down. The couple had a flight to catch. TJ interrupted the music. He thanked everyone for coming and wished them a safe travel home. TJ told them that he and Francis had a flight to get to. As they left the guest clapped. The music started playing again and the guest started dancing again.

TJ and Francis went up to a room that had been held for them. They changed clothes and gathered up their bags. When they left the room Francis called Tracy. Tracy met them in the lobby. Francis gave Tracy her dress and TJ's tux. Tracy hugged them and they left. The limo was waiting outside. When he saw them the driver got out of the car and opened the vehicle door. Francis and TJ entered. The driver got into the limo and drove off. The couple was quiet throughout the drive.....

When they arrived at the airport the driver pulled up in front. He opened their door. Francis and TJ got out. The driver took the luggage out of the trunk and gave it to the airport personnel. TJ checked in. The couple walked into the airport and then followed the signs to their terminal. When they found the terminal the flight had began boarding. The couple got in line. When they got up to the door the flight attendant checked their tickets and they were allowed onto the airplane. The couple found their seats. The two were excited. This was their first time flying first class. Once the flight got on it's way the attendants began serving first class. TJ was impressed. He nudged Francis and told her that this is the way to travel....

After they finished eating TJ and Francis drifted off to sleep. TJ woke up a few times. When he would awaken TJ looked down at his bride and smiled. He pulled her closer to him. TJ drifted back off. When Francis awakened the pilot was announcing that they had made it to their destination. Francis sat up. TJ felt her move. He opened his eyes. She kissed TJ and told him that they were in Hawaii. TJ transitioned his chair in the up right position. After the plane landed TJ and Francis exited it. After retrieving their bags the couple went out of the airport where a car was waiting for them....

As the couple traveled to the hotel Francis took pictures. She marveled at how beautiful the scenery was. When they arrived at the hotel the driver helped them with the luggage. Although they didn't have much TJ was happy for the help, because he was feeling some pain from the reception. When he got to the room the bail person placed the luggage into the room. After he left TJ lifted Francis into his arms and carried her into the room. He placed her gently on the loveseat in the sitting area. He then walked back over to the door and closed it. TJ then walked back over to Francis. He sat down beside her and kissed Francis passionately. When the passion over came them TJ picked Francis up and carried her into the bedroom. Still holding her TJ pulled the covers back. All the pain that TJ had been feeling disappeared. As TJ caressed Francis body she watched every touch. Francis watched his expression. She was surprised that not only did she see desire in his eyes she saw love. Francis couldn't believe that love could be seen so clear, but she saw it and she was taken away. She was taken to a place where she floated off the earth. Her body burned with desire and melted under TJs' touch. Francis never felt such pleasure and never wanted to touch the ground. TJ and Francis held onto each other, not wanting this feeling to ever end. Before falling to sleep TJ whispered that he loved Francis. She returned the sentiment......

Several hours later TJ awakened and eased out of bed. He went into his bag and then into the bathroom. He turned on the water and got into it. The jets massaged his muscles. He laid there a while. When the tub had been partially filled TJ turned the water off. He was tired from all of his activities in the last twenty four hours. TJ drifted off to sleep......

An hour later Francis awakened and saw that TJ was no longer by her side. She looked around the room and saw that the bathroom door was closed. She got up and headed to the door. Francis walked quietly to the door. She peeped in and saw that TJ was asleep. Francis remembered TJs' first time at her place. She figured that he must have been in pain. Francis went into the lounge and retrieved the fruit that had been left for them. She took it into the room with the Jacuzzi. Francis laid the bowl on the top of the Jacuzzi and then eased behind TJ. He awakened. TJ moved up. Francis reached over and took one of the strawberries and fed it to TJ. He ate it and in turn fed her a piece of fruit. After eating half of the bowl Francis began messaging TJs' shoulders. She asked him was he in much pain. TJ told her not to worry about it, assuring that it was manageable. He promised Francis that his pain would not get in the way of them enjoying themselves. Francis kissed his back....

Chapter 11

THE NEWLYWEDS DECIDED TO STAY in their first day in Hawaii. They only ventured out to a restaurant inside the hotel.

The next three days the couple traveled to different islands. They visited some of the local clubs and took in a traditional Luau. They hung out on the beach and toured a live volcano. At night they made love and sat out on the balcony watching the waves of the ocean.....

At the end of the week the couple was exhausted, so they stayed in. TJ ordered food from a nearby restaurant and they made a picnic on the floor.

Their last day the couple went for a long walk on the beach. They kicked around in the ocean and then returned to their hotel. TJ and Francis decided to sleep out on the terrace. The sky was a beautiful blue. Only a few clouds above. The weather was perfect. Francis brought a sheet out and placed it over them. Under the beautiful moon and stars that neither one had ever seen the newlyweds made love and there they fell asleep in each others' arms.

The next morning the couple woke up to a beautiful bright blue sky. TJ covered their heads trying to block out some of the sun. After some time they got up together. TJ kept the sheet closely shielding their bodies. They went into the room. The couple took a quick shower. They didn't have much time, so TJ and Francis hurried to one of the nearby restaurants that they fell in love with. The couple couldn't eat everything so they had the food wrapped. TJ and Francis returned to the hotel where a car was waiting for them. Francis got kind of sad as they traveled to the airport. She laid her head on TJ's chest and watched as they past the island.....

When they arrived there the flight had just began calling for first class passengers. TJ and Francis walked up to the airport staff. Their tickets were checked and they were allowed to enter the plane.

The couple found their seats. As they waited for the other passengers to enter the plane TJ and Francis talked about their honeymoon. They became quiet. Francis laid her head on TJ's shoulder. She thought of her life with TJ. She wasn't especially concerned about her relationship with Tommy Jay. Things had gotten better. While they weren't very close Tommy Jay didn't act like he disliked her. Francis looked over at TJ. He was still awake. She brought up them having children. TJ reassured Francis that he wanted children with her. Francis took comfort in his words. She closed her eyes and after some time Francis fell asleep.

After a while TJ closed his eyes, but did not fall asleep. He thought about all that had happened in just a short period of time. TJ thought it remarkable how he and Francis had been reacquainted after so many years of being apart from each other. He thought it astonishing how much they loved each other and now married. TJ recalled the night before the wedding. His friends had given him a bachelor party. Tommy Jay was TJ's best man so he was allowed to come to the bachelor party so he could toast his father. He was only allowed to stay an hour because of his age. Thomas informed TJ that once he and Tommy Jay get home he was going to stay as well. After he had given his toast Tommy Jay got ready to leave. Thomas told TJ that he had decided to stay home. Thomas thought that since this was his son's last night as a single man and all those who were attending the bachelor party was his friends, TJ might feel uncomfortable with his father being there. He hugged his son and told him to behave himself. .....

After his father and son left one of the friends who helped plan the party turned the channel to on demand. He scrolled through the pornographic movies. The friend stopped at one he thought was interesting. All the guys watched and joked with TJ about some of the position the actors were in.

As it got late there was a knock on the door. TJ excused himself and went to open it. To his surprise it was Rosalyn. She asked TJ if she could speak with him. He went out into the hallway. Rosalyn told him that she didn't feel comfortable out in the hallway. She informed She asked TJ if she could speak with him. He went out into the hallway. Rosalyn told him that she didn't feel comfortable out in the hallway. She informed him that she had a room down the hall. He looked at her curiously. He followed her to the room. Once in the room Rosalyn asked him to have a seat. TJ sat in the chair next to the window. They were both quiet for a few minutes.

TJ broke the silence, "So what's going on?"

"TJ what happened?"

TJ looked confused.

"What do you mean?"

"We had something once."

"Rosalyn we were kids."

"You and Francis were kids too, but we're sitting here on the eve of your wedding."

"Rosalyn I asked you about having a relationship and you told me no. You and I are like family now."

"So you're not attracted to me at all?"

" I will always have a special place in my heart for you. You and I lost our virginity with each other."

Rosalyn smiled.

"I never knew that. You seemed so experienced. TJ no one have ever made me feel the way you have. I don't believe anyone could. TJ it's not too late." TJ couldn't believe what he was hearing. "TJ I watched as you and Paula had a child. I wanted that with you. If I had gotten pregnant I would never have left you to raise it alone. I wanted to help you. But you never asked. When Ana graduated and we went on that cruise I wanted to spend time just you and me, but you spent that time with Francis."

"Rosalyn why are you telling me all of this now?"

"Because I love you."

"Rosalyn I love you too."

Rosalyn face brightened up.

"So we have a chance?"

"No. I love you, but I'm not in love with you. Maybe you're confusing the two."

"No. I want to be with you."

"Still, why did you wait until now?"

"I thought you would have called me that night we ran into each other at the club. Besides I thought each time that we ran into each other I thought you would have called."

"I guess my signals were off. Our possibility went away when you told me that you weren't interested in a relationship."

"That was so long ago. TJ can we please try?"

"Rosalyn it's too late."

Rosalyn went into the bathroom. TJ waited patiently thinking that she went in there so he wouldn't see her cry. He felt bad for her. He couldn't believe what was happening. When Rosalyn came out of the bathroom TJ turned from looking out of the window. TJ couldn't believe his eyes. Rosalyn was now standing in the room in nothing but lingerie. She had on red lingerie with black lace trim; stockings attached to her panties and had let her hair down. She had put on makeup accenting her beauty. Rosalyn smiled knowing that she had TJ's attention. She reached into her bag, pulled out a radio. She plugged it into the wall socket and turned on music. TJ remained seated as Rosalyn walked over to him. Rosalyn came up in front of TJ and began dancing provocative. He moved his chair back and then stood up.

"What are you doing?"

"Don't I look tasty?"

"You look very beautiful."

Rosalyn moved closer, making herself barely touching TJ.

"TJ let me show you how good I am."

TJ moved away from her. He began walking towards the door. Rosalyn moved in front of him.

"Where are you going? TJ you're not married. Please let us have this one night. It'll be our secret."

"I don't need any secrets in my marriage."

"This is your bachelor night. It's expected for you to have on last fling."

"No it's not expected."

"People do it."

"That doesn't mean I have to."

Rosalyn cornered TJ by the door. She positioned herself in front of it. She unhooked her bra which had one snap in front. She then took off her panties leaving only her stocking on. TJ had to admit that she had a beautiful body. He was turned on. Although he tried to conceal it Rosalyn could tell that he was turned on. She moved closer to him, not leaving any space between them. She took his hands from his side and put them around her. TJ did not move. Rosalyn placed her arms around his neck. TJ did not move. Rosalyn placed her arms around his neck.

"Rosalyn what are you doing?"

Rosalyn laid her head on TJ's chest. TJ remained still.

"Just hold me."

TJ couldn't believe here he was holding this beautiful woman, who had a drop dead gorgeous body and who he had lost his virginity with.......

Turbulence jolted him back to the present. He opened his eyes. The turbulence also woke Francis. The pilot announced that it was just turbulence. Francis was hungry. She opened her bag and took their left over food out. She offered some to TJ. He told her that he wasn't hungry. Francis began to eat her sandwich. She teased TJ with the sandwich. She noticed that his mood had changed. Francis questioned him, but he just said that he was tired. TJ closed his eyes. He drifted off to sleep.

He began to dream:

"TJ and Francis exited the car. TJ picked Francis up and carried her into their home. Once in the house TJ put Francis down. He picked up the luggage and began carrying it into their bedroom. As he entered the bedroom there laying on the bed was Rosalyn. She was naked, not even wearing stockings. Rosalyn was laying on top of the covers, leaning on his pillow and legs crossed. She was smiling. When TJ asked what she was doing there Rosalyn told him that they weren't finished. He told her that she was going to have to leave. Rosalyn got up and moved close to him. He moved back, bumping into a wall. There was no where for him to go. Rosalyn placed her arms around his neck. She kissed his neck. TJ tried to move her gently. She nibbled his ear and whispered "I won't tell anyone." She then took his face in her hands and held it. She kissed him. When he didn't respond she stuck her tongue in his mouth. TJ put his hand on her waist moving her away from him. Rosalyn walked up to him again and put her hands to his belt. She began loosening his belt buckle and unzipped his pants. TJ grabbed her hands. She

managed to pull them open. Rosalyn smiled when she saw him aroused. Rosalyn touched him infusing TJ even more. He allowed his pants to drop to the floor. Rosalyn kissed TJ again. This time he didn't protest. They were now in the bed with Rosalyn moving on top of him. TJ watched himself as he made love to Rosalyn. The heat from her body made him sweat. As they made love sweat dripped from his forehead. As he went to wipe his forehead Francis walked into the room. She began yelling wake up. Rosalyn smiled at her and continued moving above him. As his body craved more of this feeling TJ knew he needed to stop. He sweated as their bodies continued moving together. The bed began to shake. TJ looked over at Francis. Seeing fear in her face and hearing it in her voice. He drifted away from Rosalyn. He became one with himself. TJ felt a jerk."

TJ woke up. Everyone was screaming. Francis was holding onto him. He put his arm around her. The plane shook and then they heard a crack. The pilot told the passengers to prepare for a crash landing. The plane continued to rock.....

After an hour the plane came down. The pilot came out of the cockpit and the flight attendants jumped into emergency mode. Because they were right at the door TJ and Francis were first to be helped out of the emergency door and down the shoot. Emergency vehicles were at the scene. TJ and Francis were taken to the hospital. While TJ was being examined they discovered that he was running a high temperature. The doctor asked him questions, but he couldn't remember anything that could cause the fever. The doctor ordered test and blood work was taken. Next to him was Francis. She was doing fine. The doctor ordered blood work for her as well. While they were waiting for the results Francis wiped the sweat from TJ's head. She was worried. Francis called TJ's parents and let them know what was going on.

Margaret and Thomas immediately got ready to leave. Tommy Jay asked to go. As Thomas drove to the hospital Margaret cried. The plane had crashed right outside of the airport so it wasn't a long ride. As Thomas drove to the hospital they could see where the plane crashed. The three tried to see the damage. When they arrived at the hospital Thomas dropped Margaret and Tommy Jay in front. Margaret wiped her eyes. When they entered the emergency room Margaret gave TJ's name. She was told the room number. When she and Tommy Jay got to where TJ was resting Margaret's heart went out to Francis. Francis was wiping the sweat from TJ's forehead. He was unconscious. Margaret walked over to Francis and hugged her. The women stayed locked in each others arms trying to gain some comfort.

Tommy Jay walked over to his father. He touched his hand and said, "Hi dad." TJ remained with his eyes closed, but acknowledged Tommy Jay's presence with a squeeze of his hand. Margaret released Francis. She walked over to her son.

Margaret bent down and kissed TJ. The heat from his head burnt her lips. An alarm went off and the medical team ran into the room. They wheeled TJ out of the room.

Thomas was coming in at the same time. He asked what was going on. The nurse told him that TJ's temperature had risen to an alarming rate. She further told them that they were taking him to try to get it lowered.

Margaret walked over to Thomas. He held her. Francis saw Tommy Jay standing where his father's bed had been. Francis put her arm around his shoulder. Surprisingly he put his arms around her and held her. The family stayed that way until the doctor came in to see Francis. The doctor told her that they were still working on TJ. He then said congratulations. Francis thought it was a strange statement and it showed. The doctor said you're pregnant. Francis continued to stare. The doctor realized that Francis wasn't aware of her pregnancy.

Margaret walked over to Francis and hugged her. She told Francis congratulations and that things were going to be fine. Francis sat down. Thomas walked over to her and asked if she was hungry. Francis told him that she had something not to long ago. The family was quiet during their wait......

An hour later the doctor taking care of TJ came into the room. He explained what they had done and that TJ had been admitted into the hospital and he was in intensive care. He asked who would like to see TJ first. Francis spoke up and said that she think his son should be allowed in first. Tommy Jay gave Francis a curious look. The doctor asked him if he was ready. Tommy Jay kissed Francis on the side of her face and then followed the doctor.......

When he entered the room his mind flashed back to when he and his father had been in the car crash. Tears ran down his face. As he walked toward his father Tommy Jay's face was drenched with tears. TJ opened his eyes. He saw the tears streaming down his son's face. He held his arms up. Tommy Jay went into them. Although TJ was weak he held his son as tight as he could. He murmured, "I'm fine." Tommy Jay didn't say anything. He remained with his head on TJ's chest. Another doctor came into the room. He figured Tommy Jay must have been TJ's son so he allowed him to stay. The doctor checked TJ's vitals. They hadn't changed. His temperature was stable, but he was not out of danger. TJ was kept in the hospital......

TJ remained in the hospital for several months. After some time past TJ started getting stronger. Francis spent much of her time at the hospital. She had not spoken of her pregnancy. Francis wanted TJ to get well before she told him. The family kept her secret as well. Francis wanted so much to tell TJ, but she didn't know whether he would try to push himself and make himself worst. She hoped that he would get better before she began showing.

Month after month Francis prayed for TJ to get well enough to go home.

Francis was in her sixth month when TJ was strong enough to be released. He was put on bed rest. Francis still couldn't bring herself to tell him because now she was afraid he would be angry......

A month after TJ had gone home, he and Francis were laying in bed, he had gotten his color back and was up to doing things for himself. TJ looked at Francis. He smoothed his hand over her face. She felt that familiar feeling. TJ moved closer to her and kissed Francis. She held him missing this feeling. TJ caressed her body. Francis had missed his touch. She whispered it. TJ looked into her eyes and told her he was sorry for it being so long. Francis smoothed her hand over TJ's face. She and TJ became one. As they made love TJ felt something. He stopped moving. Then he felt it again. He moved off of Francis. She was still in a tranquil state, not realizing what happened. She looked up at him. When she went to reach for him she felt the baby move. She looked at TJ and then realized what had happened. Francis sat up.

"Francis what's going on?"

"TJ I'm pregnant."

"When, How?"

"When we were taken to the hospital they did blood work. I'm seven months."

"The first five were the boring months. You're here now and these are the best."

"Why didn't you tell me?"

"I didn't want you to rush your recovery."

"What about when I came home?"

"I didn't know how. I'm so sorry."

TJ placed his hand on Francis stomach. The baby moved again.

"The baby is active."

"Yes. It moves all the time."

TJ got a concerned look.

"How are we going to tell Tommy Jay?"

"He already knows. They told me at the hospital, in front of everyone. The doctor thought I knew."

"Everyone knows?"

"Yes."

"I can't believe no one told me."

"We all wanted you to concentrate on getting well."

"I can't believe all of you."

"Are you angry?"

"No."

As time past Francis had a baby girl. Jay as he would have people to call him now was seventeen. He adored his baby sister. Jay was a good student and earned a scholarship to a four year school. He decided that he wanted to go away. TJ did not argue because he himself wanted to go away, but decided not to because of his son......

When August came TJ and Francis took Jay to school. They stayed the weekend and then left on Sunday. Jay had a friend who was also accepted into the school, so he did not feel alone. Jay also thought that he was being noble, giving his father and stepmother time to be a family without a teenager.....

Jay did well in school and came home for the holidays.

In his second year Francis gave birth to his baby brother. He came home for Summer to see his kid brother. Jay enjoyed the time that he spent with his sibling.....

When Summer was over Jay returned to the dorms. He began his sophomore year.

Jay had grown to six feet and looked identical to his father. He enjoyed school. There was one class he dreaded taken. That class was history. He liked history alright, but wasn't so interested in taking it in school since professors made it boring. His first day in class Jay sat waiting for the professor to come in and wanted to get it over with. As he sat there Jay began reading the assigned book. The class began to fill with students. The professor began speaking. Jay looked up. The teacher's voice was not at all what he expected to hear and then after looking at her, he couldn't believe what he saw. This woman professor was absolutely gorgeous. Her voice sounded like a song. Jay sat up straight in an attempt to be noticed. When she began calling out everyone's name he couldn't wait for her to get to his.

When she did Jay could have sworn the professor stared at him. For the next three months Jay looked forward to those two days that he would see this professor. When it came time to select courses for the next semester Jay looked for the professor's name, but she was only teaching that particular history. Jay decided that he was dreaming and that she was out of his reach. He went on to his regular activities.

One night Jay decided to go out to one of the friends. He knew how to dance, but didn't go out much. Once there he leaned against the wall and watched others dance. Hours into the night a young woman walked up to him and asked him to dance. He decided to go with her. He could barely hear her voice because of the loud music. As he began to dance with her Jay recognized her. She was the professor. He couldn't believe that it was her. He tried not to seem excited. She danced up on him. Jay tried not to get arouse. She danced erotic. Jay touched her hips as they got into the music. After several dances the woman thanked him for the dance and then left. The rest of the night he watched the floor, but did not see her again......

For the rest of the semester Jay went with his classmates to the club hoping to see the professor again.

On several occasions she showed up and they danced....

When Spring break came Jay told his father that he wanted to remain at school and take additional classes. TJ gave him his blessing.

Jay worked and purchased a small car. Jay went to the club every weekend in hopes of seeing the professor.

On one hot spring night in early June Jay saw the professor. This time he saw her before she saw him. Jay walked up to her and took the professor by the hand. He didn't know her first name so he called her professor. He asked her to dance. They danced close and slow although the music that was playing was fast. Jay held her close with one hand wrapped around her waist. As they danced Jay asked her name. She smiled and told him she liked the sound of professor. She asked him if he would like to go somewhere. Jay said sure. She walked him to her car. He informed her of his. The professor told him that she would bring him back to his vehicle. She assured him that it would be alright. Jay was impressed with her BMW. As they drove the professor asked what did he like to be called. He told her Jay. She asked him about his family. Jay told her all about his family, his father's recent illness and his new family. Jay thought it amazing how interested she was in him and his family. Jay looked around when they came to a stop. They drove into a townhouse complex. The professor turned the car off and as she got out of the car she said, "Here we are." Jay got out of the car and followed the professor into the house. She led him to the living room and told him to have a seat. She asked if he would like something to drink. Jay told her no. He was nervous. Jay had never been in a woman's home before , not a stranger. The professor excused herself.

Jay sat there wondering if she would let him kiss her. He couldn't believe that he was sitting in an older woman's house. He couldn't believe that she was attracted to him. Jay sat nervously in the chair as he waited anxiously for the professor to return. She had been gone a half hour. He wondered what she was doing. Jay heard foot steps. He looked up and coming down the stairs was this beautiful woman with a short black dress on. She had shoulder length hair that hung loosely. She had taken her jewelry off, but refreshed her make up. He went down her body, noticing her full breast, small waist and hips he remembered touching while they danced. He continued his observation. She did not have stockings on and Jay didn't think she needed any. Her legs were perfectly shaped and didn't have a scar on them. He imagined himself starting from her perfect feet, caressing all the way up her body.

His thoughts were interrupted by the professor. She asked if he wanted a drink. Jay tried to compose himself. He had become aroused and it showed. The professor noticed and smiled. Before he could answer she walked over to the bar and poured them drinks. Jay admitted that he had never had an alcoholic drink. The professor told him to try it. Jay sipped the drink. He put it on the table. The professor sipped hers and then placed it next to his. She patted the seat next to her and asked him to come sit next to her. Jay obeyed. He sat nervously next to her. She looked at Jay. It was obvious that he was nervous. It kind of reminded her of how she felt her first time. The professor placed her hand on his leg. She then placed her other hand under his chin and then asked if he had ever had sex. Jay looked away. The professor told him not to be embarrassed. She stood up. The professor stood in front of Jay. He looked up at her. She took his hands and placed them on the top of her thighs. Jay tried to compose himself. He did not move. The professor told him that he could rub them. Jay couldn't believe that this is what he was just thinking of. He gently caressed her legs. He could tell it was turning her on. He got brave. Jay moved his hand up her dress. He felt lace and silk. This turned him on. The professor lifted her dress up allowing her underwear to be seen. Jay looked at them in amazement. He had never seen a woman's panties on them before. The professor told him that he could touch her. Jay looked up at her. He continued to just look. The professor asked him if he had ever heard of oral sex. He shook his head embarrassed. She asked him if he would be willing to try. Jay shakily placed his hands on her behind. He brought her closer. The professor couldn't believe that he had never done this before. Jay could tell that he was doing it right because the professor moaned. The professor loved the feel of his huge soft hands. She abruptly moved back. At first Jay thought he had done something wrong, but then the professor lifted her dress over her head. She placed it on the arm of the chair. She held her hand out and Jay took it. When he stood up he tried to shield his arousal. The professor smiled and told him not to be embarrassed. She led him upstairs and down the hall to her master bedroom.

When they entered the room the professor began undressing Jay. He stood without moving. When he was completely naked the professor smiled at Jay acknowledging that she was impressed. She took his hand and led him to her canopy bed. She moved the curtains back and then got into the bed. Once she was in she patted the bed for him to get in.

Once he was in the bed the professor moved up and lightly kissed him. She looked at him and then kissed him again, being more invasive. He returned the kiss. She took his hand and placed it on her breast. Jay squeezed it gently sending chills throughout the professor's body. They continued to kiss. As if he had done this before, as they kissed Jay seemed to know what and how to touch the professor. After they had kissed and he caressed her body for a while the professor stopped kissing Jay. She looked at him with a look that told him that she was thoroughly turned on. She kissed him lightly on the lips and then his chest. She touched and caressed his body making him experience sensations he had not imagined he could feel. Jay caressed her hair. Jay wanted this feeling to never end.

When the professor knew that Jay could not take any more she moved up his body and kissed him. The professor moved up and pulled Jay to her. They began kissing again. The professor coached Jay to lay on top of her. He clumsily laid on top of the professor. The professor adjusted her body to fit comfortably under Jay. She held his face in her hands and kissed him. She moved underneath him. Jay moved with her. When their arousal had reached to where they couldn't stand being apart, after a few tries the professor guided Jay. The professor caressed Jay's muscular body. The professor guided Jay's movements. The professor griped his body tighter and called out his name. Jay lost control of himself. The professor held Jay tight and took delight. Jay moved off of her. He asked if she was okay. The professor told him that he was great. She laid her head on his chest. The professor soon fell asleep. Jay lay there with his arm around this beautiful older woman. He still couldn't believe that she was interested in him. Jay thought about all of what hey had done. He became aroused again. He began caressing the professor's body. After a few minutes the professor awakened. She smiled up at him. She said, "Oh we're ready so soon?"

Jay responded, "Is it too soon?"

The professor said, "I was joking. I'm always ready for more of you."

The professor placed her hand behind his neck and pulled him to her and began kissing Jay. This time she didn't have to instruct....

Later when they awakened the professor told him that he was an excellent student and lover....

Their relationship went on throughout the Summer. When he began school in the Fall Jay returned to the dorms. He stay in them during the week. He stayed at the professor's home on the weekends. Jay didn't know when he'd been happier.....

When the holidays came he asked the professor to come home with him. She declined. The professor told him that she wasn't ready to meet the family. Jay hated leaving her, but he hadn't been home in months. When he got home he decided to keep his relationship to himself. His family noticed a difference in Jay, but couldn't pin point what it was. His grandparents figured that it was him being away.

Thanksgiving Francis announced that she was pregnant. Jay congratulated them, but couldn't believe they were having another child. He was happy to see his father so happy. When they returned home Jay was happy to get his father alone. It seemed as if it had been so long since they talked. They caught up on things around the house. He asked when Ana was due. He was told any day. He asked how did his grandparents feel about all the children. TJ told him they were enjoying everyone of them. TJ and Jay got quiet for a while. TJ told him that it was good seeing him. TJ told Jay that he missed him and asked how was campus life. Jay was quiet at first. TJ looked at his son. Then it hit him. TJ smiled. Jay asked him what was he smiling about. TJ told him that he knew. Jay asked TJ what did he know.

TJ said, "Man you lost your virginity."

Jay had a shocked expression on his face.

"What are you talking about?"

"Man I know the look. Who is she?"

"Dad I don't want to talk about it."

"Why? How was it?"

Jay couldn't resist smiling.

"Oh it was good."

"Yeah dad. It was better than I could imagine."

"So she's experience?"

"Yes."

"How experience?"

"She's older?"

"Older! How old?"

"Dad, come on."

"How old."

"Just a few years. I met her in class. Let it go."

TJ figured it was a classmate and that they must have broken up, so he didn't press. He didn't want to bring up sore feelings so TJ left it alone.

Saturday Jay flew back to school. At the airport waiting for Jay was the professor. He hugged her tight. The professor whispered "So you missed me?"

Jay kissed her passionately. The professor took him to her home. When they got into the house Jay picked the professor up and carried her up to her bedroom.

After making love the professor laid in his arms. She began asking Jay about his visit home. Jay couldn't believe how interested she was in him. After they were quiet a while the professor asked Jay how did he feel about children. He told her that they were okay. She asked him if he ever thought of having children. Jay said yes, that one day he would like a family. The professor climbed on top of Jay and began kissing him....

Jay and the professor continued their relationship quiet, not seeming too familiar when they ran into each other on campus.

As Christmas came closer Jay asked the professor to come home with him. He confessed that he was in love with her. Jay asked her to tell him about herself. The professor told him many things about herself. She told him that she cared for him as well. The professor told him that she couldn't go home with him, but she would be waiting for him when he returned. She told him that she would have a surprise when he got back. He tried to pry it out of her, but she wouldn't tell him. Jay told her that he would return after Christmas. The next week the professor dropped him off at the airport. She kissed him passionately and then said good bye....

When Jay got on the plane he thought about his relationship with the professor. He wondered if she felt the same way he did. Jay thought that maybe her surprise would be her confessing her love for him. He smiled and laid his head back. Jay fell asleep....

When he awakened the plane was landing. Jay put his seat in the upright position. After the plane landed he rushed to the baggage area, where his father was waiting with his sibling. They ran up to him. He loved his sibling. They hugged their big brother. Jay spin them around. He hugged his father and then they headed to the parking area. After helping buckle his sibling in the car he and TJ got into the car. TJ asked Jay about school. Jay told him that he was doing fine. Jay told him that he had been thinking about remaining at the school after graduation and completing his master's there. TJ was happy that his son wanted to go further in school, but didn't like the idea that he didn't want to come home. Jay assured TJ that he liked the school and independence. TJ left it alone.

During Jay's time at home he spent a lot of time with his sibling and visited with his cousins. At night and especially weekends Jay missed the professor. He wondered if she missed him as much. When he was alone, which wasn't too often Jay would call the professor, if it wasn't too late. During his time home Jay spent some time with Francis. He discovered that he liked her.

Christmas came and Jay enjoyed watching his sibling open their presents excitedly. On their way to Margaret's home for Christmas dinner Ana called and asked if someone would meet them at the hospital because she was in labor. Jay offered to pick up his cousins....

When he arrived at the hospital the staff was helping Ana out of the car. Jay walked over to Ana and kissed her. He then walked over to Marcus and shook his hand. Marcus helped Jay transfer the children to Jay father's car. As Jay drove the children to their grandparents they chatted. Jay wondered if when he was their age talked as much as these children. He laughed at some of the things they said....

When they arrived at their grandparents the children got excited. When Jay pulled into the driveway the children tugged at their seat belts. Jay got out of the car and then opened the back seat. Jay unbuckled their belts and then lifted each one out of the seat. Jay took their hands and they walked up to the porch. Jay opened the door and the children ran into the house.

During dinner Jay watched his sibling and cousins. He wondered if he would have been a different person if he had sibling and cousins to play with when he was a child. After dinner he amused the children playing with their toys.

Jay decided to return home. He was missing the professor. As he was walking out the door the phone rang. It was Marcus. He informed

Thomas that they had another grandson. The family was thrilled. Jay volunteered to watch the children. It was already bedtime for the children, so Jay made an area on the floor in the den and had the children lay down. After they fell asleep he called the professor. When she answered the phone he could hear it in her voice that she had been sleeping. Jay felt bad for waking her. She told him that she was happy to hear from him. They only talked briefly, because he wanted her to get back to sleep. Jay told her about his aunt having the baby. It surprised him how thrilled she seemed in response to the news. Jay told her that he was returning the next day. The professor told him that she would be at the airport. They said good night and Jay blew a kiss to her.

When his father returned to Margaret's home Jay informed him as such. Jay saw the concern and then asked how was he staying in the dorm. Jay told him that he had cleared it and if that didn't work out then he had a friend that he could stay with. TJ had reservations, but since Jay was twenty-one he let him go and told him that home would always be here.

The next day Jay got up early. He ate breakfast. TJ came into the kitchen. They talked a little while. TJ knew something was going on with his son, but couldn't figure it out. TJ heard Tia. He went to check on her. He dressed and fed her. TJ took Tia with him to take Jay to the airport. Jay told his father to let him out at the curve. TJ did as Jay asked. When Jay got out the car Tia asked when he was coming back. Jay was surprised. He looked back in the car and told her he would be back soon. Jay hugged his father and then went into the airport. He checked in and went to his gate. As he walked Jay thought about his little sister. He smiled thinking about what his sister said. Jay got a warm feeling thinking of his sibling. He thought of how he was a big brother. Jay thought of how he would like to see his sibling grow up and be close, but wasn't sure if he would return to Jersey. He was in love with the professor and didn't think that she would want to move to New Jersey. When Jay boarded the plane he fell asleep. He was exhausted from the night before. He slept throughout the flight.

When he awakened the flight had landed and passengers were getting out of their seat. Jay jumped up and was able to maneuver his way through the some of the passengers. Jay walked quickly through the airport. Once he was pass airport security he saw the professor waiting. She had never looked more beautiful then she looked right then. He walked faster. When he reached her Jay put his arms around the professor, lifted her up into his arms and kissed her. They walked to her car. The professor drove him to her home. When they arrived there Jay noticed she had set the dinning room table. Candles were lit and food was on the table. Jay asked her what was it for. The professor explained, "I told you that I had a surprise for you." Jay went into the bathroom. When he came out the professor was sitting at the table. Jay walked over to the table and sat down. She served him. After they were finished the professor placed her hand across the table. Jay took them. Jay looked into her eyes. She glowed. Within a few seconds Jay's world had made a dramatic turn. Jay just stared at her. She asked him what did he think. Jay continued to stare. The professor let go of his hand and walked over to him. She stood in front of him. The professor took one of his hands, lifted her blouse and placed Jays hand on her stomach. He did not try to move it. He felt something. He looked up at her. She told him that it was the baby and informed him that she was six months. Jay continued to just stare at her. She let go of his hand and wrapped her arms around his neck. She bent down and began to kiss him. Jay placed his arms around her. As they kissed the professor began removing his clothes. Before he could think they were making love.

After they were finished the professor got up, took Jays hand and led him into the bedroom. They laid on flower petals she had placed there earlier. As they layed there the professor questioned Jay about his trip home. Jay told the professor about Ana having the baby before he left. He thought about the professor saying that she was six months pregnant.

"Professor."

"Yes?"

"Do you really want to have a baby by me right now?"

"Why not?"

"I'm not established. I don't even know where I want to live."

"Jay you are special. You're perfect for me to have a baby with."

"I don't understand."

"I chose you Jay. You are perfect to be my baby's father."

"Do you want to get married?"

"We're fine the way we are."

"Are you sure? I want to do the right thing."

"You've done everything perfect. Let's not talk about this right now. I missed you. It's just you and me right now...."

Jay was mesmerized by the professor. They made love day and night during his winter break. Whenever he tried to bring up the baby or the future the professor changed the subject or cause him to become distracted. Jay couldn't believe how great a relationship could be. It was perfect. He didn't know that women were so sexual, but maybe that was it, the professor was a woman, not a girl and knew what she wanted. She brought so much pleasure to him. The two spent all of their time with each other.

Jay called home occasionally, only talking for a short time. He didn't let on who he was staying with.

When school was back in session Jay returned to the dorms. He and the professor returned to their arrangement. Being from under her constant distraction Jay began thinking about the professor's pregnancy. He didn't know what she wanted from him. He was surprised at her not seeming to expect anything. He thought again, that's the difference in a girl and a woman. He wondered how his father would react especially having a child the same age as his grandchild. Jay lay in his twin bed upset with himself for not using a condom. His father had told him about sexual intercourse. Jay had thought about using one the first time, but didn't have any. He wasn't dating, so never thought about purchasing any, when the professor didn't mention using any he figured she was using some sort of birth control. She was a woman. He figured she would have taken care of that. Jay wondered if his father would be angry. Jay wanted to call TJ, but was afraid to tell him. Jay decided to wait until the baby is born....

The months seemed to go by quickly. His father made plans to come down without Francis. She was due in April. Jay spent more time with the professor. He went to stay with her in her last stage of pregnancy. He was amazed at how active the baby was, moving around in the professor's stomach. The professor was so happy. Jay wondered if the professor had planned the pregnancy. If she wanted to get pregnant. He wondered if she thought that she was getting old and couldn't wait for a proposal of marriage. Then Jay questioned why him. He wished that he could call his father, but then it was only a short while now....

All week the professor had been having Braxton hicks contractions.

By the end of the week the professor was feeling more pressure. She tried to rest, but couldn't.

When the professor got up she felt pressure. Her water broke. Jay ran over to her. He helped her to sit down. She instructed him to get her bag. Jay helped the professor to her car. He drove her to the hospital. When they got to the hospital Jay parked in emergency and then went into the hospital. The professor was checked and then taken to the delivery room. Jay stood by the professor's side watching in amazement as his child was being born. Jay coached the professor. She pushed for a while and then after an hour the baby's head crowned. Jay was in awe. The doctor instructed the professor to push again. She pushed a few more times and then the baby was out. The doctor, said congratulations you have a son. Jay eyes filled up with tears and pride came over him. He bent down and kissed the professor on the forehead. After they cleaned the baby up the professor was given to hold her son. She held him to her breast and then brought him to her lips and kissed her son. Jay looked at the professor and saw how much she loved the baby.

The nurse took the baby and left the room. The professor was taken to her room. Jay kissed her passionately once they were alone. He touched her forehead with his hand. He told her that she felt warm. The professor told him that it was just that she had given birth. A few hours past and the professor fell asleep. The nurse brought the baby in. Jay walked over and looked at his son. He was beautiful. Jay picked him up. He walked out of the room. Jay called his father. TJ was happy to hear from his eldest.

"Hi dad."

"Hi. You ready for next-month?"

'Yes. Dad I have to tell you something."

The baby began to make sounds.

"What's that?"

"Your grandson."

There was silence.

"I didn't understand you."

"Dad my son was just born."

"Jay what are you talking about?"

"The lady that I told you about just gave birth to my son, your grandson."

"Jay."

"Dad I know. I didn't think, but he's here now."

"I want to come down, but Francis is due any day."

"I know dad. I just had to call and tell you. I'm sorry I didn't tell you before now, but I didn't know until she was six months."

"Who is this girl?"

"She's not a girl dad. She's a woman. She's around your age."

"Jay. I thought you met her in class."

"I did. She was my professor."

"Jay."

"Why do you keep saying my name?"

"I can't believe this. I knew something was going on. I can't believe you felt you couldn't confide in me."

"It's not that."

"I can't believe your professor took advantage of you."

"She didn't. Dad I am a man."

"But she's twice your age."

"It doesn't matter. She is beautiful and she picked me."

"Jay was she your first?"

"Dad."

"Jay."

"Yes."

"I can't believe that woman."

"Dad I feel privileged. She picked me out of all the guys she could have had. You would find her attractive. If you were single you would probably want to date her."

"I doubt it. It appears she likes younger guys."

"She said that I was the first and only younger guy she's ever been with."

"I find that hard to believe."

"Why?"

"I just do."

Jay took a picture of the baby and text it to his father. In a matter of seconds TJ got it. Jay told him to look. TJ looked at the picture. He told Jay that his son looked like he did when he was born. TJ asked his name.

Jay told him that he was the forth. The baby began to cry so Jay got off the phone. He went back into the room. The professor had awakened. She smiled seeing her son. Jay brought him to her and said he thought that the baby was hungry. The professor tried to feed the baby, but he wouldn't latch on. He began to cry. She was sweating. Jay called the nurse. She checked the professor. She was running a high temperature. They brought formula for the baby. Jay fed his son….

Two days went by and the professor was still ill. The baby was released. Jay took his son to the professor's home. He came up everyday to visit the professor. She was unconscious most of the time. Jay kept in contact with his father. TJ worried because he could hear the stress in his son's voice. Francis had not yet had her baby. Ana decided to take the trip to see her nephew.….

When Ana arrived at the airport Jay picked her up. She had him take her to a hotel to get a room. After dropping off her luggage in the room, they went to the hospital. She told Jay that his son looked just like he and his dad.

When they got to the hospital Jay got the passes as Ana held her great nephew. When they entered the room Ana stepped back and gasped. Jay asked her if she was alright. Ana told him no. She walked closer to the professor. Ana stared at her. She couldn't believe her eyes. Ana asked Jay her name. She had to check. Jay wondered why his aunt was acting so strange.

"Jay."

"Yes Aunt Ana."

"Do you know who this woman is?"

"Yeah."

"No. I mean do you know who she is?"

"I don't think that I understand your questions."

"Jay that's my sister."

Jay looked at Ana.

"Are you alright Aunt Ana?"

"Jay that's my half sister. She is my father's daughter. Her name is Rosalyn."

Jay looked at her in disbelief.

"Is she related to me?"

"No."

She could see some of the worried look wash off his face.

"I can't believe this. She knew you as a kid. She baby-sat you sometimes."

"I don't remember her looking like that."

"Well it's true. Did you tell her about your family?"

"Yes. We talked about our families all the time."

"So she knew our names?"

"Yes."

"Then she had to know who you were. I can't believe it. I don't understand why."

"Maybe I was too irresistible."

"I don't know. I have to tell your father."

Ana left out of the room. She called TJ. He didn't answer the phone. Ana returned to the room. She told Jay that she wasn't able to reach his father......

The next day TJ called Ana. She was still at the hotel. TJ informed her that Francis had a girl. Ana congratulated TJ. Then she told TJ about what she discovered. TJ was quiet for a few minutes. Then TJ said that he was coming out in two days.

Jay was happy that his father was coming out. He needed the support. The professor wasn't getting any better.

Two days went by....

Jay woke up and got the baby fed and dressed him. He had fallen in love with his son. Jay placed the baby in the car seat. He went to pick up Ana and they drove to the airport. When they pulled up in front of the airport TJ was coming out. Jay pulled up and then got out of the car. He hugged his father and took TJ's bag. Jay put it in the trunk. TJ sat in the back seat. He looked at his grandson. Jay smiled. He hoped that his father would accept him. As they drove to the hospital everyone was quiet....

When they arrived at the hospital Jay parked the car. The group got out of the car and walked into the hospital. When they walked into the professor's room the doctor was in there. He told Jay that if the professor had family they should be notified. Jay looked at his father and aunt. Ana told the doctor that she was her sister. The doctor began telling Ana about Rosalyn's condition. He explained that she was very ill and what they were doing to get her stable.

As the days went by Rosalyn was in and out of consciousness.

Two weeks went by....

Jay, Ana and TJ watched over Rosalyn. On one particular day the three came up to the hospital. Rosalyn seemed to be alert. Jay sat next to her bed. He held her hand. TJ felt sad for his son. He watched on. Rosalyn looked at Jay. She smiled.

"I've always loved you."

"I love you too."

"I've waited so long to hear you say that. You see our son? He's as beautiful as I thought he would be. Why did we wait so long TJ?" Jay sat up and looked at the professor. He was confused. "Remember the night before your wedding? Why did you leave me? Why did you make me wait so long? Remember our first time? You were so gentle. I never suspected that it was your first time too. I was a fool back then." Ana looked at TJ surprised. He looked sad. "TJ we should have gotten married. I should have had all your babies. I'm sorry I didn't wise up earlier. But I have one now. He's ours. Hold me TJ." Jay got up. He walked closer to the professor. He bent down and then took her into his arms. He cried as he held her. "You don't have to cry we're together now TJ."

Ana walked out confused and with tears in her eyes. She dialed her father's number. When he answered the phone Steve couldn't understand what she was saying.

"Ana?"

"Yes."

"What's wrong?"

"It's Rosalyn."

"What is it?"

"Rosalyn is very ill. The doctor wants her family to come to the hospital."

Ana gave Steve the address of the hospital. He told her that they would be there as soon as they could get a flight.

When Ana got off the phone with Steve she called Marcus. Ana filled Marcus in on everything. He tried to comfort her. Ana hung up with Marcus and then called her parents. Margaret heart went out to her. They talked a while and then Ana said that she was going back into Rosalyn's room. Rosalyn had fallen back to sleep.

Margaret called Marcus. They talked a few minutes and then Margaret suggested that he go out to be with Ana. He thought it was a good idea and told Margaret that he would get the children things together. Marcus said that he would bring them over when he gets a flight out.

That night Marcus brought the children over. When he returned home Marcus called Ana and told her that he would be there the next morning. Ana felt comfort in knowing that he was coming....

The next day Marcus got up. He quickly dressed. He had arranged for a car. It was waiting outside. Marcus thought about all of what Ana had told him. He felt bad for Jay. When he arrived at the airport Marcus ran into Steve and Shirley. They happened to be on the same flight. They happened to be seated next to each other. Rosalyn parents' expressions were strained. As they waited for their flight Shirley talked about when Rosalyn was a baby. Marcus thought that she appeared to have had a stable childhood. Steve talked about her when she was a teenager. Steve admitted that he was happy when his daughters met each other.

The plane started boarding. The three of them rose when their seat number was called. When they found their seats the couple continued talking about Rosalyn. Marcus was tired, but he didn't want to fall asleep, because he knew the Wares needed to talk. He listened intently. Marcus realized that Rosalyn's parents didn't know where their daughter was living. He wondered what happened to cause her to move away from her family and not keep in touch. He wondered if she lost it when TJ got married. He wondered what would make a person go to such measures to be close to someone....

An hour into the flight the Wares became quiet. Marcus closed his eyes and drifted off to sleep......

When Marcus awakened the plane was landing. Once the plan had landed Marcus readied himself to exit the plane. He called Ana. Ana told him that she had Jay's car and would be waiting outside of the airport. Marcus asked the Wares if they had transportation. They admitted that they had forgotten. Marcus told them that Ana was picking him up and they were welcome to ride with them. They accepted. When they exited the airport Ana was waiting outside of Jay's car. When she saw them Ana walked up to Marcus and hugged him. They stayed locked in each other's arms for a few minutes. Ana then went to her father and hugged him. Tears filled her eyes. Ana's father held her tight. Marcus interrupted them by saying, "I think we better go." Marcus volunteered to drive. They all got into the car. Ana gave directions. At Ana's direction Marcus dropped the Wares in front of the hospital. She gave them Rosalyn's room number. They got out of the car and Marcus pulled off. Ana leaned against Marcus, and told him that she needed to be alone with him. Marcus placed his arm around her shoulders. After he parked Ana began telling him the latest in Rosalyn's condition and about her state of mind.

Steve and Shirley walked up to the receptionist. The receptionist gave them two passes. Steve put his arm around Shirley's shoulders. They walked towards the elevator. When the elevator opened the two entered. Steve pushed the second floor button. When the door closed Shirley turned towards Steve. He held her in his arms. When the door opened again Shirley tried to wipe the tears from her eyes. They walked towards Rosalyn's room. When they walked in Jay was sitting by Rosalyn's bed, TJ was sitting by the window holding a baby and Rosalyn was unconscious. Jay looked at them. Ana had told him that they were coming. He did not remember them from Ana's wedding. Then it dawn on Jay that Rosalyn was in Ana's wedding. He was young so Jay didn't pay attention to her. Steve walked over to Jay and shook his hand. TJ walked over to Steve and shook his hand. TJ hugged Shirley. Jay spoke to her. Jay moved away from the bed, giving Rosalyn's parents room to visit with her. Shirley kissed her daughter. She sat where Jay had been seated. Steve bent down and kissed his daughter. He stood next to his wife. Everyone was quiet....

An hour later Ana and Marcus entered the room. Ana put her arm around her nephew. TJ got up and shook Marcus' hand. Marcus looked at the baby. After doing so he walked over to Jay and shook his hand. He whispered congratulations. Jay said thanks. Ana told Jay to give Shirley and Steve time alone. The group left out of the room. They went down to the lounge.

Rosalyn woke up. She looked around. She called out for TJ. Her father sat on her bed and took Rosalyn into his arms. She continued to call out TJ's name. Steve tried to comfort her by saying that daddy's here. The monitors began going off. The hospital staff ran into the room. They asked Steve and Shirley to leave the room.

When Ana, Jay, TJ and Marcus returned they saw the couple standing outside Rosalyn's door. Ana walked over and asked what was going on. Steve told her. Marcus told them that they should have a seat. Shirley didn't want to leave the door, but Steve convinced her to sit. They sat not far from the room….

After an hour Steve looked at TJ. He asked him who the baby belonged to. TJ looked at Jay and said that it was his grandson. Steve congratulated them both. Steve inquired further, asking why did he have the child there and why was he there. TJ spoke for his son.

"It's Rosalyn's son as well."

Steve didn't speak. He just stared at TJ. Shirley sat up.

"You're not serious." Shirley looked at TJ as if he would take back his words. When he did not she turned her attention to Jay. "Jay right?"

"Yes."

"How did you?"

"Mrs. Ware your daughter was my professor."

Steve and Shirley stared at Jay.

"She was your professor?"

"Yes."

"How did this happen?" Shirley pointed to the baby. "I mean."

"I know what you mean. I was out at a club and ran into her. We danced. After that we met a few more times and then she took me home."

"Didn't you know she was your aunt's sister?"

"No. I didn't remember her."

TJ interrupted, "Excuse me, but I don't think it's my son who should be questioned. I don't mean to bring this up, but your daughter knew who my son was and prayed on his naivety."

Ana said, "TJ, don't."

"Ana, she come in here questioning my son, what about her daughter?"

"Dad I'm an adult. I knew what I was doing. I knew about birth control. Let's not do this. This isn't the time."

Everyone was quiet. The doctor came out. When he walked over to Rosalyn's parents they knew. Jay didn't wait. He ran to Rosalyn's room. Rosalyn's body lay there as if asleep. It was quiet. No more machines beeping. Jay walked slowly over to the bed. When he reached Rosalyn's bed Jay sat on it. He picked her up into his arms. He held her close. Tears drenched his face and her hair. His body shook. He began to talk to her.

"Why couldn't you stay. I love you. What are we suppose to do now? Your son needs you. Professor."

The group walked into the room. TJ's heart went out to his son. As if he knew, the baby began to cry. Jay looked back. He layed Rosalyn back down, walked over to TJ and took his son. Jay held his son close and walked out of the room. TJ walked over to Rosalyn's bed. He bent down, kissed her on the forehead and then smoothed his hand on the side of her face. TJ said goodbye and then left the room. He caught up with his son and put his arm around his shoulders.

Back in the room Ana walked over to her younger sister. She sat down beside her. Ana smoothed her hand over the side of her face. Ana fixed her hair. "I'm sorry I wasn't a better sister. I'm sorry I didn't look after you better." Ana caressed Rosalyn's face. Tears flowed down her face. Marcus walked over to Ana. He sat next to her and placed his arms around her shoulders. Ana leaned back on him. Marcus held her tightly. He continued to hold her as he stood. Marcus moved her away from the bed. Shirley turned to Steve and began to cry. Steve held her to him. The social service person came into the room. Shakily Shirley signed papers. Steve explained that they wanted Rosalyn's body transported back to New Jersey. They were taken to Rosalyn's townhouse. Ana helped them clear the house out....

Two days later the Wares returned to New Jersey. Ana and Marcus left the next day. TJ and Jay packed his things. Jay informed the school that he would not be at the graduation and where to send the degree....

When they arrived back in New Jersey they just made it to the funeral. Jay said his last good byes. He placed a picture of the baby in the casket. Jay bent down and kissed Rosalyn's lips. TJ held his son. Jay went into his father's arms and cried. Francis looked on. She wanted to comfort her stepson, but was afraid of his reaction.

Later on after they had returned home Francis hugged Jay and told him that she was sorry. She was surprised at his embrace. He held onto her a few minutes and then went to his room. Jay laid down and held his son close to him. The baby rested peacefully......

As time past Rosalyn's parents reached out to Jay and asked if they could be a part of the baby's life. Jay was finally able to talk with his father about Rosalyn. Jay told his father all about his relationship with Rosalyn. TJ couldn't help thinking how malipative Rosalyn had been. He wondered how long or when she began suffering from mental illness. TJ told Jay about his encounter with Rosalyn. TJ confided in his son that the night before his wedding he was tempted, but because of his love for Francis he resisted. He told him that he always thought that a relationship with Rosalyn was taboo. He didn't want to cause any ill feelings between him and Ana.

TJ discussed Rosalyn with Ana. He saw sadness when he talked about her. Ana asked if he ever had a relationship with Rosalyn. TJ admitted that he and Rosalyn had sex a few times when they were just kids, but never as adults. He admitted that they lost their virginity to each other. Ana couldn't believe how ironic things had turned out.

As Jay struggled to get on with his life he entered a nearby graduate school. Jay met a woman in grad school......

After dating a while they fell in love and were married a year after they graduated. He and his wife had a son. Thomas the forth was very happy with having a baby brother....